BEHOLD A PALE HORSE

SALLY SPEDDING

The right of Sally Spedding to be identified as the author of Behold A Pale Horse has been asserted by her under Copyright Amendment (Moral Rights) Act 2000.

All rights reserved.

Copyright © Sally Spedding 2017.

This book is a work of fiction. Names, characters, businesses, organisations, places, events and incidents are either the product of the author's imagination or used fictitiously. Any resemblance to actual persons living or dead, events or places is entirely coincidental.

No part of this publication may be reproduced, stored in or introduced into a retrieval system or transmitted by any other form or by any means without the prior written consent of the author. Also, this book may not be hired out whether for a fee or otherwise in any cover other than supplied by the author.

ISBN: 978-1548644833

Published by DEATH WATCH BOOKS

Front and back cover images from original watercolours by Sally Spedding
Author photograph by Jeffrey Spedding

PRAISE FOR SALLY SPEDDING

'You may not have heard of Sally Spedding, but you will, you will... This is a ghost story handled with real assurance.'
- *Barry Forshaw (Wringland, 2001)*

'Beautiful, clever and haunting... Cloven was a treat to read.'
- *JA Corrigan, author of 'Falling Suns' (Cloven, 2002)*

'An alarming story of surprises and shocks.'
- *Gerald Kaufman, reviewer for 'The Scotsman' (A Night With No Stars, 2004)*

'An excellent, creepy chiller. The perfect gift for all those tiresome people who boast about the French idyll they're about to live.'
- *Carla McKay, fiction reviewer for the Daily Mail (Prey Silence, 2006)*

'Taut, dark and nail-bitingly suspenseful, this story is fiendishly clever and packed full of unexpected twists and turns.'
- *Booklist (Come And Be Killed, 2007)*

'This vibrant collection of short stories will draw you into a dark, pulsating world that is easy to pretend doesn't exist... Her writing is so distinctly unique, it will truly chill you to the bone.'
- *Sally Meseg for Dreamcatcher (Strangers Waiting, 2008)*

'This is a thriller that will not surrender its hold on my mind.'
- *Mallory Heart Reviews (Cold Remains, 2012)*

'A stunning book with vivid characters and a gripping story… Not recommended for the faint-hearted, but recommended for everyone else.'
- *Christoph Fischer, best-selling author of the Three Nations Trilogy (Malediction, 2012)*

'What a fantastic how-to book. I couldn't put it down. Pure joy from start to finish. Highly topical and such an easy read. Thanks to this author for sharing her secrets with us. We are so lucky. Highly recommended.'
- *An Amazon customer (How to Write a Chiller Thriller, 2014)*

'Chilling. Seriously chilling. Fully 3D landscapes full of menace in themselves… A very compelling read, hard to put down.'
- *Thorne Moore, author of A Time for Silence, Motherlove and The Unravelling (Cut to the Bone 2015) Now optioned for a feature film.*

'The landscapes, the houses and hovels, the cold ice and damp are all very tangible… and of course, the cliff-hangers which kept me reading through the night.'
- *Timeisariver (The Yellowhammer's Cradle, 2016)*

OTHER BOOKS BY SALLY SPEDDING

WRINGLAND

CLOVEN

A NIGHT WITH NO STARS

COME AND BE KILLED

PREY SILENCE

STRANGERS WAITING

COLD REMAINS

MALEDICTION

HOW TO WRITE A CHILLER THRILLER

CUT TO THE BONE

THE YELLOWHAMMER'S CRADLE

SALLY SPEDDING was born in Porthcawl and studied Sculpture at Manchester and St. Martin's, London. Having won an international short story competition, she was approached by an agent and in 2001, Wringland, set in haunted Fen country, was published in a two-book deal with Pan Macmillan. The Yellowhammer's Cradle, her tenth chiller, was published in 2016.

Her short stories and poetry have been widely published and won major awards, and when not writing, she enjoys researching hidden aspects of Wales and France.

Sally lives in Carmarthenshire and is married to the painter, Jeffrey Spedding. Their bolthole in the eastern Pyrenees has, for many years, provided yet more inspiration.

www.sallyspedding.com

In loving memory of my parents, Dulcie and David Wolff,
who first showed me the south of France.

Grateful thanks to our daughter, Hannah Spedding,
for her proofreading skills.

Also to my equally literary cousin, Elisabeth Parks for reading the early
manuscript and for her encouragement over the years.

Hats off, too, to the inspiring poet and crime writer, Dave Lewis
of Publish & Print - as ever, the skilled 'midwife'.

'He who had done more than any human being to draw her out of the caves of her secret, folded life, now threw her down into deeper recesses of fear and doubt. The fall was greater than she had ever known, because she had ventured so far into emotion and had abandoned herself to it.'

Anaïs Nin

BEHOLD A PALE HORSE

PROLOGUE

'In the beginning is the end... '

The sound of the incoming tide pounding against the rocks, enters the tiny church to accompany the threadbare congregation's Evening Prayers. To the right of the altar in his own arched recess, lies the Knight, Mordiern Guyon, in green, mildewed repose with a whippet coiled at his feet.

They think him dead, the good singing folk of Manorcastle, but to his ears the waves that crash over their living tongues becomes another song. The song of distant seas gone by, of a love far greater than man for his Maker. And is it a sigh that the Reverend Adam Vitello Ash can hear from those sandstone lips as the dust-choked nostrils take in once more the scented hills of Roussillon?

I

'And I looked, and behold a pale horse: and his name that sat on him was Death, and Hell followed with him.'
(Revelation.6.v.8.)

Autumn in Normandy. The year of Our Lord 1271, where winter's bleak breath had blown the trees bare too soon overnight in the fiefdom of Pierre D'Alençon. By vespers, the leaves around the *Château Doucelles* were merely trampled stains in the bright early frost.

Suddenly, heavy footsteps neared the bedchamber from where a woman's screams filled the pious air above the evening prayers to Saint Denis as she lost her blood. The blood her firstborn had shared for two hundred days, and in turn would shed when another cooling autumn came around. And at that doleful season of his death, the infant slipped early from his refuge into a vile and restless world. Pure white against white, more a tiny corpse than a life begun. Fruit of old seed warmed for too long in the shade-less desert lands, his red eyes opened innocently to his father's face. From that moment, Jean Corbichon, the *Châtelain* of Doucelles, vowed never to look upon him again.

"See how I have sinned!" He cried. "And this is my penance. On the suffering of Our Lord, I shall make reparation." At this, the infant turned away to the wet nurse's breast, and clung like a maggot to its providing fruit. Not in shame, for it knew nothing of its deformity, but for the pull of warm, sweet milk.

"I should never have returned." Jean Corbichon knelt by his wife who lay inert, depleted, unable to give suck. His hand on hers, but not for comforting. "Others were dying while I found safety."

"You had to bury the King." She murmured. "That was noble enough." Her lips barely moved on invisible breath.

"The Comte d'Alençon begged me to help carry his bones. How then could I refuse?"

"You could not. His land is our land. He puts meat in our mouths."

For a moment her husband fell silent and covered his face with two brown hands. "But this... this creature... cannot bear Lord Louis' name as I'd planned. That would be sacrilege."

"In time to be sure, Rome will find enough to make him a saint," muttered his wife, weary but steadfast while the October evening iced the outer stones, and within, the candles set at either side lightened her spread hair and small, oval face to alabaster. "He is our child, and for that very reason he will have the best."

"He is a monster no less." Jean Corbichon was beside himself; on his feet now, striding back and forth around the birthing bed. "Borne like a plague on the wind. Why? How?" His brow had knotted like the wreathing limbs of old trees. "There is no such terata amongst my antecedents. Nor yours. So it is God who wreaks his revenge!"

Rage excluded all reason in the man well past his middle years. Tall, still agile, Governor of the castle whose huge, extended keep crowned the surrounding plains of Mayenne. This former Master of the hordes of Turcoples and Sergeants *en route* from Caesarea, and confidante of the King, had had no control over what had left her womb or any authority on her resolve.

"My husband, you blaspheme." Marguerite Corbichon spoke quietly. "That which I have not heard from you before."

"This aberration will not be nourished under my roof. Take him to another hearth, give him another name. From here on I deny him mine and that of my Holy liege Lord!" His words exploded like unseasoned sparks from a hungry fire.

"If that is your wish." She restrained her tears, all the while, in great turbulence of mind, making those meagre plans, those slender choices that are the lot of the dispossessed.

Once the child was weaned, they would repair to Froissy, north of the Garonne, where Marthe, her sister, newly betrothed to one Hilaire Roland, kept two flocks at St. Just. There he would be baptised in the names already given and learn not just the arts of manhood, but her grandfather's songs. The *Minnesinger* Friedrich Holz had left her a legacy not in *livres* or bezants, but in Latin lyrics of love that he'd sung from castle to castle on feast days and holidays throughout the German Empire. One of the envied *Herrenlos,* masterless men. Slaves only to their art. These words were now collected, all of a piece, for a grandson who would understand. For with a mother's knowing, she knew that few enough things would so enrich his singular life.

"He is to be gone by *Toussaint.* I have my soul to guard." Jean Corbichon pulled the curtaining roughly around her bed, excluding her from his torment. "You may have a horse with a small '*charet*' and every month, you may send for ten livres. That is not ungenerous."

His military voice faded from the chamber and Marguerite Corbichon was alone save for her own darkly distorted shadow that moved with the draught on the thin, enclosing drapes.

The light had faded to a stillness stirred only by bats who had long usurped the *pigeonnier* outside. Marguerite shivered, not from any puerperal weakness, but in the awful knowledge that this act of birth, their joint creation, had at a stroke, rendered her and her son as lepers.

She'd seen them often enough, scuttling from hedge to shack, any shelter, any hole, where afterbirths lay scattered amongst the litter of vermin bones gnawed to the marrow and charred dog husks. In memoriam of a life without charity on another's hostile land.

"*Pater noster, qui es in coeli. Sanctificetur nomen tuum...* " She crossed herself upon hearing her son's plaintive cry and, having called out in vain to her erstwhile provider, submitted their futures to God's will.

*

Some three hundred leagues away while the calling rooks flew north, and this young albino helped his uncle Hilaire pen the moulting Landes sheep near the farm, new mother Nolwenn Guyon was also delivered of a son.

Born on the light Pembrokeshire wind that ruffled the tall grass above the sea and made the new lambs leap and twist in delirium, he smiled at the world, and not an hour passed that was not blessed by his pleasure.

"He will make a true knight," his father said, bearing him proudly to the lowest field which, on stormy nights sometimes caught spray. "You are destined for great things in the Lord's service. Over the water and far away, the infidel still hold the Holy City. The great king's work is still unfinished." He looked into those replica eyes. Grey and blue intermingled. The colour of winter's sky, and the little body's warmth touched his.

By summer's end the Knight Guyon would have left the rutted sand-blown paths and the sturdy farm whose narrowest wall faced the wind. Gone to the warmth and colour of Constantinople, freed from the ravages of a northern winter. He pressed his son's tiny hands into a prayerful pose, and closed his own eyes.

"Lord God, grant that we may so despise the prosperity of this world that we stand in no fear of adversity... "

Saint Denis' prayer once invocated by the dying king, was now addressed to the springing sea. It was for Louis not Edward, that he had surrendered his best acres. For him and his sacred memory, they both would die. The Spaniard's husband who had harassed and tortured the Jews before their ultimate removal, who after Pope Clement's death had imprisoned the aged Bacon for his mind, was not worthy of any man's sacrifice.

Caught by the glancing sun, the child smiled such a sweet-lipped smile that his father held him close. Tightly crushing, flesh on flesh, this most precious burden, soon, too soon, to be a widow's blessing.

II

London Docklands. January 1983.

"Right, Ladies and gentlemen, let's take it from the top." Daniel Madox's left hand hovered imperiously over his choir, whereupon Catherine Ash, pale from the city air, dutifully opened her mouth again, for it was not her nature to refuse.

'... *Vous ay encherie*
Tresdont que premiers
Vous vi
Jusqu'au morir
Vostres demour... '

"More *feeling*, please! Come on now. This is far too insipid!" The choirmaster impatiently laid down his tuning fork. "Look here, this is a desperate plea for love. Mordiern Guyon was a stricken man." He stared at the small choir in front of him, still in their working clothes, and in particular at the young woman in front whose Titian-coloured hair fell smoothly burnished under the artificial light.

"Catherine, you *must* bypass the throat. Bring the air from down here... " He gripped both sides of his lambswool stomach, straining, spoiling his fine, classical features. The only reason why the ladies in particular, were willing to endure that draughty room every Tuesday evening.

"I'll try." Catherine hated the attention, and glanced nervously at the bass on her left." It's been a bad day, that's all," she explained. Besides, the bruise under her left armpit was hurting.

"Ah! But we must rise above such things in the great pursuit of love." Madox raised his arms for a fresh start.

Catherine had almost 'phoned him at his school to say she was too tired for *ballades* and *virelais* after a long shift at the Fertility Clinic, but she was never one to let anybody down, and now her voice was weaker, self-consciously so. He always had that effect.

'... *S'ay si dur a endurer*

Que durer

Ne puis mie longuement... '

"Hopeless! Hopeless." The conductor looked up at the ceiling and the Early Music Balladeers fell sullenly silent. "It's not as if I'm even paid to do this. Goodwill has its limits, you know."

He pouted his full, sculpted lips, reminding Catherine Ash if such a reminder were needed, how her husband did the same with less excuse.

"Forget the concert. Fine by me." He gathered his things and ferociously zipped up his briefcase before striding, unfocussing, through their midst towards the outer door.

*

"Oh well, a problem shared is a problem halved, I suppose," observed a British Telecom baritone, slapping shut his songbook.

"What do you mean by that?" Catherine was curious.

"Er... who's for the jolly old *King's Head* then?" Jack Tanner, a bass, deflected. His face the colour of a weathered countryman despite years spent in a Shoreditch shipping office. "My round."

"Never say no to a G and T." Jane Bowlby fellow soprano in a loud angora sweater, gave Catherine a hefty nudge. "Come on."

"No thanks. Really." Then she turned to see Daniel Madox vanish into the dark January night. "Is anything the matter with him?" She asked the soft marshmallow face next to her, whose myriad chasms moved under the weight of powder, heaped like sand on a living body.

"Ah ha. Tell you when you're twenty-one," it laughed and walked over to flirt with the few remaining men.

*

Nearing Moorgate tube station, Catherine could see that the choirmaster was still agitated by the way he snatched up the aerial on his battered Saab. She waved, but he turned away to force his key into the lock.

"Clement sends his regards." She shouted, and suddenly he spun round, mouth open. Then it melted to a smile, and she smiled too that she had calmed him.

"Bloody cold," he said, getting in. He checked in the driving mirror. She was still there, the wife, but not yet mother, with the east wind teasing her golden mane around her head and blowing the day's debris into a dervish at her feet.

*

"Good news!" Clement Ash was home first, and behind the door the moment he'd heard her key. "Guess what?"

His face with its shock of dark hair, peered round the frame.

"Greenbaum's opening up in France, and he wants me to get the whole shebang on the road. My *Carte Professionelle* came through today..." His large, brown eyes seemed even more enormous, as though they belonged to someone else, and in his excitement, he bobbed up and down on hard, sprung calf muscles that never tired. Then he shut the door on her, almost trapping her shoe.

"I won't let you in until you've said Wow! How wonderful and well done."

Catherine sighed. It was one of those silly games again. But the cold wind was lashing her face. Tearing her raincoat away from her legs.

"Shit... "

"No, that won't do at all. Come on now. Say you're really, really pleased for me."

"I'm really, really pleased for you." She knew when to obey, seeing in an instant, like the moment before death, her whole life thrown into a kaleidoscopic spin.

"Well, I think we can do better than that, don't you?" He was on a high. Unpredictable. Besides, the pavement behind her was deserted, for theirs was the only occupied house in the Chute Street docklands development. A narrow oasis of lit, un-curtained rooms, offering not comfort, but fear.

Time was up.

"I think it's fantastic," she murmured, so he let her in. Fresh and strong in his flexi-time lemon yellow tracksuit with a leaping gazelle appliquéd over his left breast.

"The *Carte de Séjour's* O.K. too, so the old Jew wants me down there ready for the summer trade and all that."

"Where?"

"Collioure... on the *Côte Vermeille*... When you walk in the garden, the Garden of Eden, with a beautiful someone... " He sang and laughed at the same time, his eyes rolling lasciviously at some private thought.

"Can I come too?" Catherine interrupted sounding like a little girl who's forgotten the latest punishment, and remembers only the nice things. Like the little blue and red boats that edged the Mediterranean shore and the rose-tipped bell tower, become orange against viridian in Matisse's eyes. Drawn beyond his balcony, to the bright, polychromed sea. "I've some Tate Gallery postcards, somewhere." She then frowned, thinking, not noticing how her husband's face had changed and how his mouth bore that ominous downturn at the sides. But danger, like some murky insoluble slick never far from the surface, had been swept away on his high tide of expectation.

"We'll cross that bridge when we come to it. This one's mine and it's a real biggy."

His syllables came in jerking lifts of the voice as though he was still working out in Canary Wharf's subterranean gym. Men amongst men, straining their pectorals and bulging glazed biceps. Brawny, sweating sinews stretched to the limits. Raised veins, taut tendons and firm, hip-hollowed buttocks which he desired for himself more than anything.

Clement jogged into the kitchenette and returned with a full bottle of milk pressed to his lips. "Mind you, I'll have to brush up on the old *parlez-vous*." A white droplet trickled down his chin. "*Reçevez Monsieur'dame mes sentiments distingués* and all that crap... Oh well, down the hatch... " He drained the bottle's contents and smiled a mischievous, milky smile at the future.

"Did you say the 30th?" Catherine pulled her diary from her bag.

"Yep."

"Well I've eighteen I.V.Fs that day. All desperate."

"Seen the state of the M25 recently?"

"It's natural to want a baby... "

Clement sidled up to her making infantile noises, his lips puckered level with her nipple.

"I'll be your baby, baby... " Her jumper smelt nice. Besides, he wanted to play.

"I'm still sore." She pushed him away, and he feigned hurt that she could bear a grudge for so long. His gym mates were different with their men talk. Bare arm banter, and *risqué* gossip after a few drinks - then all forgotten - *tabula rasa*. He liked that.

"How's Hermes these days?" Clement bent down to tie one of his laces; his bottom shaped like two yellow bon-bons.

"Who?"

"Mr. Music Man, you know… "

"He's fine. I told him you sent your regards... Why did you ask?"

"No reason." And with that, he bounded past her and out through the door to snort and grimace his way yet again around the latest Sparkes and Collett Docklands project.

*

After only two winters, their light, terracotta bricks were already grimy. Anarchically so, conspiring with the scarred, primary-coloured pipework and railings to defy the Greenbaum Estate Agency hype. Nevertheless, number 4a, Chute Street - 'Enterprise Penthouse *par excellance*' - was all theirs and paid for, with its mini-stairs and mini space soon filled by even one modest chair.

Plush, ivory-coloured, carpeted levels led off in all directions to the different lifestyle areas that they never lived. It was gardenless, pathless, neighbourless, but still a sound investment amongst the weather-stained high-rise blocks permanently decked out with damp washing and stained satellite dishes.

Clement, being in the trade, had been able to buy it cheaply, with money over for all the little idiosyncrasies that make a house a home. He'd installed a landscape of rings and pulleys in his bedroom. Exercise for supple, limbrous dreams, while Catherine was allowed to hang a job lot of Italian porcelain masks, as white and smooth as she, around the door to greet their few callers with a cluster of hollow, hermaphroditic smiles. Or post-coital, so her best friend said. And she should know. Lusty, fearless Serena Dicks who was all the things Catherine was not, and flaunted them so readily that after just one minute of meeting her in *The Cockerel* in Holborn's Shoe Lane, Catherine felt she'd known her all her life.

She stepped out of her clothes and walked naked to the bathroom as a high, wailing Muezzin call to prayers from a nearby Mosque mingled with the wind outside. The late Franco Vitello's daughter was no voluptuous pink, nor succulent puce. The Flemish masters from Cambrai would never have asked her to recline amongst their busy, patterned interiors. For she was of an earlier age - of albumen thickened with pale pigments for hair and skin, but bearing now in sheltered parts, dull, purple bruises.

Or Ophelia. She'd been called that too, and taken it as a compliment. 'A martyr,' Serena said. So now she too, lay with slender, aquatic grace in the oblong of water; her tresses covering first her breasts then reaching to the fierce, bright bush between the top of her thighs.

Clement would be sweating by now, she thought idly, raising a foot to the cold edge. Exorcising, only temporarily, all his surplus perversities. Leaving dark underarm stains on his tracksuit.

"Bloody fool."

She lay more still than those hide-and-seek ova and sperm in their little Petrie dishes, only four streets away.

"Have *you* got children?" Mrs. Munroe, Mrs. Egerton and Ms. Branch had asked in the same voice only that morning, as though somehow her affirmative would change their misfortune.

"One day." She'd lied, as always, smoothing the pillows and making them comfortable on their paper sheets. "One day."

Then suddenly, the 'phone rang and wouldn't be ignored. The

bathmat was out of reach and water coursed down her legs, wetting the carpet as she reached the receiver.

"Hi! It's me, babe," came the other voice. "Were you busy?"

Her friend invariably chose the worst moments to call. Catherine shivered.

"Damn you, Serena. I'm soaking!"

"That's a bit harsh coming from a Catholic. I'm sorry."

Catherine heard a distant door slam.

"Mike's just arrived. It's not the same talking to Miss Veal when he's around."

She shivered again.

"Don't call me that. You know I hate it."

"But it's so perfect for you, darling. Pale, indoor skin, and those long, tawny eyelashes... "

"At least I don't crap on the floor." But even this crudeness failed to dislodge Ms. Dicks. In fact it had the opposite effect. Serena roared her mirth all the way from Ladywell Court, South Kensington.

"Well, now that stencils are so passé, brown's all the rage for pseudo-rustic bathrooms, didn't you know?"

She was on her interior design hobby horse again, and Catherine knew she'd been drinking. "I'll 'phone you tomorrow," she said bluntly but not unkindly, and was about to replace the receiver when Serena broke in.

"Hey, I hear Clement's buggering off to the south of France."

"How did you know?"

"Ah! The trans-City grapevine," Serena laughed again. "Are you going as well?"

"Er... "

"Well I'd watch him if I were you. All that sun, sea and sand, and topless bimbos, not to mention *le* lovely *vin...* "

"But he doesn't drink..."

"How can you honestly say you are totally *au fait* after only two years?" Serena was being deliberately contentious. What did she know? Or was she jealous? It was preferable to think so.

"Of course I am." Catherine replied, hearing the latest boyfriend's voice, then Serena tittering in collusion.

"I'd better go now. See you around." Her flirty friend had clearly lost interest as other things beckoned.

"OK."

"Ciao. Ciao."

"Bloody cheek." Catherine replaced the receiver and stared at it before running back for the bath towel. "At least my marriage is twenty-two months longer than anything she's ever had. Miss New Dick every week... My marriage... "

She repeated those two words as if this would somehow imbue them with meaning as she rubbed baby oil into her city skin and put a jumper on over her nightdress. Then, settled warm, secure, and open to love, she returned the gramophone stylus to the 'Songs of Mordiern Guyon' and sang along.

'*Tuit me penser sont cesser en vous amer...* '

The mysterious man's longing floated as if reborn from that sweet tenor's throat and their voices arched and dipped as one while her hand slipped down to where her husband never touched. All the while, she stared out at the small patch of dark sky between the M.F.I. warehouse and Latimer Court's tower block, aware that all too soon, Clement would be back, pulling and trawling his body through a final act of homage before plunging into his own single bed.

III

'Because thou sayest I am rich and increased with goods, and have need of nothing; and knowest not that thou art wretched, and miserable, and poor, and blind, and naked.'

(Revelations.3.v.17.)

Marguerite Corbichon, wretched mother of The Whiteface was taken for a witch by the vigilantes of Froissy on the eve of the *Fête d'Épiphanie*. January 5th 1296. She had been alone, preparing candles for the dawn when their welcoming flames had flickered and died as the farmhouse's main door succumbed under twenty forcing bodyweights.

It mattered not that she was barren. Or for five summers since her only son had journeyed north to Lison, there'd been no blood, and since the *Châtelain* of Doucelle's last invasion into her body, no other man.

"Her womb is evil! Kill the she-devil!" Came the cry, for they feared she would bring forth a second albino. Thus was she dragged, two men to each arm, from the tiny altar set in the room corner out into the silencing snow and thence to the *Place des Oies* in La Baume. To the makeshift mountain of sticks and storm debris hauled from the Vignague.

While her tall, moon-coloured son with the Saint's name was praying for his soul and for all who had given their lives to Christ, she was roughly tied, skin and damp wood indivisible, ash to ashes already, her mouth quietened by a linen rag steeped in bitter aloes.

"...for the monks of the Order of Penitence... the White Mantles and Brothers of the Holy Cross, let us give humble thanks... " Girard Corbichon's white head was bowed reverently towards his knees, as his mother's turned to the sky, only to find in her terrible moment of need, nothing to believe in.

*

Every year, on that Feast of Light, celebrating God in Christ - first visible to a waiting world - the *Commanderie* of St. Loup at Lison, welcomed new brother monks to the service of God. Only the undeveloped young or the very old had shared its discipline since the fall of Acre, thus to receive men was a time of joy tempered with solemnity.

Its preceptor, Raymond de Savigny, having long recognised brother Girard's special gifts, appointed him as one of the receiving monks. His smooth tongue, his large, gentle hands, those rare eyes that both magnetised and drew fear, made him the perfect host.

"These are all lusty sons of knights." The Preceptor broke silence after Compline. Wine on his breath. Its redness rimming his lips. "However, the weather is against them. Pray God they be safe."

"I shall be prepared." Brother Girard smiled." For that is my calling."

Thus they parted. One to the horses, the other to the simple cross to pray for the travellers' deliverance on the treacherous tide.

*

Girard liked the fragrant darkness of the stable, with its memories of the farm at St. Just. But here, unlike the peasantry of his youth, these beasts of burden showed no alarm at his countenance. Nay, they fed trustingly from his hand, exchanging their warm breath for his. The dark also hid his other desires, for in all his life, he'd touched no ripening girl, no woman of older years. But still he burned, hidden in the furthermost gloom behind the manger. Lonely stroking himself to thoughts of longing and a sudden silent gasp as the straw received his miracle of molten seed.

Light-headed, he stumbled to the clothing store to make ready the rations for the new recruits. Two shirts, a tunic and jerkin divided below the waist, two pairs of shoes, felt and cotton caps, then towels and blankets. Girard arranged a wide leather belt across each pile, his finger lingering on the clasp. A noble, bearded head. Then finally, the under-drawers, spun from soft, kemp-free fleece. Fresh and lightly scented, soon to bear headier man smells from days *en chevauche*. Reluctantly, he folded each apiece, filled with a quiet yearning that only one of his songs could assuage.

'L'amour embraser et aviver
Et ay a souffrir
En doleur trop dure
Car partiroit mon cuer d'ardure... '

*

The ewes were restless, not because of the fierce night wind that buffeted the lambing barn, or their stirring, kicking young, but because the boy slept amongst them, and they were unaccustomed to such human intimacy.

As the New Year moon rose over the English Sea that the 'unquiet Welsh' would never claim, Mordiern Guyon whispered farewells to each, and the unborn soon to lunge and suckle on the new spring grass. By next nightfall the wide water would have come between, and the familiar warm-woolled bodies that harboured sea salt deep in their lanolin fleeces, would be just another memory.

*

The next day, mist blurred cliff and rock against the sky, fusing the Fleming's Head summit amidst the lowering clouds. This short, sturdy young shepherd's footprints deepened with each step towards the trickling sea, and at the water's edge, the cold wet sand secured his ankles fast. The same effluvium, but baking dry, that had held his father's armoured, unmarked body for five years in Damietta under a faraway heathen sky.

Now France too, lay south, beyond the waves, beckoning his willing heart to do that *chevalier* honour. His only child of sixteen summers, tanned from an outdoor life, was lithe and strong, well grown on his mother's love. Now he faced the sea, ignoring the glancing rain that weighted his cloak and darkened his full, golden curls. A sudden shiver passed through him, not from the air, but his spirit forever shaking free his youth from the wide, curved fields and the widow's comforting hearth.

He brought her back a shell so smooth and pink. Fine lady-skin, still full of ocean music. But she was not to be comforted.

"You will die too, Mordiern," she said in the kitchen smoke, setting his gift aside. "And there is only so much loss a woman can bear."

"We must all die, mother. I am not afraid, if it is the Lord's will."

It was time for the child-man to put away foolish things. Besides, he was no longer hers to keep. He'd drunk his fill of her shrunken breasts and had left her sheltering womb bare of secrets. Cold as the ancient limestone caverns hollowing the shore. She held him close, just like his father and all those others helpless before the power of God. Felt his heartbeat, quick and young on hers. When he was gone where she could not follow, leaving only the unloving wind's empty song carried south to tease and jostle the heretic's sluggish pyre, she re-traced her steps home.

As the tide returned, Mordiern Guyon scrambled up to St. Agnan's Church, set high on guard over the smuggling cove. Alone on that Epiphany eve, he prayed for his mother and the flock. That his poor, simple cousin Hagard would tend them as well as he, and there would always be bread in the oven. Then he prostrated himself on the damp, cold flags to offer body and soul to his Maker.

IV

"Morning Mr. Greenbaum." Clement smiled. Heads had rolled recently in the wake of the recession. But not his.

"*Bonjour.*" The large man, mottled pink and brown was always amused and not a little touched by his protégé's eagerness.

"*Comment ça va?*" His left shoulder bore the remains of bird shit topped by a torn piece of pink toilet tissue.

"*Bien, merci.* I say, can I give you a hand?" The mess spoilt an otherwise immaculate suit.

"No, no my boy. You just concentrate on English to French for the next few weeks. Word perfect remember. What's 'septic tank?'"

"*Fosse septique.*" Clement promptly obliged.

"'Land registry'?"

"*Cadastre.*"

"Fine. Fine. We must be ready for all eventualities, not forgetting possibly troublesome *Notaires.*" This addendum took the gilt off Clement's gingerbread. He looked peeved.

"I've asked Lianne to leave two more files out for you. All goodies under eight thousand francs, plus an advanced technical vocabulary which I want learnt a s a p." Then Harold Greenbaum turned away to another matter, and for the moment, Clement Ash was excluded.

The young estate agent returned to his desk vaguely discomfited despite the winter sunshine that flooded his Holborn office and the fresh coffee that Miss Bourton had left on his blotter. His workspace adjoined the main reception area choked from floor to ceiling with property photographs, and as no potential client had stepped over the Happy Homebuyer mat since nine o'clock that morning, he could give

Greenbaum's latest offerings his undivided attention.

The first folder disgorged darkly photocopied sheets of detailed maps covering the entire Languedoc Roussillon area. Busy, linear overcrowding of unpopulated tracts of land included the Fenouillèdes, the Canigou and Albères, when suddenly, colour brochures of southern beaches, Cathar fortresses, mountain villages, gorges, vineyards, set under azure skies, fell to juxtapose with the monochrome material in a curious Cubist assemblage.

His keen hands then burrowed deep into a big manila envelope for a bulky paper-clipped batch of properties, gratefully rejected by an assortment of other agencies. Some large, filling their allotted, smudged frames, others small. Then barns, hovels, old town dwellings - all *'pas habitable'* - written in miniscule print.

"First and foremost, our punters want something cheap." Greenbaum had said authoritatively only the day before. "Unlike us, the natives aren't into D.I.Y. They think we're nuts. So that leaves rich pickings." Except that he and his wife, unbeknown to anyone in the agency, had chosen a white wood dormer bungalow near Fort Lauderdale as their holiday home. Thus abandoning their origins in mainland Europe to increasing portents of unfinished business. "You can sell them anything if it's hot and sunny, that's for sure. A smart fellow like you could really hit the big time."

Words that had lodged in Clement's mind. But he hesitated as he sorted those with rooms for animal shelters from those with *caves* and *greniers*. He saw rotten shutters, crumbling walls, door-less weed-blown heaps which no clever camera angle or poor focussing could disguise. Here one bedroom, but no *cuisine*, there an earthen floor and a hole at best. No land, no terrace, not even a balcony amongst these disintegrating clusters.

His heart sank. The Chute Street house came painfully to mind with its chrome and mock marble virginity - a perfect foil for his measured, physical life. As functional as a climbing frame... But these sad relics of de-population whose pasts wept through the walls in the damp bleak months, yet burnt and scoured by the sun, who'd want them? He shoved them all into his briefcase and went to knock on Greenbaum's door, marked PRIVATE.

"*Entrez.*"

The room smelt like a saloon bar. The man's wide back turned towards him.

"Er... Mr. Greenbaum, sir, I'm not too happy... "

"I don't employ you to be happy, young man."

"If these," Clement tapped his case, "constitute a typical selection, then God help us."

His boss slowly swivelled round, and his eyes slid up and down Clement's body as though he might change his mind about the trip at any moment. "My dear *garçon*, people just haven't got the money. Have you? Can you cough up twenty grand for one of life's little luxuries? Just like that?" He snapped his fat fingers and Clement blinked. "*Who* is borrowing these days?" He spun back to his papers. "Do tell me."

Silence.

"Remember, our post-war inheritors haven't scored yet... when they do, it'll be a different ball game... until then, we build our portfolio; get ourselves noticed," Greenbaum concluded.

Clement stared at the brown, bald sphere of his head, honey-glazed under the strip-light and tried to visualise the bloodied matter lying beneath that orchestrated and sustained his well-heeled life. "Point taken."

Greenbaum was no fool. It was best to concur gallantly.

"Better get cracking then." A puff of cigarette smoke rose up. "By the way... what about your wife... ?"

"Catherine?"

"Ah yes, the lucky Catherine!"

Clement didn't like his tone.

"Not sure."

"Is her French good?"

"Very." Came out without thinking.

"Let me know her decision by the end of the week. Remember, nervous buyers on holiday often find a woman reassuring."

"Will do."

*

"Bad news." Lianne Bourton handed Clement a sheet still warm from the copier. "The pound's lower again." Her newly glossed lips pursed together in mock concern. Her exposed thighs close by. "And it's dropping, so it's Shit Creek if the Brits don't bite, and you'll carry the can." She clearly wanted him to look her way. To show interest, but soon walked off, deflated. He was never interested.

Clement got up smartly and barged through Greenbaum's door. This time, without knocking.

"For Christ's sake, we can't do it!" He shouted. His ears bright red. "What can we offer for 85,000 francs? There's nothing on those lists for less than 120."

"You'll have to box clever, my boy." The other man didn't even turn round. "Very clever."

*

"I don't know." Clement Ash sat by the tiny *trompe d'oeil* balcony whose window looked out on to Cranmer Tower - a ziggurat of coloured curtains with no signs of human life. Unusually, he was still in his office clothes. "I've got to somehow believe in all this. I reckon I can even sell a piece of used bog roll, but these! Look at these!" He waved the papers at Catherine who, at the end of her morning shift, was silently ironing a pile of tracksuits. She kept her head down; her thoughts tight inside.

"Would you cough up for this?" He barked accusingly. "Well, would you?"

"Maybe," she ventured, "the photos don't do them justice."

This was getting out of hand. He wanted support, not her opinion.

She looked up. "I'm coming by the way." The iron banged down in its holder.

"What!" Clement sprang to his feet, scattering the hidden ruins of Roussillon at his feet.

"Serena says I must."

"That fat tart?"

Catherine kept a wary eye on his fists. If they began to clench she'd have to move. And quickly.

"We could let this place," she suggested. "There'd be regular money coming in. Anyway, I love the south of France. I'd open like a lily flower… " She folded up the ironing board.

"The fucking bitch." His rage stifled by his hands.

But Serena Dicks was useful. She knew someone called Jasmine in Sotheby's for whom the Chute Street house would solve the problem of temporary homelessness. It would also save hours of interviewing potential tenants, and enslavement to the 'phone.

*

"Jasmine's a dear." Serena said, forty minutes later. Her eyes flirting with Clement over her Malibu and Coke, in Holborn's '*The Cockerel*,' refusing to accept his indifference.

They were the only women in what was predominantly a young man's haunt, but Serena always enjoyed a challenge and proceeded undeterred.

"She's got the sort of *café au lait* skin that I'd kill for." Her wide legs crossed and uncrossed in full view of the window causing several passers-by to stop in their tracks. Catherine also stared, mesmerised by the red wetness of her lips and the dark ravine dividing her breasts, while Clement searched for something suitable to write on. A handsome dark-suited man passed him a beer mat.

"Thanks." He grinned, and Catherine noticed. "Can she manage a grand a month?"

"Sure. This is someone who's just helped shift a Vlaminck for six million you know. Not your usual sort of gallery person."

Under normal circumstances he'd have lingered in that crowded lunchtime, gay bar, jostled by good-looking strangers. But he had Catherine, and other problems.

"Got to get back." He drained his milk and stood up, pushing the shock of straight brown hair off his forehead. He was aware of the barman's eyes on his crotch. "People to see, places to go... "

Catherine blushed, embarrassed. They hadn't invited Serena home since the previous Christmas. It might look as though there was something to hide. She tried compensating by smiling.

"Hey, I hear your choir chappie's having a bit of bother." Serena winked before reaching for her bag. She studiously lit up another cigarette and inhaled, waiting for the response. Clement duly sat down.

"Oh?"

But Serena turned to Catherine. This was women's talk.

"Jane Bowlby, the one in your choir... Well, her aunt is one of my best clients. Small world eh? Apparently, he's right off his wife. *Chambres séparées*, and all that. Or so I believe." She tossed her dyed, black head to direct the smoke upwards.

"That explains it." Catherine said to herself. "Might give him a ring." Clement was glad his admirer had his best profile.

"Us men must stick together." Clement got up.

"Don't know if I like the sound of that." Her friend teased, and Clement glared with his full, brown eyes. Bulls' eyes, black-fringed ready for the *'humillar.'*

"He's got some sort of French test this afternoon." Catherine apologised.

"Ah, are you the favoured mentor then, Miss Veal?" The designer laughed twisting her cigarette butt in a little dance of death in the dirty ashtray.

"My French is just as good as hers thank you." Clement was near the door.

Catherine touched her friend's hand. Her face seemed drained of blood.

"I'll be in touch before we go."

"I approve of the 'we'." The red lips beamed. "*Bonne chance.*"

They left her ordering another drink, and made their way to Holborn Underground, coats tightly wrapped against the cold river wind. Two youthful profiles, two carefully groomed and striking individuals walking - but only walking - in unison.

"Damn." Clement saw the sign first. **BOMB SUSPECTED KEEP CLEAR!** Red on white. Blood on a shroud. Catherine gripped his arm. Policemen frightened her, and these looked tense, waiting, shouting at people to move. She pulled him across the road to hail a taxi.

"Fucking nutters. Why can't they foul their own nest?" He shouted. "Sod the lot of them!"

*

The slightly depleted Early Music Balladeers sat waiting for their conductor in the Monkwell Community Centre's chilly hallway. Outside, a clock's eight chimes coming from a nearby Barbican courtyard, were almost drowned by the sound of heavy rain on glass.

"We must be bloody bonkers, what with all these bomb scares going on." Jack Tanning, now the only bass, folded his racing rag while Catherine exchanged small talk with some of the ladies.

"Pssst! Here he comes!" Whispered Jane Bowlby, whose little, busybody eyes scoured those of the conductor for any outward sign of his recent troubles. But the downpour had disguised him, unravelling his curls to lie flat on his forehead, giving his face the gloss of wet stone. Hermes of Praxiteles come tardily amongst mere mortals, he shook his red and yellow umbrella over the floor, creating little pools on its chipped, lavatorial tiles.

"Bloody climate!" He unlocked the inner door and the choir duly followed his drips into the bare rehearsal room.

"Oh dear. This doesn't augur too well." Jane Bowlby looked nervous. "He's not happy you know."

"Who is?" Catherine declared, keeping her eye on him.

"Things are definitely iffy. Know what I mean?"

"I had heard." The younger woman passed her to sit nearer the front than usual.

When Daniel Madox had regained his composure, he briefly smiled at them all over the pile of books on the piano.

"I'm prepared to give this whole thing one more go. So, let's have more control, better breathing and less vibrato." He focussed on Jane

Bowlby whose hot flush had deepened to magenta. "Hit those top notes on the dot."

Catherine grinned as their eyes met. She'd sing like an angel for him tonight - and she did.

At the end he applauded, and for the first time in weeks he seemed genuinely pleased.

"Right. If you can get your diaries out for confirmation of April 21st, St. Giles, at even thirty prompt. Friends *et al*, all welcome." Catherine realised he'd avoided the word 'family'.

"Is there anyone else who can't make it?" He looked at Catherine. The only one not writing.

"Actually... I don't think I can," she blushed. "We're off to France."

An uncomfortable silence followed, with all eyes suddenly on her. Their best soprano deserting. Escaping…

"Collioure... you know," she elaborated. "Derain, Matisse... views through the open window... " When all she could see so far from that treacherous, wet London night.

"It's alright for some."

"Got any room? I'm only a forty hip." Someone said.

Daniel Madox inclined his ear to his tuning fork and hummed a B flat.

"By the way, nice of Clement to 'phone'." He said without looking at her. "Much appreciated. Oh, and if anyone's interested in going to the Last Night of The Proms this year, I might be able to wangle a few precious tickets. Let me know."

A buzz of interest greeted this announcement, and Catherine's news was quickly forgotten amidst noisy speculation as to who the singer and conductor might be. Then, with the raising of his hands came the opening bars of "Fins cuers doulz chieri." sung as though their very lives depended on it. But Catherine's voice had already died in her throat.

*

4a, Chute Street lay ready and waiting for its new incumbent, bereft of the porcelain masks around the front door and anything else at risk of being pilfered during the day. There was no one in sight. No neighbour to wave and wish her well, for those in work had long gone, and for the rest, morning television was on. One last look, then Catherine started her new, silver Renault's engine.

"*Arriverderci... solamente sei mese... six mois... au revoir...*"

Despite having recently immersed herself in French, she was nowhere near as good as Clement who seemed quite at ease with his new 'target culture'. His motives were clear - business through the slick of the tongue. Hers were not.

Catherine manoeuvred the car into the Mile End Road in front of a Guildhall bus. It suddenly loomed large and threatening, filling up all her mirrors.

"Just jealous," she muttered, resting her delicate elbow on the window ledge in defiance. The bus driver could obviously see her fresh G.B. sticker and the polythene still covering its seats. Symbols of salaried success and a blue-sky future, while he was doomed to navigate the Capital's filthy streets all day. She put to memory the familiar, dingy sequence of station, market, Post Office, betting shop as though she'd never see them again.

Then the anonymously modern St. Mark's Clinic took her eyes from the road up to the second floor where her mothers-hoping-to-be would be lying in wait, legs apart. But their absconding nurse could summon no guilt, for even in their prodded barrenness, they were better off than she. And Serena, clever, colourful Serena. Doubtless she'd be busy at Byzantium amidst bales of muslin and damask, choosing this to go with that...

The overbearing bus finally veered off as she parked near the Agency alongside a British Gas van, leaving her hazard lights on. She ran into the mock busy brightness of the front office where Lianne Bourton looked up, hostile, from her word processor.

"Clement?" she snapped, moving her coiffed head to one side. "Someone to see you."

There was no time for Catherine to be hurt at her exclusion, for there was her husband, on cue, radiating confidence and *bonhomie*.

"Hi." He was carrying two large briefcases and a Michelin map of France. Harold Greenbaum followed, sweating above his tight collar. "Think I've got everything." Clement looked smart and cool in his beige safari suit - the one he'd worn when they'd first met at 'Properties for Singles' exhibition at the Hammersmith Novotel. The girl at the desk stared at his well-shaped legs as Greenbaum handed him a large, manila envelope.

"We've got your *Cartes de Séjour* sorted out - for both of you, and Lianne here has organised your work permit." At this, the girl smiled smugly. "The Embassy was a bloody disgrace. Still, *tout est bien qui finit bien*. It's up to you now."

"Thanks Lianne." Clement leant over to dutifully peck her cheek, but she held him there, kissing his mouth. He quickly disengaged himself and wiped his lips on his sleeve, leaving a pink stain.

"Good that you're driving rather than flying," Harold Greenbaum sensed unease. "Help you get a better feel for the place." He proffered his hand. "I'll try and get down early May sometime. Hope there's good news by then."

"I'll do my best." Clement was at last free, but not so Catherine, the object of the older man's liverish eyes roaming loose in his head as his vast, pulpy palm swamped hers.

V

'And I saw a new heaven and a new earth: for the first heaven and the first earth were passed away; and there was no more sea.'
(Revelation.21.v.1.)

Mordiern Guyon's first hours in France were spent under a coarse, vile-smelling blanket, sheltering from the battery of hailstones that assailed the *charet* on its way from La Chappelle to Moncelet. Gales had driven the boat to seek refuge near the Pointe de Barfleur on a small, shingle beach set hidden between huge barricades of unhewn granite. It was a miracle that the craft, with its leather and human cargo, hadn't been tossed like a plaything back into the roaring sea, and on landing, breathless, salty prayers from twenty seasick lips were offered up to La Sainte Marie. *Le Manche du Mer Brittanique* had spared them.

The pale stallion snorted disdain at the onslaught from the sky. A massive creature, tight between the cart's shafts, he tossed his massive head this way and that, and his mane, like a woman's hair let loose, flew back into the travellers' eyes once the storm had cleared.

"What's he called?" Mordiern asked the tall, rugged man who swayed like a drunkard above him on his perch. Whip held high, not that there was need of it. The boy knew an entire from a mare, and expected all creatures used thus by man to bear a name.

"Druide. A fine name, after the stones at Les Gemmes." Robert Sagan, the sharp-boned farmer and small-time breeder of *Boulonnais*, growled from inside his hood. He'd discovered the dishevelled Welshmen whilst outside setting wild boar traps, and knew that certain welcome perquisites would be coming his way, should he deliver them safely to their destination. Mordiern fell silent. How that name enhanced the creature's noble vision. Ears pricked, tail arched, unstumbling over every kind of ground, the stallion bore the now depleted party through the marshy flats around Issigny, and south towards Lison.

*

A feeble winter sun edged the clouds low on the horizon, gilding the high, trotting rump an even lighter gold, which blocked out the young traveller's view.

"And I looked, and behold a pale horse... And his name that sat on him was Death... " Mordiern struggled to remember the rest, and failed.

"Let's hear no more of that," reprimanded the farmer who sat with the reins slack in his lap. "'Tis a bad omen, to my mind."

Mordiern stared at him, puzzled. He'd been brought up to learn and pay heed to St. John the Divine. Those winged beasts who consume the new-born, fire, plague, earthquake, could all be summoned by unholy thoughts. For nothing is secret from the Lord.

*

The stony road became a deep, muddied track through a desolate landscape. No farm, no barns or prosperous *messuage*. Beyond all human habitation, the St. Loup *Commanderie* stood bare of trees, perched on a wide, earth plateau. Its octagonal keep starkly silhouetted, proclaiming nothing other than a life of rigour and severity. The horse suddenly whinnied, recognising his own kind as they approached the gates. The walls beyond appeared to stretch forever on either side, bulked out by clusters of different offices and the adjoining chapel. The Rieu river, swollen in turn by the Vire from the sea, passed in front, forming a natural but problematical barrier. The water lapped against the wooden bridge and the horse suddenly stopped as though to ponder his own reflection.

"Allez, Narcisse!" The man shouted, slapping his stick against its thigh. The animal lurched forward, swinging the cart perilously close to the fast-moving current below.

"Mater Christi!" Someone screamed.

"See what your damned Bible curse has done!" Sagan shouted spittle, and Mordiern hung his head. Shame replaced any pride in the fact that this was where his father had once bathed his face in the summer stream, or walked the very same length of greensward that led up towards the arched, stone entrance. For the first time, in a brief moment, he felt the hollow ache of homesickness.

*

The *Boulonnais* eventually came to a halt, sweating despite the cold, while the three youths with their meagre wet belongings disembarked. The elderly Preceptor of St. Loup appeared, flanked by two brother priests heavily mantled, sheepskin-lined. They stood as still and straight as candles. Disciplined, mortal flesh in the bitter wind. Three blue noses and six hands turning slowly to marble. The youngest one with a face as white as the rising moon, and eyes the like of which Mordiern had never seen before.

"We have to thank the good Lord for your safe keeping." Raymond de Savigny's finger made a brief sign of the cross as the horse was unharnessed. He then offered the farmer a bed, and a share of the meal that awaited. "Take the horse to the stable and give him two rations." He ordered one of the monks who moved all too readily. But "Druide," suddenly freed from the restraints about his loins, gambolled about like a foal, his huge, plated feet leaving a pattern of deep, muddied crescents in the sodden ground.

"Whoa!" The farmer, flushed and short of breath, caught him, then fixed his black eyes on the Preceptor and monks as if the time had come to ask an already prepared question. "What price will you give me for him, good sires? He's too much a young man's horse for me."

Mordiern's mouth slackened. He forgot his own discomfort, the hunger and his freezing, clinging clothes. Instead he looked imploringly at the monks, who seemed to be conferring.

"We have need of another, certainly," replied Raymond de Savigny. "But our mounts have rather more Barb in their veins. Besides, they are uniformly black."

"Yet he has travelled without fault. Like an arrow." Mordiern spoke out, and all eyes were fixed on him. "I would take him tomorrow, had I the chance."

"And I can tell that the son of Robert Guyon has his father's voice." The old Preceptor said not unkindly. "Come, enough of this night. We will talk in the morning."

The little party wound its way up the hill behind the horse's bulk that shielded them from the worst of the weather. Their deliverer held back to take Mordiern's arm, smiling uneven teeth.

"Some say, *mon hommet*, that this is a strange calling for a man in his prime. That all is not as it seems."

Mordiern's cold cheeks flushed in anger.

"Do you call me a dwarf?" he challenged.

"Why not? You barely reach my breast."

The man was close. His breath unclean. Their steps in turn eager and weary. As one. And not to be thwarted by the other's silence, he then asked in a wheedling tone, the whereabouts of this Welsh youth's hearth. The exile from Manorcastle pulled his cloak tighter round, and trustingly obliged, recounting his brief life. The flocks, the neighbouring sea, and how, of the thirty Castleton Farm fields spread south of the Landsker line, some fifteen had already been donated to the Order.

"That is no surprise." The ambitious, opportunistic Robert Sagan whispered. "These are leeches who gorge on the blood of their hosts, while we break our backs in toil, only to lose it all. And they say it is for God! Pah!" His laughing sneer issued a puff of warm steam into the air. Mordiern wanted to ask why then had he taken pity on them, but the Preceptor was waiting, signalling silence before leading the way in the gathering dusk towards the chapel's mighty rotunda.

VI

"What's the woman's name again?" Catherine ventured once the traffic had eased near the Dartford tunnel.

"Tavernier. Rosa Tavernier. *Numéro huit*, Rue des Templiers." His accent was good. "She's got a butcher's shop." Clement kept his eyes fixed ahead and patted his pocket where he knew the keys to be. This made her feel safe, for the moment at least. They had a place to go and a face to meet them.

"Has the flat got a 'phone?" She asked, suddenly thinking of his father.

"No."

"What about your office?"

"Not connected up yet." That brief security faded like the winter sun now lost under the murky estuary sky.

"I've fiddled some more commission, by the way," he said as they entered the tunnel's bright orange opening. "Beat the old bugger at his own game... "

Catherine closed the window on the fumes, and the intimacy of that enclosed space made it seem right to touch his thigh. The muscle froze under her fingers.

"Lianne Bourton was dying to do this, couldn't you tell?" She said playfully. "And Serena."

But he clamped her down with the dead weight of his hand.

"She's just a whore."

So Catherine withdrew to sit demurely restrained by the seat belt. Head bowed, knees together, warily quiet as daylight appeared. Clement met it with a surge of speed and a grin on his face.

"Talk about a Crusade. This is it! For God, read Brits. For the Temple, read *Maisons du Soleil*. Got it?" He laughed as the speedometer nudged ninety. "And incidentally, I've done one good deed before leaving. Well, ask me what it was then... ?" His tone changed. Just for her. But she was magnetised instead by the southerly pull of sky and tarmac to the distant horizon line. Caught, trapped, in the close company of container lorries and fleets of identical-looking cars.

"Ask me!" He demanded, fidgeting in his seat.

"I'm asking."

"I've written to Dan."

*

The next stage of their journey on the ferry, was spent in stifling silence as Kent's fields gave way to the sprawling, untidy port huddled beneath the cliffs, and the doubtful promise of its dark ferry-strewn sea. Flocks of noisy, scavenging gulls filled the quiet, layered sky above the passenger deck. They swooped and soared in big dipper flight over newly opened sandwiches and detritus trapped under damp seats from the previous crossing. Opportunists all, Catherine thought, watching how her husband at the deck rail, dapper amongst the crumpled shell suits and anoraks that strolled closely by, seemed self-absorbed.

Like her, the 'Maid of Dover' was childless, it being the wrong season for souvenir trips and study visits. At least she could stare unencumbered at the sea, thus spared the awkwardness of youngsters coming too near. Replicas and lookalikes of mothers whose wombs had been no less ready than hers... No, this was obviously a voyage for honeymooners, Art Tour rubbernecks and hypermarket gluttons hung about with foldaway trolleys, and in this mixed but unmixing company, the Ashes were borne inexorably towards their only consummation. With the south.

VII

'And in the midst of seven candlesticks one like unto the Son of man, clothed with a garment down to the foot, and girt about the paps with a golden girdle. His head and his hairs were white like wool, as white as snow, and his eyes were as a flame of fire.'
(Revelation.1.v.13.)

"Do you seek the company of the Order of the Temple and the participation in the spiritual and temporal goods which are in it?" Luc Fossard, aged Preceptor of the province, asked the small group assembled in the chapel's anteroom after high Mass. A murmur of concurrence rose up, no-one wishing to sound louder than his neighbour. This Preceptor was then joined on either side by the same two brother knights, silently as ectoplasm from the very walls, but to a collective gasp of astonishment. For the taller man's extraordinary countenance was now fully illumined and neither his beard nor cap could disguise it. An albino possessing skin of the palest new-born, yet with eyes that swam in their orbs like liquid pools of blood.

Mordiern, awestruck, barely heard the initiating words that followed. Nothing in his meagre shepherding life had prepared him for this. And now the man looked his way.

"You seek what is a great thing." The Whiteface began. "But you do not know the strong precepts of the Order. For you see us from the outside, well dressed, well mounted and well equipped, but you know nothing... for when you wish to be on this side of the sea, you will be beyond it and vice versa."

Mordiern detected a faint smile and the tips of yellow teeth.

"When you wish to sleep, you must be awake, and when you wish to eat, you must go hungry. Can you bear these things for the honour of God and the safety of your souls?" The young men all fervently agreed, avoiding his gaze, as more questions came to each on their faith, any secret infirmity, debt or knowledge of simony. Finally, drawing closer, and lingering the longest on the young widow's son, the knight repeated his question.

"Are you are married or promised to another?"

Mordiern looked to his left and right rather than at what resembled two spy-holes of a furnace.

"I am my own man, sire." Words that belied his bewilderment. The other smiled again, giving him the sign of the Cross.

"We command that you turn towards the chapel and pray for God to grant your petition... " Then on a sudden draught of the opening door, the two brothers and Raymond de Savigny left the newcomers kneeling on the cold flags, deep in their own conflicting thoughts.

*

"Brothers in the Lord, you can see how the majority is favourable for Mordiern to join us, to serve God and Holy Mary. If there is any amongst you who knows of any crime or wrong-doing, he must speak out." Luc Fossard lightly touched the boy's hair. "Better now than later." His dark, southern face spanned those assembled, but all remained silent except for the relentless wind outside bringing its own plainsong through the fissures and orifices of the ancient stones.

Then Raymond de Savigny stepped forward to administer the oath of obedience, tall as a pillar from their humble position. Gaunt and sallow, the colour of ancient amber, lips indistinct. The rules overflowed from his abundant source, smothering, binding. No hunting or other sport. No chess, no dice. No song no jest, no extra raiment or nourishment unshared. No galloping of horse or unpermitted *sorties*. No money or property, and lastly, the greatest sin of all, and forbidden - the love of a man for a woman...

Mordiern closed his eyes and swayed, but someone was there, quick to take his arm. Brother Girard - The Whiteface - in ermine. His outgoing breath herb-sweet, ready to bless.

"He is fatigued. May he stand?" He asked, still holding him.

And so with his companions, Mordiern was invested with his mantle, and kissed on the mouth, hierarchically, first from Fossard, then de Savigny, cold and moist, before Girard, warm and full with a touch of his tongue. After them, the remaining knights in swift succession.

"Go. God make you worthy men." Fossard ended. "Brothers Girard and Etienne will furnish you with your garments after hearing thirteen *Pater Nosters* in the chapel. Seven for Our father, six for the day. Then you may rest until dinner."

*

Thus was Mordiern led past the laundry and bleaching room to the tiny chamber where two low, rough pallets were set next to each other against a curving end wall.

"Yours," said Etienne, turning back the thin, black and white blanket. "And his."

Mordiern glanced quickly at brother Girard. Unsure. He'd never shared a room in his life.

"You may also use this on your horse." The other picked at some long, dark hairs trapped amongst the blanket's fibres, then bent down to sniff it. "Someone else has done the same. That is how it is." And Mordiern remembered how he'd saved a small twist of sheep's' wool as a memento of his farm, but nothing from his mother's head.

"Be sure to rise on the bell, whatever the needs of the body." Girard helped remove his sodden outer cloak of dirt and brine combined. He too, touched the other's golden hair and for a second, let his fingers curl the locks above an ear. Skin still as browned by the summer sun as his was white. Young and taut with no trace of un-worked fat.

"Tomorrow I will shave you," he said, as would a loving sculptor to his art. And Mordiern saw without fear now, how the man's irises widened and deepened to a burning, red ember, as if in admiration.

"There is one other rule." The albino turned away, hesitating. "Your breeches must not leave your body during sleep."

"But I've never worn clothes in bed!"

"Sssh! That is the order."

"Er... can you ride?" Brother Etienne asked, suddenly embarrassed.

"For ten years I have sat a horse." Mordiern's effort at their language caused welcome amusement, but it was not the time for laughter.

"We will ride together then." Girard said, folding his clothes. But the boy was already falling asleep, his fair lashes fringing his cheeks, pink lips apart, as the faraway pony bore him once more over the sea-blown grass, drawing the straggling flock in to the fold.

*

On the very night that her son found his Saviour, Nolwenn Guyon, grieving for her greatest loss, abandoned Him, denying Him her presence at the Holy Day service. Instead, she stayed in her cold marriage bed, her desolate tears glistening her only son's empty shell.

VIII

Once on French soil, Clement re-set both their watches and returned his own to his smooth, brown wrist.

"Would have been on the Isle of Dogs this afternoon." He mused, following *Péage* signs for Paris. "Old Greenbaum missed out badly there..."

To Catherine these names were already faded, overlaid now by bright posters awash with azure skies, promoting homes on the windy Côte Atlantique.

Suddenly, a large, white Citroën drew alongside, laden with fragile, spinning sports bikes and bare feet dangling from its windows. The crowd inside waved and cheered at the striking young woman with the mane of auburn hair and were rewarded with a regal salute. Then they passed on.

"Sixty two... Pas de Calais... " She checked the Michelin map for their *département* number, but when she looked up, that car had gone.

"They'll get done for speeding," Clement said bleakly. "You'll see."

The autoroute meanwhile bore them through undulating copse-covered hills to spacious farmland punctuated by pylons and tiny, clustered villages, then on to the Valley of the Somme whose very name seemed to stir the wet mist and clogged, stinking soil of war. Also those feet from another time, the colour of clay, without skin, tucked up under stones, hard flints without cloth, without sinew...

Catherine shivered as concentration set Clement's face fast as the traffic increased near the *Périphérique*, and slowly they were engulfed on either side by endless bulk transporters... animal... vegetable... mineral...

the whole world on the move, it seemed, hurtling round in a fumy fog. Catherine gripped the map for fear of losing her place and her finger - gnawed down around the nail - carefully noted each exit sign.

"We need the *Porte d'Orléans*. There'll be a sign soon." She then panicked as half-hidden roadside directions appeared then vanished. A passing lorry driver stared in at her pale anxiety and then at her long legs entwined together like a plait. He made a gesture she didn't understand then, like all the others, was swept up in the man-made tide.

"Drancy." She announced suddenly, recognising the grimy sign from somewhere. White on navy, half-obscured by trees.

"What?" Clement barked, tight and tense.

"Nothing."

More livestock trucks shuddered by, stuffed with living meat half-strangled by worn ropes, tongues flailing, choking for water...

*

The second cargo that month seemed more crowded than the first, yet it was still a carefully counted one hundred victims who swayed and jostled together meekly in the darkness, where eight horses should be. Touching, breathing in each other's shallow breath, then with every lurch of the iron wheels, a sudden fall, and Joachim Kreisler, piano teacher from Nice's Mediaeval Rue Droite apologised profusely to his poor neighbour who'd borne the brunt of his weight.

Little civilities, incongruous but necessary, he felt, to preserve some degree of dignity, even in that stinking, frightened hole. And as his destiny bore him east, or was it north or west, along the rumbling, rubble track, he wondered numbly in his animal pain, where Joseph Weiss was now. Had his pupil's blood smeared Brunner's walls like his own? Had he also been dragged from desk to door by the scrotum, then whipped for names he wouldn't say. Then the pole worn so smooth just like the one his mother used to move her boiling washing about. Herr Doktor had liked his toy, but more than that, his status as '*Soldaten Käfer...* '

The big man sobbed silently in remembering. Amongst the cries and the dying, he heard again the sweet notes of the last scherzo as the Milice had invaded and fouled his music room, half-drunk on rain and wine... They'd called him 'pederast,' and now that sharp, little label dug deep into his neck...

Trapped in this heaving misery, he saw once more his beautiful ebony piano. How the narrow window's light had made it shine. And how the sixteen year-old pupil's long, elegant fingers had charmed its keys to sing...

*

The Orléans section of the *Péage* stretched out in front and the bulk carriers, concrete mixers, large cars, small cars, pillion riders and cyclists were all left behind. But it was another perspective that came to Catherine, and stayed too long. Railway sleepers and stones, not tarmac and trees. Wire and lights and the smell of rubber. Lookout towers, not freedom...

"Bloody caravans!" Clement was resentful now of anything else on the road. Spoilt by the spaciousness of it all.

"Services in forty kilometres." Catherine compensated as he pulled out smartly behind an unmarked lorry that had entered too quickly from the right. As for that animal transporter, she saw noses and tails squeezed through the cracks, and diarrhoea dribbling down its sides. Pembrokeshire sheep - mules and half-breeds, wethers, tups and killing ewes, rounded up from gentle fields to die under a Mediterranean sun.

She tried to turn round in her seat.

"Did you see that! She repeated its number plate until she found a pen in the glove box. "Poor little things."

Soon the grim cargo was just a speck in her mirror, out of sight but not out of mind, and the empty road was once more his. Lulled by the monotony of the new engine, Catherine reclined her seat, letting her hand dangle unthreateningly between her thighs. Then she began, softly at first, to re-rehearse her *ballade* of love.

*

The travellers were now well past Saintes, and the mist that had begun to blur land with sky, thickened as the silver Renault neared the Gironde. Clement duly flicked on the fog lamp and his stomach, unfilled by an earlier salad baguette, rumbled loudly,

"I could eat a bloody horse!" he announced, just under the speed limit.

"We're getting on." She tried, like she always did, to smooth, to assuage. Her map lay open at section 121 and she'd found Lormont which seemed a suitable place to stop. The thought of a dining room full of appetising smells and candlelit tables, spurred him on, almost into the rear of a Spanish tomato truck with inadequate lights.

"Fucking Dagos!" His face was pure anger as he crouched over the steering wheel.

Catherine applied deodorant under her shirt and then wiped the windscreen with a tissue. Next, she would sort out her eyebrows.

"At fifty kilometres an hour, we should be there by nine," she encouraged, noticing something familiar had drawn up alongside, making no effort to pass. "Clement! It's those poor sheep again!" Their bleating was muffled yet insistent, and the stench of urine pervaded the neat, orderly car. She swivelled her air vent in his direction.

"Thanks." He was still in a bad humour and not just because of the fog. "Fuck off!" He shouted up at the obstruction. "There's plenty of bloody road!"

As if on cue, a dark green deposit hit Catherine's window and trickled down to the ledge. Opaque become translucent bits of Welsh grass, as the truck sped on, followed by a police car's sudden siren.

Heard but not seen.

"Oh Christ. An accident. That's all we bloody need!" Clement's sourness was total. "There aren't any bloody signs either!" He frantically fiddled with the car's lights to make some impression on the road, but he and she were now enveloped in an eerie silence amongst invisible traffic. Marooned eight hundred miles from the cheery little Docklands home where Jasmine Khan and her Filipino partner lay comfortably ensconced on the moleskin sofa.

Clement tried the radio, but it only offered a crackling distortion of voices followed by what she felt to be a faraway, rhythmic stamping.

"Can you hear that?" She switched it off, but still the noise of running feet grew louder. More distinct, interspersed with angry oaths and the call of hungry dogs on the scent. "Oh my God!" As heavy reverberations filled her head from the dried, echoing earth. Portent of a famine to come while freebooters, mercenaries, men of the Church, thirsting for blood, gave out their hue and cry.

"Jesus!"

The car was off the tarmac, cushioned instead on roadside grass. And then as suddenly as that din had begun, all was quiet. As empty as the grave. On guard they sat, anxiously alert. A Henry Moore King and Queen in their silvery, metallic sarcophagus lined with vinyl.

Catherine was shaking.

"Look! Lights!" Clement suddenly craned forward. "Fucking

great!"

Sure enough, several coloured blurs pierced the gloom and the fog lifted. Instantly the evening sky was clear above urban and industrial sprawl. Also the thinning traffic heading for the *Autoroute de Deux Mers.*

"We've missed Lormont... but this'll do... Gradignan... *Zone Industrielle...* " Catherine still trembling, read diligently everything she could find. "We must have come over the river. Strange. I don't remember that." Then, amongst the plethora of billboards and flickering neon displays of furniture warehouses and wholesalers' showrooms, glowed a welcoming sign of the *Hôtel du Coq Rouge.* Safe harbour for commercial travellers plying their trade between north and south. Brand new, it was still set in sand, littered with builders' equipment. Constructed on the same treeless, inhospitable terrain that had almost given up the fleeing Mordiern Guyon to his pursuers.

*

Its foyer was stuffed with artificial plants of every description. Ivies, vines, palms and wide-leaved ficus creating a nest of silken green in which she and Clement stood momentarily disorientated. Judging by the quizzical stares of those in the small, adjoining lounge, tourists were rare. Especially before Summer. Catherine smiled politely at the receptionist, starched in dress and every movement. By comparison she felt unkempt and travel-soiled and wanted only to hide. Their booking-in was further complicated by the woman mistaking them for Germans.

Finally she plucked a key from a bank of hooks.

"*Numéro vingt huit. Avec douche. Deuxième étage.*"

Not a syllable wasted. She then pointed to the lift, and Clement strode forth clutching the heavy orb-like key ring. Their room was also strictly functional. Brown on brown - covers, towels, picture frames, horsehair rugs. Even the long curtains that shut out the darkening sky were patterned umber and the walls carpeted a warm caramel to deaden any sound.

It soon became filled with their things, kicked, thrown, scattered, not at all in their usual careful way. Anonymous become personal - his and hers inter-mingled. Then Catherine collapsed spread-eagled on the low bed, white and etiolated against the humus tones. But Clement in his boxer shorts, was more
taken with the notice behind the door than her uselessly provocative pose.

"Dinner's 'till ten. Let's get a move on!" He jogged into the bathroom while she still lay inert, listening for the sequence of minutiae that constituted his noisy ablutions. Sounds of paper pulling, of caps unscrewed, neck, armpits, groin, a foamy fart, detached and highlighted, but gradually lost as that mysterious sound of marching returned with yet more feet, more shouting in a language vaguely familiar, crowding into her head...

"Clement!" She screamed covering her ears, rocking from side to side. But too much water flowed in defiance of the bloodied sac, which had once contained him, and killed his mother just two hours after labour...

*

"You can't go down looking like that!" He was standing over her, sprinkled with *Homme Liège* and wearing a clean, white shirt. Catherine slowly slid to the floor, dragging the cover with her. "For God's sake, there'll be nothing left. You know how they stuff themselves over here." His face was darker now beneath the light, and his fingers tightened into fists. She knew that one wrong word, one false move, and those clever, selling hands would pump more unseen contusions beneath her skin.

"I'll only need five minutes."

51

"I'm going." His pouch purse swung like an incense burner. His jacket askew on his shoulders.

"Wait." She smoothed her hair, fastened her skirt then followed, as always. A veal calf to the long, sweet knife. "My shoes!" For her feet were bare. Then he suddenly turned, eyes on fire, quite at odds with his pale, new suit. He threw her the heavy dungeon key and it caught her knuckles. Brass on bone. An uneven contest. She let out a cry of pain.

*

Her unworn white shoes were on the wrong feet as they entered the dining room, hands lightly touching as all eyes were upon them.

"Seems to be the only watering hole around here. We certainly struck lucky." Was his public conversation, as he smiled at the young waiter who led them to their table still littered with another's remains. Assorted stains, crumbs and screwed-up napkins. And "*Merci*," as his chair was pushed in first before Catherine's. She gripped the room key in her lap while the *garçon* in tight, black trousers and matching waistcoat deftly cleared the debris with the grace and co-ordination of a dancer. He leant over, legs brushing. Clement touched his arm.

"You seem very busy," he said, The familiar '*tu*' was deliberate, and the Frenchman flashed a row of bright, even teeth, before waltzing away, tray aloft, leaving the couple in silence. Clement followed his every move towards the kitchen, until something else caught his eye. Small flames flickering on the ceiling in the far corner, behind a bank of plastic shrubs.

"Odd." He got up and sauntered over to investigate as the smell of roasting meat intensified amidst a series of sudden, sizzling explosions. "Hey! Get this! They've got a barbecue!" His voice carried over the cutlery clatter, and again, people stared. All except Catherine who scrutinised the menu to hide her embarrassment. "That's really neat."

But hardly neat was the end wall, out of the diners' view. It glowed vermilion streaked with dark, burnt blood, like the private insides of public lavatory cubicles, against which dripped and spluttered whole sheep and pig, touching shank, skirt loin and flank of horse, or was it beef, he couldn't tell. Flesh become food in the kissing flames. Fat to crackling to lodge between teeth and cause a mighty thirst. Perfect *Bratenfett* - far too good for soap or candles...

The heat drove him back as the fire increased, licking and circling, sometimes green, sometimes blue - like a living *Fauve* painting. Catherine ignored his swaggering return.

"I'll try it. You've convinced me." He flattered, tucking his napkin into his collar as the waiter hovered attentively, pencil poised. "But only if it's *très bien cuit. Comprends*?" He winked and the young man winked back, then turned to Catherine whose decision was delayed in horror.

"*Escalope de veau avec légumes*." She whispered her order.

Clement suddenly roared, tilting perilously back in his chair.

"You bloody cannibal!"

People stopped to listen.

"You have chosen well, Madame. The calf has been raised in - how shall I say - fresh air... " The waiter threw his arms wide, as if to embrace the whole of Limousin and Quercy, the Landes and Rouergue, then fetched a wine list.

"We don't drink, thank you." Catherine was down but not out.

"Oh yes we fucking do," Clement countered. "I think a nice, rich red would go with my horse." He gave a grotesque neigh... "Mmm, *j'ai tel envie du cheval!*" He laughed and coughed simultaneously. Meanwhile, the waiter had returned, his fly almost touching Clement's arm.

"*Numéro de chambre?*" He pressed closer.

"*Vingt-huit.*" The other's eyes invited.

"*Attendez...* " Then he was gone, but soon back, obviously neglecting other tables, and bearing a large, oval platter whose fibrous burden wept rivulets of blood into the surrounding garnish. Catherine's stomach heaved as it was set in front of Clement and the '*Medoc*' then opened. She suddenly got up and ran out, past startled buffet staff; her shoes adrift of her feet, while the waiter intimately filled Clement's glass. The Londoner stayed put, too settled to move. Besides, his mouth was busy, silenced by a young draught gelding from the Mayenne. The last offering from the doused and dying flames.

*

Meanwhile, above, in that quiet private room, Catherine lay surrounded by the litter of her city clothes, the bedspread taking what little warmth she had. Its short tufts became grass as her eyes closed. Hot, summer grass alive with rasping *sauterelles*, and the wild, overgrown cherry swayed their ripened bulbous drupes... Mordiern Guyon was panting. He parted the branches - his mouth dry. No spittle, no water from any source for this man on the run.

"*Je sui vo chevaleis... mais je seuil plus ne chant...* " His words seemed close, so close. Words she'd already sung before she could understand.

"*Pour ce que tuit me penser sons cesser... en vous amer... tresdont que premiers vous vi...* "

He knelt down, obscuring the light, his face full on hers. A young, strong face, but weather-beaten and edged by a clipped beard of Celtic gold. The dreamer's eyes met his, lodged between fair, curled lashes, and as he noiselessly shed his heavy cloak she made ready to receive him.

"*Ah... belle... passes en douceur...* " Quick bursts of breath engulfed her narrow, bruised hips that were lifted upwards to fuse and tangle with his chin. Then, his mouth was there with a soft and subtle tongue, as he'd been taught, tracing the unfamiliar virgin valleys, and like the cherry flower suddenly touched by the sun, she opened to a sweet succulence that he could not, could never leave...

"*Pulcele... O pulcele...* " He murmured, and faded as the moon rose to hover over the neon-lit commercial centre and a heavy dew veiled the uncovered window.

*

"For Crissake! Let me in!" Clement was pummelling the door and Catherine leapt in terror. She found her skirt, too quickly and put it on back to front, while her blouse collar's tag nudged her throat, and both arms were encased too tightly. A captive, she felt dizzy.

"Coming!" she mouthed, before he lunged into the room, soaked red with meat and wine. Every pore alight. Her shoes were in his way so he flung them at the television.

"This is the fucking life! Fucking great!" His body crashed on the bed and to her relief, lay instantly comatose, straight and rigid, like that verdigris sleeper, who on ordinary weekdays such as these, had the little coastal church in Manorcastle all to himself.

Catherine felt it safe to go and brush out her dishevelled hair, softly singing her dream lover's unfinished verse.

"*... Amours me fait desirer et amer, mais c'est si folettement que je ne puis ésperer...* " Then she remembered that he hadn't told her his name.

*

It was an altered Mrs. Ash who sat alone in the empty dining room helping herself to leftover coffee and unwarmed rolls - alone amongst tables heaped high with breakfast remains and muted, piped music coming from the bar.

She should leave him. Finally. Retrace her steps through the expanse of western France and north again. Leave him to his own devices and desires - for he had never desired her. The butter was hard and quarried into the bread instead of spreading, but the jam was the sweetest she'd ever known.

'*Confiture des Cerises, mûrit dans La Réole...* '

Catherine wiped her mouth and got up to pass the manageress with a brief greeting. The corridor outside the bedroom was blocked by cleaning trolleys and aproned women caught amongst billows of used sheets. Adjoining bedrooms were now clinically bare in the day's brightness - only their room held secrets and Catherine sidled in allowing the maids no glimpse, no inkling of what lay beyond.

*

After a brief stop near Carcassonne, Clement felt ready to drive again. The rest, on a scrubby slope under a plane tree had revived him, and soon the Docklands Renault was cruising along *La Languedocienne,* heading for Spain.

Sunshine from a cold, wide sky, made him squint, changing his profile from city slicker to anthropoid. Or so Catherine thought.

"I think the first European settlers might have come here." She observed, looking around at the scrubby hills. "*Homus erectus*. In caves, somewhere behind that lot."

"*Homus erectus*, eh?" Clement smiled, then reached for his sunglasses and set them on his nose. "Well let's hope this flat we're getting isn't some bloody cave. Greenbaum did say 'all mod cons.'"

"Meaning a tap and a hole." Catherine again scoured the dry, heaped hills of the Corbières to the right, and the flat, blue shoreline to the left. Then came a moment's panic. Where were all those houses to be sold? For there was nothing except an empty landscape as far as the eye could see.

North of Perpignan, the traffic increased, and the Londoners crawled nose to tail with other seasonal visitors, giving Catherine the chance to observe neighbouring privacies. Sleeping heads thrown back, open-mouthed. Arguments, eating, car games and, in a new Mercedes cruising by, a young woman was having her breasts fondled.

"Baccarès." She said blandly. "*Hypermarché.*"

A white BMW then drew alongside, where two tanned youths sat close, as one, their fingers interlocking on the wheel. Clement's shaded eyes left the road to dwell on their every movement. Music throbbed from a stereo. A rhythmic jungle beat pervading the English couple's quiet space.

"'The *Autoroute d'Amour*," she muttered to herself as Clement posed, tapped the beat on his wheel. Then as suddenly as they'd come, the young males were gone, in a screech of revs, leaving the foreigners in a cloud of exhaust.

Clement shouted obscenities, soon reverting to form. The fumes were choking and sweat trickled from his forehead like that barbecued meat. "Better give Rosa whatsername a ring when we next fill up." He coughed twice, looking grim.

"Tavernier." Catherine was good with names. She'd had to be in her job in case fertilised egg Jones was passed into vagina James.

"Watch out for a garage, then." He ordered, licking his salty top lip. "Looks like the whole of bloody France is down here. Doesn't anyone do any bloody work?" He hooted aggressively at anything that managed to scrape by.

"You've been given that rude sign four times now." Catherine felt distinctly uncomfortable and tried not to look anyone in the eye. "Petrol's on the right."

She was glad of a diversion, and checked again the outspread map whose red, yellow and green veins bisected the three valleys of the Eastern Pyrenees. "Only twenty kilometres." She added. "We're nearly there."

VIX

'That ye may eat the flesh of kings, and the flesh of captains, and the flesh of mighty men, and the flesh of horses, and of them that sit on them, and the flesh of all men, both free and bond, both small and great.'
(Revelation.19.v.18.)

"He's ours now." Girard led the way into the dark stable, whose narrow windows beamed the dawn light on to the row of ebony rumps of the horses. Then, finally the cream.

"Druide!" Mordiern called out.

"Ssssh!" The Whiteface glanced around nervously. "It is silence time remember?" But the mighty beast knowing nothing of such things, had swung round, loose in its stall, neighing and pushing its huge head their way.

"What did you call him?" The older knight then whispered in alarm.

"Druide. Robert Sagan who brought us here, had already named him after the stones at St. Gemmes, so he said. Why, what's wrong?" Mordiern offered his hand to the quivering, velvet-like muzzle.

"Never say that heretical word again," warned Corbichion as red eye met animal brown, and nostril breaths mingled, until other brothers joined them after Prime to feed and water their own. The moment for intimacy had passed.

"He must have a name." Mordiern protested.

"Like us at St. Loup, he becomes anonymous. Now then," the taller man leant closer. "Between dinner and nones we shall practise in the *enclos*. I will ask permission to be released from my other duties." He patted the mass of equine bone that determinedly faced the food store, all the while calculating his strategy for the sleeping hours between Matins and Prime.

*

Mordiern's stomach disagreed with the full meat meal set so early in the day. At home, in winter, no-one sat at table until dusk, and then only once the pigs had been bedded, the goats milked and the sheep penned securely against marauding wolves. Besides, much had occurred at the dinner to disturb his other sensibilities, apart from seeing how a penitent brother knight was forced to squat and pick his food from the floor.

Girard had sat opposite, a world between, but still while the priest at the Preceptor's table continued reading aloud from his text, he had felt the heat from those eyes, ever on his face, and the man's smile fixed despite his eating and drinking. No-one else appeared to notice, yet something warmed within the sixteen year-old. Something he'd neither given nor received from anyone his age.

He was blushing uncontrollably, his hand trembled on the knife. And worse, but mercifully hid from view, his young manhood stirred, remembering the recent, calming night.

*

Next morning, it was time to try the horse, and Girard authoritatively led him out. Mordiern then brought the blanket that served as his bed cover, embarrassed by the stallion's mottled penis lengthening below its belly.

"Put it on evenly," said Girad. "I've got him held." Brisk words to hide a sneaking smile.

Immediately the stallion began a dance of defiance - his huge, feathered hooves dangerously close. His member swinging, darkened by flies.

"I'll ride to the fore." The albino said. Then suddenly he was aboard, catching the horse unawares, his mantle billowing about him like a sail.

"Hey up!" He extended his hand to the boy below who had neither the stomach nor the experience to follow, but was not to be disgraced. He landed tight up against his partner, feeling even on that chill morning the other's welcome body warmth.

They circled this way and that, under the curious gaze of those planting in the kitchen gardens. First a walk, then a trot which soon became a three beat canter - a high, rocking gait that threatened to unseat the pillion.

"Hold me if you wish!" Girard called out, and Mordiern in fear and relief, obeyed, for he was unused to stirrup-less riding, and the ground was a man's height away. The horse took them out of the compound and along a woodland path framed by bright clusters of early leaves. Girard kept him on a firm rein, his thick neck arched high in front, with the undressed mane tossed by the breeze. Snorting thunder rolls, starting skittishly at the smallest thing - it felt good to be alive, and at one with so much.

"He has such a beautiful mouth." Girard relaxed the reins, and Mordiern, hearing those words so softly spoken, felt a momentary tinge of jealousy. "It's a wonder that old fool didn't ruin him." The other man in front bent his supple body low under the canopy of overhanging branches, at the same time keeping them from striking the boy behind. Then, they were clear with flat, green pasture either side of the path to Bellefois.

"We shall be guarding pilgrims first of all, because they are always easy prey." He half-turned, his face, dazzling like fine, blanched paper in the sun.

"What about widows and orphans?" Mordiern asked, for of all the many regulations and responsibilities set down by the Order, this seemed the most pertinent and what he remembered most.

"As we can." Girard smiled at his innocence and the pleasure of such comely company. "For I know you are a widow's son." The track narrowed into another copse, and they passed two peasants from the next commune fixing squirrel snares to the even lower branches of nearby beech trees.

"Miniver pelts." Mordiern said, trying to appear a man of the world. The men hastily gathered their sacks and scuttled for cover at the brothers' approach, not from any guilt, but fright at the apparition. A truly white man on a pale horse.

"You would relish your prize more if you had gained it honestly!" Girard called out, unabashed, and Mordiern couldn't help but marvel at his wisdom and courage. If the Order had shaped a man thus, he thought as they made a wide turn for home, then he could ask for no more.

X

"*Bienvenue à Collioure.*" The butcher's huge, ringless hand extended from a blood-stained, black sleeve. It was a massive appendage even for such a substantial woman, and not entirely free of mince trapped under the fingernails. A smell of stale meat accompanied her movements.

"*Enchantée.*" Her teeth were mere bone fragments. Her lips thin and dry.

"*Nous aussi. Us, too.*" Clement smiled with difficulty, then indicated Catherine. "Ma femme."

Black-olive eyes passed up and down her body, missing nothing. Her gaze rested on her breasts. "*Mon plaisir, Madame Ash.*"

"*Merci.*"

Then Catherine noticed in more detail what hung in her window.

The traffic in the *Rue des Templiers* drowned any further exchanges, as the cool, sea wind penetrated their travelling clothes.

"My English is not good." Rosa Tavernier raised her voice. "I also have a little of Italian *und irgen Deutsch...* " She suddenly stopped. "There is your apartment." She pointed to a grey stone portion housing two windows and two tiny, rusted wrought-iron balconies set above one half of the *boucherie*.

"It's pretty." Catherine lied, nervously, seeing how paint had peeled from the shutters and a tangle of old cables hung from the roof.

"I am *à côte*." The old woman indicated the two other, newer, wider windows alongside and unlocked the narrow front door on the street. "You have *une cuisine, salle de séjour, deux chambres, das Klosset und Dusche...* "

"Thank God for that." Clement fumbled in the dark for one of

Greenbaum's plastic wallets. He handed the woman a sheet of headed notepaper bearing his boss's signature.

"Ah." She had switched on the electricity and now studied the letter while Catherine picked up the old, damp junk mail strewn on the floor's dusty tiles.

"Yes. Harold Greenbaum. *Un Juif, n'est-ce pas*? He had my details from the *Syndicat... Venez.* Come this way... "

She led the couple up the tight, curving stairs, her wide dark hips filling the space, quite unrelated to the small neck and head beyond them. Suddenly, daylight flooded in as she forced open the old shutters, and in that uncompromising brightness, the Londoners could see that no-one had lived there for a very long time.

"*Viola*! And there are metres for water and electricity." The butcher was giving them little time to react. "When I receive *les factures* I pass them to you."

"Thank you." Clement said absently, casting about with an estate agent's practised eye.

"Remember, it is *me* you must pay!" Rosa Tavernier banged her chest, and then proceeded to un-jam the apartment's two inner windows. They crashed back against the shutters, and when it was safe to do so, Clement obligingly craned his head out over the second balcony as she tied back the limp, stale curtains.

"You have a good view, *hein*?" She said. "Whatever the season."

"Indeed." He replied, the wind trapped in his mouth, blocking his words, while Catherine seeing no respite from the depressing dinginess could only think longingly of what she'd left behind. Brown flowered wallpaper sagged from the walls and the bare light bulbs hung lopsided from black, twisted wires. The furniture - what there was – probably belonged to the dead long gone. The smell the same.

"What's that?" Catherine then spotted an old photograph in a pewter frame, mounted on the nearest wall above eye level. For a moment the butcher seemed discomfited.

"Family friends, that's all." She then quickly led Clement to the furthest rooms, out of sight.

Catherine meanwhile rubbed the photo's dirty glass to bring into focus an obviously prosperous middle-aged man, handsome and strong-featured with a small, fair-haired girl sitting on his knee. In the background, blurred and mysterious, stood what seemed to be a table bearing a game of chess in progress, set in front of a large, black grand piano. The child looked steadfastly at the camera, her puppy-fat limbs straddling the grey-suited leg. And she was smiling, proud perhaps of her new muslin dress extravagantly decked with sewn-on flowers. The man, on the other hand, seemed uneasy, so close to her warmth.

"*Le bourgeois et sa fille.*" Catherine murmured, hearing Rosa Tavernier's voice coming from the bathroom. She went to investigate.

"... *eau potable,* but never put so - *les serviettes - dans le W.C.*" The old woman mimed the removal of a sanitary towel and Clement averted his eyes.

"So this the loo?" Catherine peered down a stained hole at the top of three, tiled steps.

"Loo? Loo? What is that?"

"She means *toilette.*" Clement gave his wife a withering look.

"Ah yes. How shall we say - *fur die Gesundheitslehre.*"

"Hygiene," hissed Clement as they stared at each other, and he suddenly laughed to relieve the tension." As long as I watch the old trouser legs I'll be O.K."

"*Vraiment.* Now the bedrooms." The butcher revealed two small rooms shrunk by their bulky beds and heavy, wooden wardrobes, more suited to a larger house. The now familiar smell was more intense.

"I want to go home." Catherine said.

"For Chrissake!" Clement spat, trying at the same time to smile at their guide. "I've got a bloody job to do!" He puffed and reddened like he always did before he hit her. Instead he kicked and caught her shin.

Rosa Tavernier missed nothing.

"I am always near if you want something." She tapped the wall, carefully, as if it was no load bearer but served instead as her listening post. The couple voiced their thanks in unison, but the moment she left, they parted. Catherine to the window, Clement to the door. Too much had gone wrong for either to say what they really felt. She shivered and suddenly realised she'd not seen the kitchen.

"I'll unpack the car." He took the initiative. Something Greenbaum had always praised him for.

"Ought to go and look at the office. Are you coming?"

"I'm fine," she dissembled, for it was with a frightening sense of alienation that she stared at the teeming street below, drawing the crowds down to the harbour and its coloured boats perched on the shingle crescent of beach.

Maybe because people were laughing, roistering, holding hands, perhaps because their skins were already brown from the early summer that she felt so apart from their world. Skateboarders, dog walkers, two-to-a-bike, young fishermen, honeymooners kissing in a pony and trap. All lay busily beneath her as it had never been in Limehouse, and the remains of her happiness lifted away on the southerly wind, leaving her cold.

And then she saw him. An old man in grey. Motionless under the

Bar Tabac's coloured awning. What did he want? she wondered, as first he watched her husband burdened with luggage, and then fixed his pale eyes upon her balcony.

*

"Are you bloody well coming?" Clement shouted from the hallway, as she suddenly dived to one side, crouching on all fours. "What the hell's going on?" He was suddenly behind her with the dirty washing bag. She could smell his sickly clothes inside.

"Someone's out there. He keeps looking up this way," she said. Clement leaned over the balcony and checked in all directions, his smooth mop of hair blown back off his forehead. "I can't see anything."

"It's some old man. Are you blind?" Was risky, unchecked, and straightaway she looked at his hands.

"Sod it then." He sulked to the bathroom and closed the door behind him. It was safe, so Catherine got up carefully avoiding the window, yet curious enough to venture outside. The brightness struck her eyes to a squint, but everything had changed. Even that watcher had disappeared, temporarily obscured by people emerging with newspapers or choosing postcards outside. Then she noticed her husband framed by the doorway, stripped to inner-city white, clutching a towel. He also looked furious. A young man nearby wolf-whistled as her hair and skirt were lifted simultaneously by the sharp sea breeze, and three bronzed youths passing too close, with fish on their breaths, chanted lewd Spanish. One lingered to take her photograph, but mistakenly caught Clement instead - his face and fists purple because it was she, not him who was the object of desire.

"You bloody tart!"

She scuttled back to the apartment as people turned to stare, and so engrossed in her affairs was the old man inside the *Tabac* that he forgot to collect his change. Wounded, she just wanted to hide, to be invisible in the shade. To go home. Her hot hands received her rubbed tears. But Rosa Tavernier's hardened eyes were dry, and brightening with each purchase. She was more than happy with her lot, for between the *boucherie*'s slow-moving customers there'd been plenty of entertainment. To the next in the queue, after the English interlude, she handed over a huge cockerel, loosely wrapped in stained paper, its neck dangling free, maroon and yellow. Fat and blood blotched on its bald, quilted skin. Feathers, fleece or body hair was strictly *verboten* on any of her creatures, and under her own dark clothes, her pudenda was as hairless as that of an infant. Twice a week she smarted from depilatories, and twice a week the grey stubble re-appeared.

She'd glimpsed the *étranger's* smooth, toned chest between the marbled Charolais carcasses, and approved. Too many of his sex paraded their noxious, hirsute bodies past her window. Too many stopped to stare in, rubbing their fur against the glass. And if they entered to buy, she could not refuse, but did her business with eyes averted. The dead-weights gashed and ripped by the ceiling hooks swayed imperceptibly each time the shop door opened. Today, however, something else had triggered her memory, and now she could think of nothing else. Matted, bristly, overgrown... everyone's pubic hair was on the move, flattened and smooth. Disguised.

"*Bonjour Madame Piquet*," she acknowledged her latest customer. "*Un kilo de foie?*"

The other woman nodded.

Hers would be darker than the mouse-brown on her head, thought Rosa Tavernier as her hand slid into the slippery bank of offal and she did her best to smile. For this was a customer she could not afford to lose.

Mrs. Ash was different. At least her colours were decorative, unlike those that had once so shamelessly processed in front of her. The first, like all who followed, black and coarse. The most dominant element, once heads were bald. So much so, they'd made her physically ill, and she'd quickly sought permission to erase them. Once these threatening *Buschelen* had been shaved away, reduced to harmless little heaps, she could proceed with the job she'd been paid for.

With the till's eager jaws finally closed, the butcher turned the sign on the door to '*Ferme*' between the cluster of lambs' heads and brimming baskets of tiny, featherless songbirds. She could hear the *Anglais* slam the outer door and race up the stairs. Her weighted fly strips moved as though in a breeze. He was now in the bathroom, she could tell, shouting above the water that thundered first from the taps and then the cistern, swamping his trousered ankles.

"Fucking hole!"

Then silence as Rosa Tavernier crept up to join the newcomers with only thin plaster-board between them and her, wondering idly which of her nutritious stock would make the most appropriate welcoming gift. He finally emerged naked but hardly new-born, and from her hiding place Catherine could tell that the rage had passed.

"Talk about bloody Belsen," he murmured and sulked into the bedroom.

"Shall I leave a shadow or a flame?" Were words from some song, from somewhere. But it was another voice that seemed to make use of the former nurse's lips.

"What?" Clement barked, vigorously drying his behind.

"Nothing."

*

By playing baby again, a fresh, clean powdered baby, he managed to persuade Catherine to go with him to see the estate agency's office. So, armed with Greenbaum's street map, the young couple joined the crowds that browsed and clustered on the dusty gravel pavements. Overhead, a plethora of signs for hairdressers, Loto, restaurants and parking - all vying for attention against the still blue sky. All made her forget the old man.

"Twenty-three Rue d'Escabènes... twenty-three Rue... " Clement kept repeating, patting his pocket to check the key was safe. "Hell, these numbers are all cockeyed... twenty three... come on, come on... " So pre-occupied was he that he failed to notice the bleak *Fort du Mirador* set high amongst vineyards above the patchwork of new, orange roofs. He also missed the vast solid ramparts of *Le Château Royal*, and how Catherine hung back with little interest or involvement in his mission. But something else did catch his eye.

"Ah!" Clement stopped. It was the pink-domed bell tower rising erect, straight from the lapping waters of the *Port d'Amont*. "Very pictureskew, I must say." He smiled to himself, and one or two passers-by mistakenly said "*Bonjour*."

"*Voila!*" He then proclaimed. "We have the street." The hum of nearby voices coming from the beach grew louder. "Can you see it?" He strode up and down past doorways and windows, tall, narrow, wide, squat, squared and oblong, tiled, shuttered, covered by grilles. Every colour, it seemed. "Catherine!"

But she was gone. Drawn instead to the noise and to a huge white flipchart headed "*Soleils et Cendres*" which unfurled its pages like sails to the wind. She frowned in the translating.

"*Veuillez-vous ecrire un quatrain?*" A dark haired student interrupted, placing a thick felt pen into her hand. "*C'est à dire, quatre* vers... "

'Suns and ashes... suns and ashes... ' the title wouldn't leave her. She felt dizzy as the words flowed forth...

'Shall I leave a shadow or a flame?
And, marked by bruise, or burn
die, harbouring men's souls,
Crowded into mine?'

Then as suddenly as they'd been born, came the burial by thick, oblique lines, at odds with one so pale and slight. For something else had impinged on her mind above the clamour. Words from *le frère de la Milice du Temple*, tense and plaintive.

'Dont ma joie est fenie
Se pitié ne vous en prent
S'ay ne peor de buscherie
Ne de soleiller... '

Her hand obeyed in small, unjoined letters and when it was done, the crowd that had gathered fell silent. Several jostled to get closer, for amongst all the other scribbled outpourings, it alone seemed to cast a spell.

"Catherine!" Clement's frantic, faraway voice was unheard, as at that moment, deftly and surreptitiously, an elderly man had moved to the front and picked up the same black pen to begin its tremulous journey across the page...

'Ce fait doubler et embraser
Et aviver
Par desirer
Mon amoureuse ardure... '

Words of a tune he'd sometimes played. But ignorant of its origin. A clever hand, she thought. Tanned and well-shaped. His grey-suited back broad and strong; a girth curved like that of a draught horse. He was bald, but not cleanly so; grizzled without clear boundaries, and his neck concertina'd in dark folds above his collar. She noticed his shoes; more formal than anything else that walked the promenades, and buffed to a mirror shine bearing no trace of the day.

"*Ah! Il est amoureux!*" Someone laughed indulgently.

"One is never too old," smiled another, and on that bright, Mediterranean afternoon under a swathe of circling gulls, the young English woman felt a surge of happiness.

"For Chrissakes, Catherine! I've found it!" A foreign voice yelled from a nearby side street. Everyone, including the old poet, looked up at the intrusion.

"*Anglais.*" Said one.

"*Plus ça change...*"

XI

'Therefore rejoice ye heavens, and ye that dwell in them. Woe to the inhabitors of the earth and of the sea! For the devil is come down unto you, having great wrath, because he knoweth that he hath but a short time.'
(Revelation.12.v.12.)

The habitual and thus expected warmth of May had come late to Normandy, still cooled by westerly winds over the Cotentin. Undeterred and well prepared for the weather, the straggle of pilgrims from St. Lô had swelled to over two thousand by the time the Forêt de Fougères was reached. The two brother knights bringing up the rear, accompanied the singing, for the chants were holy, not of the flesh, and Druide, unaccustomed to such numbers kept his large ears on alert. These were men and women in equal proportion, mostly workers from the land, not yet impoverished. Also artisans who still held their *livres* and their faith. Enough to endure a summer's journey to Santiago di Compostella by boat to la Pointe Barbe, and thence south through Spain.

The duties of the Templars from the St. Loup Commanderie extended to the port at the mouth of the *Sèvre*. For brother Girard this was the tenth such excursion, since Malec el Asseref held sway in Palestine, and suddenly, despite the boy close behind him, felt his whole life bereft, without true song. Without close human love, reduced now to a ritual more tedious than the canonical restrictions at St. Loup.

He had once, upon return from the coast, taken the road westwards through Ernée, to see again the place of his unwelcome birth. But his father had long since gone as a hermit to the forest, leaving the Château near La Motte abandoned. Picked at, laid waste through the years by vultures of the air and the land. Nothing left for him, the son, to claim. Only the distant view to the Mayenne with mares and foals grazing on its nurturing pastures.

"Saint Nazaire will be six nights away at this pace." He complained, although careful to smile down disarmingly on those who still stared at his difference. "And then what? More menial *travaux de routine?* I haven't even got my viol. They took that on the first day."

Mordiern was discomfited to hear this fine man suddenly speak so. For him, to be a pilgrim guard was his first adult and selfless role within the Order, albeit less hazardous than any expedition of war. His dead father would have been proud of his noble mission, and the *croix pattée* emblazoned across his young shoulders. Besides the desire to please and appease the Holy Trinity with prayer, fasting and other abnegations of the flesh, extended now in a simple, loving way to his new companion.

"Can you make music then?" The young admirer asked simply.

The heavy sigh that followed was taken up by the evening breeze, and the older man's hand reached back to touch his.

"It never leaves my head." He said. "My songs are my soul."

"What songs are those?" The innocent's eyes widened. He knew little apart from the music of the Church and a few shepherds' snatches.

"Of love." The Whiteface stared straight ahead, still as a statue, before adroitly crooking his leg over the horse's withers and sliding to the ground.

*

The second day of June 1299, dawned fine and clear, with news of yet more outrages against the Jews of Paris, and further peasant uprisings in the Beauce. Yet Girard Louis Corbichon still did not know he had lost his mother. He stared out at the far ocean, seeing not how the calm, easy tide bore the weary pilgrims on their way, or how the morning sun cheerfully marked their fulsome sails. His red eyes reflected another world, of fire and flame, of chaos unending. Even Thomas Aquinas was long gone and of no influence now.

"The Apocalypse is upon us." He said, turning his melancholy away from the sea. "And they worshipped the dragon which gave power unto the beast... My young friend, it is time to depart. Will you come with me?"

Mordiern dropped the reins in astonishment, and the horse, instead of breaking free, stayed close. Now part of their future.

"To where?"

"South, to the Aragon lands, where the troubadour reigns. That is where my songs shall be reborn... " The albino's hands were shaking. He clasped the boy's shoulders as tremors more powerful than any of earth or rock, passed osmotically between them, fusing the two brothers of Christ into truly *frères du sang*.

XII

The *Maisons du Soleil* estate agent office smelt of old clothes, and the lights wouldn't work.

"Fucking great!" Clement pushed open the shutters and they crashed back against the wall. He was dirty already, and like the incoming tide in the *Crique de la Moulade*, he was brewing up for a storm. "Where the hell were you?"

"Sshh. There are people outside." Catherine closed the door.

"Well, they wouldn't bloody want what I've been lumbered with." He hauled the only piece of furniture - a huge desk - into the middle of the room, causing all its drawers to fall out. "Do something useful, woman," he ordered. "Take that For Sale sign down for a start. God knows what the old Jew paid for this dump... "

"There's some mail here." Her hand was disobediently deep in the letterbox. "Something from S.A.U.R. and E.D.F.... "

"What the fuck are they?" Clement now prone on the filthy floor, was checking the telephone cable.

"Bills." She said.

"Well they can go back to H.Q. for starters," he snapped, suddenly upright and dialling a random number. He put the receiver down smartly when a stranger's voice answered. "At least *that* works." He then prowled from side to side, from back to front, touching walls, hitting the ceiling, kicking loose floorboards. "Must make a list. Money no object. Give Greenbaum the works. What do you think? Shall I get in touch now?"

But Catherine faced the other way, watching the fading light as the sun passed behind west-blown clouds moving rapidly across the sky. She felt cold and the familiar figure hovering obscured outside could surely see that although Clement's ring was on her finger, she seemed to have no part of his life or his small ambitions.

Again the angry man tried the 'phone.

"One nine four four... " He stabbed at the dial, and she strained to hear any remotely London sounds. Only a disappointing crackling filled the room.

He tried again.

"Remember to drop the nought this time." She said, tonelessly.

"Still nothing doing. Damn and blast!"

"Best to leave it for tomorrow then."

*

Impatient horns and rough engines of home-going cars had meanwhile clogged the streets outside the office, and Catherine caught snatched conversations of hotel workers and shop assistants going home to nice kitchens and proper bathrooms. Occasionally people stared in before moving on. But that old man stayed, resolutely, blurred by the dirty glass.

"Everything will be better in the daylight." She lied, as a chilling draught from the door caught her unawares.

"You talk real crap sometimes." Clement said witheringly, locking up. He suddenly pulled down the Notaire's sign, snapped it in half over his knee and threw the splinters into the doorway. He then crossed the busy road to survey his future from a distance, vaguely aware of someone nearby hastening away.

"Mmmm. Maybe some possibilities after all," he told himself. Umber could be covered over with something brighter, and an awning would lend a summery ambience. The roof and downpipe seemed sound. Mere grime was nothing. The best thing of course was the large display window, soon to be crammed with properties. Commissions multiplied in his mind, and like a wilful child with its tantrum passed, Clement clapped his hands in glee. He continued walking backwards, still imagining, until several restaurant tables positioned on the pavement for the evening's diners, blocked his way.

"You wait. This is going to be *extraordinaire*!"

"Can we eat here?" Catherine asked, exploiting this rare nugget of good humour. Besides, she was as empty as a reed. "It looks quite nice." She ventured. In fact, the *La Fontaine* was also deserted indoors and its large, glassed-in menu featuring the local speciality of anchovies, too faint to read.

"Only if I can get pissed again."

"*Excusez-moi*." An elderly waiter had appeared as if dressed for a funeral. "Would you like to eat here?"

Catherine waited nervously for her husband to protest, but instead, and to her relief, he locked the agency's door then acquiesced with a polite smile as they were shown to their table. Its position enabled late strollers to share unembarrassed their harvest of salty anchovies bedded in a wild sea of curly kale and black olives halved. Clement soon drained the carafe of Roussillon Rosé, each time raising his glass to a new set of bemused onlookers.

"*Bienvenue aux Maisons du Soleil!*" He shouted, before sticking his tongue out at a curious family who lingered too long. A shiny, dark olive perched provocatively on its end, made them hasten away into the dusk. Meanwhile, that old man of the shadows, camouflaged by the poor light, saw how she toyed with her tiny, headless fishes, leaving them untouched. Another ruse with olives came to mind. One he'd tried many years ago... and then of course there'd been the balloons... and the bets on the soldier beetles... his speciality. All tricks, all ploys, except for the legacy they'd bequeathed...

"I think you've had enough." She said to Clement, crushing her pink napkin deep into her unused glass. "Let's get back."

But to where? To what?

Her tone had suggested a home. A welcoming room, a generous bed, not what the Rue des Templiers offered. But it was to there that they returned without stopping at any of the bright pavement bars, unaware of their following companion.

*

By ten o'clock the next morning, with a bold *Maisons du Soleil* advertisement in *L'Indépendent,* Clement was feeling even more optimistic. His files lay in place on the agency's desk and a wiry young man in blue overalls was busily fixing light switches into the walls. Besides this, the telephone engineer had agreed to call at midday, *en route* to Port Vendres. The afternoon would be used to contact various builders to offer renovation deals, buy a camera and telephoto lens plus four display boards and a fax machine. Tomorrow would see the search for a photocopier. These things engrossed him, and the list grew ever longer, spawned of impatience while Catherine lay stretched out in sleep, slightly snoring in the darkened apartment.

More stationery, files and folders, stamps and envelopes. New chairs and a square of Moorish carpet... Ah, and a palm or something green and succulent to tempt the browser. Yes, the theme would be green... Clement tilted back in a chair taken from the flat, his biro clenched determinedly between his teeth. He must check the banks for the best loan deals for his clients, and find out, unobtrusively of course, what properties the local *Notaires* had on offer. For he was nothing if not a master poacher. And where other than at *Maisons du Soleil* would prices be lower?

Greenbaum had already bought space in the UK's Sunday papers highlighting bargains along the Tech, Tet and Agly rivers that met the Mediterranean near Perpignan. It was up to the inventive Mr. Ash to lure northern sentimentalists further into the arid Aude hinterland where ruins with possibilities awaited. There was little point in including the Côte Vermeille, besides, viewing on its choked roads would be off-putting to even the keenest speculators.

Clement smiled, and the electrician smiled back. No, most of the *Maisons du Soleil* properties would be secreted in tiny hamlets, or hilltop villages, locked in ancient time-warps, cocooned from all cares, except taxes and utilities, for whom the comforting Eurocheque was no longer acceptable.

He would have to detail some guidelines for new buyers...

"*J'ai fini.*" The workman flicked through all the switches before collapsing his metal toolbox, and taking an Agency card for the invoice. They shook hands, and it was then that the estate agent noticed the boy's smell. A tropical musk of animal undergrowth. His grip lingered, and the lad decorously lowered his gaze.

"*Mille remerciements.*" Clement beamed. "*Si vous connaissez des gens qui...* "

"I have a little English - from school," the other admitted, withdrawing his hand.

"Well if you know of anyone who's looking for a cheap property, I am here. *Ici.*"

"I will ask."

"Your English is pretty good you know." Clement flattered. "*Au revoir* for now." He followed the Frenchman's neat figure out to the street, noticing how the blue cotton fabric rucked up tightly between his buttocks, and how nimbly his young legs entered the van.

*

The sun basked high overhead, ruthlessly exposing the shabby stucco walls and grimy ledges, but Clement felt fulfilment. His old instincts were returning, and the adrenalin flow of his Docklands days delivered a vision that could not fail. Meanwhile, the octogenarian now sipping his regular *chocolat chaud* outside the *Café Regina*, mused on events so far and how the Englishman was showing his hand too soon. He could never tolerate the way one male of the species can sometimes look at another... His thumb pushed his drink's cold, milky skin to one side and he drained his cup in one draught. Then he stood up. Solitarily out of place amongst the casual student groups who laughed and joked with the abandonment of youth. The estate agent brushed past him on his way to the counter, but it was only a ghost's shadow that momentarily touched and turned away into the sunshine.

*

Fortified by two cherry tarts and a can of Coke, Clement rolled up his sleeves and began to clean his new workplace. The walls immediately brightened under his wet, soapy cloth, to a soft grape green, restful on the eye.

"Lampshade, desk light... " He scribbled the words, dripping dull water on to his list... "Waste bin... in tray, out tray... good, better, best. B*on, meilleur, mieux...* " He was almost singing. Things were looking up. And still Catherine slept unremembered.

The desk seemed already quite business-like by the time the telephone engineer called, exactly as the *Église de Notre Dame des Anges* pealed midday. The grey-haired man deftly dismembered the phone's mouthpiece and examined the connections, squatting agilely on his heels.

Once again, blue overalls seemed *de rigueur*.

"*C'est pas grave.*" He mumbled, straightening up. "Just wear and tear."

"*Good.*" Clement marvelled at his dexterity, and after a brief call to Greenbaum's answerphone, all was in order. "I now need a fax to make life easier...."

"Fux, Monsieur?"

The younger man then grinned poor teeth from ear to ear. "*Ici?*"

Clement ushered him to the door convinced he had drink on his breath, and watched him slap his thighs in mirth all the way to his truck. One or two passers-by stopped as if wondering what could possibly be so amusing about that still drab, empty office.

*

Catherine meanwhile dreamt on through the noonday carillon of bells and echoing traffic noise, with her mouth open and arms splayed out above her head. Dark inkblot bruises sheltered under each armpit, and her hair aflame, left her face as exposed as a bleached pebble in the light of the journeying sun.

Then she stirred.

"Mordiern!" Her lips moved in half-sleep on the name he'd never given. "*Me porroit venir,*" she sighed, opening her wide, hazel eyes and seeing instead, the swaying light bulb, host to several dusty tendrils. But there was no more sleep, for his breath was imposing on hers, panting, running, gasping, through dry, fallow fields and brittle, fire-dry copses. Over spent riverbeds, skirting hamlets hungry for news, eager for reward. Her heart pumping his very fear as he crouched down, flattening himself amongst figwort, fennel and wild clary, mindful of any traitorous breaking twig or startled lark whenever a horse and cart trundled by...

Never his horse, the ghostly Druide, foaled near the ancient stones at Sainte Gemmes. No longer his warm grass breath, instead the hot summer wind brushing his newfound beggar's clothes. But better to be *un mendi* than a *Chevalier du Christ*, and fodder for the flames. Wiser to keep his own company, trusting no-one with his story. He had kissed his belt farewell and buried it, complete with that strange, central image of Baal, deep in the light soil, as the same sun that had scorched his back now heated the land from the Golfe du Lion to the Charente, rising a little higher each day over the southerly Albères, to its apogee.

*

The floor felt warm under Catherine's feet, by the open window. She felt dizzy, exhausted, and unaware that her short, thin nightdress barely veiled what her observer had expected all along, from the street below.

Despite the dismal bathroom, and lack of storage space for her few belongings, she washed and dressed with care for her first day of freedom. Loosened from Clement's plans and uncertain moods, she took longer than usual over her hair, braiding a thin plait into each side, identical to Claude Lorraine's *'Anchoress of Lacaune,'* once seen in her teens at the Louvre. Then lilac leggings, which sculpted every bone and muscle, topped by an outsize jumper as a precaution against the stiff breeze vigorously borne in by the sea. She slowly pirouetted in the only stained mirror. *Vogue* poses with leg drawn up or draped around the other. Chin tilted, lips pouting, puckered, come-hither. She'd survived and felt hungry enough to go out in search of breakfast.

*

Lured by the smell of coffee at the *Bar Majorque*, Catherine chose to sit at one of the tables that unevenly edged the busy pavement. Her clothes had felt wrong the moment she'd stepped into the sun. Imprisoning her in heavy wool and polyester, so carefully chosen in another climate.

"Madame?" The voice behind suddenly ended her warm reverie. She looked round at the chairs behind and saw it was him. The same person who'd written that poetry by the beach. Now full face and further coloured by small red capillaries that criss-crossed his cheeks. His almost colourless eyes lay deep set, like two pockets of un-melted ice against his weathered, earth-brown skin. A mask of clay, pitted and cracked, not like her delicate porcelain knick-knacks now stored away. This had been buried, dug up, exposed against the sky-blue, open-necked shirt. A harmonica jutted from his top pocket. Its chrome end winking at her in the sun.

"You are staying in my sister's apartment? 8, Rue des Templiers?" He enquired in perfect French. Catherine blushed at his use of the 'tu.' Although she was no longer a child, he was nevertheless, a stranger.

"You mean Madame Rosa Tavernier? "

"The very one. "

Perhaps they'd had a different parent. There were no similarities whatsoever.

"I'm afraid my French isn't up to much yet." She managed to reply, aware that his gaze was fixed on her legs. She crossed them beneath her as if to hide them.

"And my English is also not good. *Vielleicht* I can improve." He stood so near she could see the weave of his suit. Then came a silence she couldn't fill. "It's very good to finally meet you." He suddenly proffered his hand. Tool of a varied life, some said, and like his life, calloused underneath, enveloping hers. He bowed, then vanished, absorbed into the ranks of lunchtime shoppers and lovers come south from colder less voluptuous parts.

Catherine returned to her gilded croissant on its white tissue bed, but her appetite had gone, so she threw it down for the bold, urban sparrows to fight over. She then headed for the Church and its pink cupola'd bell tower, wondering vaguely why the butcher hadn't mentioned she had a brother in the same town. Also, why he'd dropped in what had sounded like a German word. Just like his sister.

*

The parish church, *L'Église de Notre Dame des Anges*, abuts on to the Boramar plage, one of the small inlets which intimately pockets the sea for paddlers and nervous swimmers. Sheltered here, the currents are regular and undisturbed, but still the secretive tide lays claim to various bright rubber playthings as gifts for its more favoured southerly shore, Bejaia, east of Algiers.

Léon Tavernier saw how the girl in his sights chose to walk along the concrete ledge nearest the sea, and how her long limbs had covered the ground with the poise and balance of a dancer. He'd seen white legs like that before. Not freely pacing as the herds on the *Camargue*, but huddled and trembling, urinating in fear, like all animals in transit. He smiled at the memory, still fresh. Also, the smell...

Her hair meanwhile, blew free, un-entangled between the plaits either side, and he sighed the despair of one born too soon to ever lodge in her thoughts, and too old to recall the youth that she now possessed and so cruelly flaunted.

*

Mass had just ended, and a small group of women in black emerged into the sunlight. Catherine entered the same way, down the damp stone passageway into the holy cavernous womb where incense still hung heavily in the air, and candle clusters wavered on the breaths of rapid prayers.

But this was no place for him. The man from Marseilles should never have come, for he could no longer look upon such things or any other outward flame. Only her brazen, fiery hair, which one day he would surely bind around their bodies... He watched from afar as someone's paid-for candle illumined for one shaming moment, the massive gilded cornucopia that surrounded the altar. Angels and prophets, the Virgin and Child, slayer and slain all startled his failing eyes. He turned away, but when he looked again, others stood in her place. Strangers.

The light had gone, and in the dark, the void of sickly sweetness, there was only the shuffling of feet on the old stone flags. Suddenly he recalled how Hauptsturmführer Brunner had once flattered him after a busy and successful operation.

"Herr Doktor Ausdauer". He'd said, meaning 'Doctor Perseverance.' Thus making his sister not a little jealous. Now, having lost Mrs. Ash, that compliment came encouragingly to mind.

*

While Clement, aided by a dictionary and Greenbaum's list of commercial terms, was ordering a computer and keeping an interested eye on the young signwriter outside, Catherine had, by chance, discovered the town's market. She browsed amongst the succulent dunes of peppers and aubergines - yellow upon green, red upon gold. Her fingers stroked their warm, ripe contours, touching the soft flesh under taut, velvet skins. Léon Tavernier, missing nothing, felt himself quicken with each caress. His old thin blood drained from his head and he had to suddenly find refuge on a brick palm tree base nearby, as perspiration and excitement gilded his cheeks. His quarry finally dragged two heavy bags of produce back to the apartment, and Rosa Tavernier came out to greet her still parting a chicken from its wings.

"I have something for you." She returned with a heavy newspaper parcel that released a slightly fatty smell.

"*Bon appétit.*"

Catherine felt instantly nauseous, but smiled all the same, and as she turned the key in the lock, the young artisan in the Rue d'Escabènes was finishing the final large, bright letters of *MAISONS DU SOLEIL*.

*

By late afternoon, the estate agency looked ready to do business, decked out with properties highlighted in bold fluorescent pen. Inside, the telephone was ringing its new, updated tone.

"'*Maisons du Soleil.*" Clement answered immediately, sounding proud. His French strong. Keen. "Welcome, Madame Vilalongue... " He scribbled her name with the receiver cocked between ear and shoulder, as he'd learnt to do in London. "So, you've an old house for sale near Fanjeaux, yes? '*La Récompense?*'"

"*Oui.* It's been in my family for years, but now I have to sell, because... "

"I'm very, very interested," he interrupted. Then, with detailed directions also written down and his promise to be there tomorrow at 2 p.m. he swivelled round triumphantly in his chair. She could have gone to any of the *Notaires* or other estate agents. But no. This was surely to be the first of many enquiries from the natives themselves.

The young signwriter outside the window was now stretching up full length, and Clement couldn't help but stare. How he enjoyed the toned, tuned physiques of working men, and had always taken the longer route to the Holborn office simply to pass those building sites and their gangs of navvies, idling in the sun. "Gods in their Heaven." He'd say, slowing his car to a crawl, wishing he were amongst them instead of flaccid Greenbaum and the repellent Miss Bourton.

Noah Bouhamiet then stepped nimbly from his ladder, and Clement was there on cue to press him to a cup of coffee.

"OK," the other replied, standing back to check his handiwork. A few pedestrians joined him to stare up at the brand new name, shielding the sun's glare from their eyes.

"That looks cool," said an English teenager, as he threw the empty paint cans into his van with the abandon of one who has the rest of the day to himself. Clement could tell he was bronzed all over, from mixed parentage and a Mediterranean life. The boiler suit fitted like a second skin with, he suspected, nothing on underneath. He filled the electric kettle and plugged it in.

"*Do you have a wc?* The twenty year-old suddenly asked without inhibition.

"Of course. Follow me." Clement led the stranger into a small storeroom and pulled a sliding door open.

"Thanks," The signwriter squeezed past him gratefully, and the smell of leaded paint filled Clement's nostrils. He waited within earshot. It was this aspect of life in the Gymnasium that he missed most of all. The shared intimacy of bodily functions, but here, his companion was silent. At the pull of the chain, Clement hurried back to the office now full of steam. Noah Bouhamiet emerged, pulling up his zip then perched with legs apart on the desk corner. Clement passed him a paper cup of instant coffee imported from Chute Street and a *Petit Prince* biscuit, noticing how tightly his *bleu de travail* clung and how obvious things were in the fly area. Then he lounged back in his swivel chair, hands firmly on the arms, enjoying the gentle pull on his hips.

Suddenly, he sat bolt upright. Someone was peering in between the property sections on display. The eyes, hard, cold. Fixed.

"Pah! He's just an eccentric." The signwriter also turned, drained his flimsy cup and crushed it. "Don't worry about him. He's old. The butcher Tavernier's brother."

"Really?"

But the moment Clement got to his feet, that same window was instantly clear, as if the *voyeur* had been a ghost. Another Tavernier perhaps, if this sister was never married.

"*À bientôt*," the other man grinned, opening the door to the street just as the telephone intruded again, giving the Londoner little time for regrets. This time, his caller was a widow near Quillan with no issue to inherit her small house with an adjoining stable. It was for sale to the first offer over 60,000francs, and if that failed, it would go to auction.

XIII

'And the fruits that thy soul lusted after are departed from thee, and all things which were dainty and goodly are departed from thee, and thou shalt find them no more at all.'
(Revelation.18.v.14.)

The summer sky above the Col des Auzines had turned during the course of the close, limpid morning, to an ominous lividity, dulling all but the strongest earth colours beneath. From somewhere far away the thunder's murmur threatened the skylark's song as it fluttered high above the tall grass like a remnant of bonfire ash not heavy enough to fall.

"If only that were my voice." Girard donned his mantle and began combing through the long beard tangle that now reached past his chest. "Just think what I could pen for it... " He looked at Mordiern who still lay sleeping amongst the purple larkspur and maiden pink; wild garlands round his golden head and limbs so straight and strong, even in repose. The young man's nostrils quivered on each breath and once his fingers moved as though on an instrument. Such beauty undefiled, thought Girard, for he had never known love for any woman nor cast his eyes with any interest their way.

"*Bel et bon sans folour, tresdont que premiers vous vi...* " The Whiteface sung softly, and his fellow traveller stirred, imagining in the seconds before waking, that he stood once more with the small group of worshippers in Manorcastle's simple church by the sea.

"Time to move on." Girard leant over him, holding Druide away from eating yet more grass. "We must try and reach Saint Cernin by nightfall. Besides," as he helped Mordiern to his feet, "this is no ordinary storm." The man from Mayenne knew only too well what that heavy, quiet air could deliver, and quickly turned their mount in the direction of the *Pic de la Vièrge*. Both sat close, hungry and unrefreshed by sleep, letting their bodies slump and roll unobserved, as suddenly a lightning spear cracked the gloom overhead.

They sprung bolt upright, taut as lute strings, muscles flexed in readiness. Even the birds were silent now in the lull, attending to their fledgling young deep in the hiding scrub. For this was higher than the vine terraces, beyond any human dwelling where banks of limestone scree left narrow, treacherous paths rattling under the four huge feet. The thunder came, with an earthquake tremble that seemed to rock the ancient hills, reverberating its warning to their unplumbed depths below.

The horse threw up his head in terror, lifting his forelegs momentarily from the ground. Mordiern screamed, seeing the sharp drop away to the left, studded by large, hostile stones. He clung to the other man for his very life, as rain fell in leaden drops wetting their bare, gripping hands and sealing their mantles around them like shrouds. Suddenly they were past that treacherous col and following the track down to the settlement at Ansignan, blurred by the deluge.

More thunder, more schisms in the sky, and ever closer the dramatic, electric charge. A shepherd's simple *cabane* – open-sided out of the prevailing wind - appeared set against an outcrop of small firs.

"A miracle." Girard first crossed himself then urged their mount towards it before tying him up close. "Come." He guided the young man in to the shelter that still held a certain cloying sweetness. The smell of fleece shorn on the transhumance brought back memories too poignant for the other to put aside. Too personal to share.

Mordiern began to cry. Tears joined his other wetness, welling and falling the length of his downy cheeks. He had left two safe havens like a sleepwalker abandons his bed, and now feared what awaited. He sobbed and shivered, ashamed and vulnerable as Heaven's wrath beat on the walls and a secret, calming embrace contained him.

XIV

As was his custom each Wednesday afternoon, Léon Tavernier took himself out of the town and up the busy main road towards Banyuls-sur-Mer. One hand held his stick, the other a deep, canvas bag. His burnished leather shoes glowed below each trouser leg, and as he walked, his bowed head was focussed on nothing else. He turned right just before the *Musée* sign, into a long narrow alleyway darkened by high boundary walls and strewn with rotting produce. The *Rue des Jardins*.

A still, fetid air hung trapped, unmoved by any offshore breeze or mountain wind, another world away from the moving holiday traffic that admired the blue against blue of the open sea and sky. Courgettes, flattened by bicycles littered the gulleys and blackened tomatoes lay squashed amongst the cobbles. The former doctor used his stick to clear a yellowing cabbage from his path and other remains that threatened his pristine shoes.

His tall gate set within a walled arch was marked L.T.in black ink that had run. The wood had jammed tight, swollen by the warmer weather, so he kicked it with the vigour of a younger man, taking care not to damage his toecaps. The gate swung wide open to reveal his private kingdom. His *'Jardin du Paradis'*.

Neat rows of every conceivable vegetable plant stretched away into the sloping distance. One texture tumbled on another, and the whole luxuriant spectacle was barricaded by high, wattle fencing from the rest of the neighbouring plots. Parallel drainage channels bisected the land barely separating one species from another. Herbs of every size and colour gave up their heady scents as he brushed by, and giant marrows slumbered where the ground burned hottest, immovable under his stick. Here, his purple aubergines lay sun-bloated, larger than those Mrs. Ash had ever stroked. She had seen nothing - yet.

He pulled out an old chair from the tin *appentis* and sat in its shade with the vine behind softly framing his head. There were no qualms about the origins of this particular piece of provincial furniture, with its simply turned legs now chipped and scratched, for he had made doubly sure that no homosexual had sullied any of his rewards. Léon Tavernier's colourless gaze roamed from the furthest bed bordered by a curtain of bleached, dry reeds, to the nearest, thick with haricot bushes thriving in the dry, stony soil.

"I shall bring her here." He said to the pretty blue butterflies that had trespassed on to his shoelaces. Then he killed them, one by one, so they were nothing more than smudges of dusty cobalt, to be painstakingly removed with his handkerchief. "She will like my things." He got up and pulled a short knife from his pocket. One he had used many times before, initialled J.K, and as the young woman slept peacefully through the warm afternoon, the *cultivateur* began severing brittle heads of thyme for his sister's sausages. He also chose a cauliflower for Mrs. Ash. The biggest he could find, whose absorbed warmth would last all day and who knows, he wondered, also through the night. It went carefully into his bag. This done, he kicked away a large brick lodged near the gate, and instantly a surge of bubbling water covered his feet.

"*Gott verdammt!*" The words spat from his mouth as he stepped aside. The narrow torrent raced down between the rows before diverging horizontally to saturate everything in its path. The earth was changed from light to dark in a moment, and loose dead leaves were carried away with other spent detritus towards the hidden stream behind the reeds.

The *jardiniers*, mere mortals amongst such splendour, were permitted this irrigation once a fortnight and these were the days he liked best, when change was swift and efficient, cleansing his paradise of all things frail, without function. Thus satisfied, he wedged the bung back in place and went to dry his shoes beyond the shadow of the shed.

*

Clement strode back to the flat in a state of euphoria, not felt since Greenbaum had first honoured him with the *Maisons du Soleil* brief. Despite one or two delays, things were definitely on the up, so much so, he courted everyone he passed with a cheery "*bonjour*", and if receptive, they were given the small, glossy card with the glowing sun in its top right corner. He even passed one on to Rosa Tavernier as she moved with reverential stillness amongst her meat, parcelling up the cheaper animal parts for the local workers' evening meals. They formed the bulk of her clientèle, that is, before the camping and other self-catering hordes arrived.

"*Merci.*" She said, spoiling it with a blood-stained finger. "I have given your Mrs. Ash a little something... it will need much - how do you say - in the hot water?"

"Boiling." He obliged, keen to leave.

*

"Hi!" His three leaps soon covered the dark stairs towards the apartment. "Anyone home?"

"Home he calls it. Jesus." Catherine sat facing the window plucking her eyebrows.

"It's going great!" Clement threw himself down on the threadbare sofa, and his executive case on the floor. "Got a full day tomorrow. Out looking... Hey?" He suddenly remembered. "Have you had a present recently?"

Catherine distrusted his *joie de vivre*, thinner than rice paper. It was best to be deaf as he rarely pursued things. But not this time. This was to do with his stomach.

"The butcher gave you something. Where is it?" He was already in the kitchen, slamming drawers, crashing cupboards. "Well?"

"I couldn't face it... " The tweezers took her skin instead. "Ouch!"

"For fuck's sake, I'm starving!"

She pointed towards the bedroom.

"Underneath the bed."

"You stupid cow! That's our dinner." Clement was full stretch and straining at the package. Its weight caught him unawares and fell to the floor, unravelling as it rolled. A large, frightened animal eye met hers, then the rest. Skinned, pink muscle of a lamb's head.

She screamed.

*

The honeycombed streets were at their quietest at dusk, after the promenades and plages had cleared of lovers and plastic-bucketed young explorers. After all the gaudy windsurfing gear had been finally strapped to foreign cars. In pavement restaurants waiters obsessively smoothed down tablecloths, re-arranged chairs and set candles in place for the evening trade. Monsieur Basile of *Chez Basile* hovered over his canvas boundary, and Catherine saw how a careless, ochre smear stained the back of his otherwise white shorts. Some diners smiled as she passed, but others puzzled by her expression, stared after her. A face so grimly pre-occupied was rare in their convivially opportunist world, and at odds with her other loveliness. But she was on the run, in step with the Knight of Christ, to exorcise the last hour from her mind and what Clement had made her do.

The small *Tabac* kiosk on the corner however, was open and, rather than miss any custom, however small, the *propriétaire* was eating at the counter amongst the clutter of key rings, car stickers and slightly curling postcards. The doctor sniffed the air with distaste. Nevertheless he bought a packet of panatelas and crossed the road to avoid the *boules* players who crouched seriously on the gravel patch next to the Fire Station. They'd soon be gone, to later reconvene in the dark, under street lamps, to finish, like him, their unfinished business.

His gift weighed heavily, just clear of the ground, and he was almost in the *Rue des Templiers* to deposit the herbs with his sister, when suddenly his heart leapt. Mrs. Ash was almost upon him, her cardigan loose around her shoulders like softly folded wings. This wasn't what he'd planned at all, but he composed himself sufficiently to block her way and reach into his bag. Thus the substantial vegetable was between them, and Catherine stared as it lay quivering in his hand.

"*C'est pour toi.* For you."

She looked round, cornered, and tried to sidestep into the road, but a hooting moped forced her back.
"Specially chosen," he added. For a brief moment he touched her arm, and his bleached eyes allowed her no escape as his thumbs gently parted the enclosing leaves. "Look. *Volkommen.*" He thrust it forwards. This was foliage not skin. A crown of florettes, not gristled lamb's head. No dreadful fear. She took it and politely thanked him. His second foreign word – definitely German – lodged in her mind.

"I have more. Many, many more. In my garden of Eden there is something of everything."

Catherine then noticed his wide, gold wedding ring.

"Your wife must be pleased then," she said.

He was silent, and then in that awkward void she suddenly realised he was the same man in that old photograph. Although time had coarsened and eroded those prosperous bourgeois looks, the gaze remained unchanged. She was held, like those dying flies on the butcher's syrupy strips, unable to tear themselves away.

"Would you like to see this Paradise?" He asked, and she saw how it was only his tongue that moved, appearing and disappearing between his lips. Reptilian and shiny from its dry skin cave. "It will give you much pleasure, *je te garanti.*"

There was no obvious reason to resist for every second now seemed to draw her away from her other existence on an ever-quickening tide.

She nodded acquiescence, and felt herself blushing.

"M*ercredi prochain* I will be there." Léon Tavernier smiled a set of carefully crafted, resin teeth.

"Always *mercredi* whatever the season." But it was now that he wanted her. Now, when he desired her downy skin that trapped the sun like a butterfly's wing. However, despite his dreams, the gardener had other commitments. Besides, he needed time to prepare.

"You will find it along the *Rue des Jardins*. By the *Musée*. And bring a basket." His pale eyes were alight, and his breath came in short, excited bursts. Then he noticed her soft, suede pumps and the legs above which his empty hand ached to follow to the source. Instead it went safely in his pocket.

"The ground is dry and rough there," he added. "You will need shoes like so... " pointing to his own, narrow and shining. Coffins, she thought. Identical to those in that old photograph.

Suddenly, strong gusts blew in from the sea, stirring the plane tree leaves above and covering his feet in a film of dust. "*À toute à l'heure, mon papillon.*" He bent down, and his old blood until now, sluggish in its silent phase, filled his head.

Catherine left without looking back. Better to bask in another's longing, than see a man old enough to be her grandfather, struggling to reach his feet. On a whim, she took the road up towards the gaunt, clustered *Palais Royal*, followed by the breeze freed from the narrow streets below.

*

The curving tarmac ended at the sprawling fortifications that overlooked the town and interrupted the sweep of land from mountain to sea. Always the same backdrop of dark scrubby peaks impinging on the sky and dwarfing the latest orange ribbons of new villas that threaded their way past the vineyards. But she had no desire to climb, to explore, to see the view beyond into Spain. Other things awaited, vague and unresolved.

Several gulls swooped low for picnic crumbs, grumbling in fractious tones, as Catherine, still clutching the gift, settled herself on the hard, stale grass. She could see the Rue d'Escabènes winding round near the church and, using the *Confiserie's* awning as a guide, could pick out *'Maisons du Soleil'* without the slightest interest. That world was fast slipping away. His world that had once so impressed in the courtship display with weights and pulleys to build him up and bind him down, for others, not her. And finally, the loveless bed. Only the songs she'd learnt at choir remained, and now she sang, to re-affirm a memory, shielded by the huge arrow-slit walls, harbour of other distant echoes...

"*Ne pas conjoir, car tant vous aim sans mentir...* " Mordiern Guyon's voice seemed to come from the warmed, mellow stones... "*Je sui en dongier mais je met mon cuer, ma vie et m'onnour en vo plaisir...*"

But his words lost in time were now lost on the wind and the muffled noise of passing traffic. Meanwhile, Léon Tavernier had pursed his lips on the edge of his harmonica and was gently piping the very same *ballade* as he returned to his moribund wife in the residential Avenue Victor Hugo.

*

Re-invigorated by his meaty meal, and his wife's dramatic show of fear, Clement had, in Catherine's absence, made a start on cleaning the apartment. Although the smell of burnt fat still lingered, he'd washed the stairs, slopped out the bathroom and was carpet-sweeping what was left of the rugs when he caught sight of the cauliflower.

    She had no intention of speaking to him ever again, and bore it into the kitchen.

    "Where d'you get that from?" he quizzed. "Shops are shut."

    "My dirty old man." She countered, chopping it vigorously into sections for the pan.

    "But we've eaten!" He was aggrieved by her vigour and purpose.

    You have...

    She kept the words to herself, filling her mouth instead with crisp, white florets.

    "See what I've done out here? All this choring." It was attention-seeking time again and very tedious. Catherine slammed the saucepan on to the ring. Her cheeks full.

    "Can't you say anything?" He bellowed.

    "Plenty." She sneered. This time deliberately, to be heard.

    "And what's that supposed to mean?" He was close enough to grip her under both arms where she was still sore, and spin her round towards him. The knife was still in her hand and lowering towards his groin.

    "Give that to me!"

    She smelt the poor, dead lamb on his breath.

    "Not until you let go. Anyhow why not chop it off? It's no good to me... " She spat bits of stalk in his eyes.

"You bitch!" His face bubbled and boiled with the water. He moved one hand to her wrist, the other to her breast, and squeezed both with a terrible force.

The knife fell to the floor as her screams pierced the fabric of the old building, through to the adjoining flat and out to the evening air.

Meanwhile, Rosa Tavernier, ensconced in her shabby armchair was picking between her few remaining teeth with a safety pin until they bled. Television applause for the clowns in the Moscow State Circus couldn't disguise the cries filling the small, tiled sitting room. The same as she'd heard from those '*Krematoriumfiguren*' as no water left their rusted shower heads, and the breathed-in air became that of bitter almonds.

Next door, Catherine kicked out and missed. The pain was worse. Unendurable. She was going to faint...

"Now we'll have no more of that will we?" Clement's raddled face was the last thing she saw until a sudden darkness swamped and then released her.

*

She woke prematurely in the sunless dawn to find herself alone with the wind outside slapping loose cables against the wall. Even with the inner windows shut, it felt cold. She lay inert, curled too late for protection like her tiny, displaced embryos on their porcelain-cool cotton. She brought the blankets over her head to sleep the kind of chilled, bruised stupor the man in the photograph nearby had surely witnessed many times before.

However, Rosa Tavernier's day promised to be far more purposeful. She was always closed on Thursdays to allow new stock to arrive by van from Perpignan. On the stroke of ten, as Catherine drifted into dreams, a boy, young enough to still be at school, staggered through her doorway bent double under his load. Sweating halves of pig in muslin perched on white, veal flanks, while horse blocks - the housewives' choice - towered bleeding from his arms. But the old woman could better his strength and had no trouble hoisting the carcasses up to their ceiling hooks. While he checked off his cargo in a childish hand, she felt each newcomer expertly and swiftly for muscle and fat. Like hair, the latter was unacceptable. Waste, she called it. *Der Abfall*. And to see how often it distorted and shamed a body was something she could never abide.

There'd once been a lot of those. Well-fed women, professors' wives, idlers of the meritocracy who could only breed, already standing close, but not close enough. She'd preferred them touching, tightly in a squash of sebaceous, sweaty skins. Bursting with subcutaneous cellulite - fatty cells run riot in their hosts. Lardy, shuffling shells coaxed into quietude. Sallow, tallow wax for candles which had sold well enough in the early days.

'*Der Osche*' had done her work even better than 'The Mare of Majdanek,' and prosperity followed her after the peace, to the ancient fishing port chosen by her brother. He'd also chosen new names. Others, more honestly had changed their money. Old francs surrendered and any wartime revenues accounted for. But Léon Tavernier - formerly Dr. Pierre Arnajon - had managed to pass on their joint fortune through Louis Bonbois, bank official and money launderer from St. Laurent. His brother-in-law, a man of few scruples. The doctor had established a fine reputation in Marseilles as a specialist in the treatment of tropical diseases, waterborne from the colonies. Schistasomas which invade the skin to lodge in the intestinal and urinary tracts delivered him a reputation far beyond the Vichy borders whilst enabling him to live in some comfort with his sister, his wife and their only child Agathe.

*

Their house, a large *Maison de Maître* in the Boulevard Monricher near the zoological gardens, was now a crammers' college for the study of modern languages. His consulting rooms had occupied the ground floor and the shy, blonde little girl would often sit out of sight on the stairs watching the array of seafarers who passed through his doors. Thin men, brawny, reddened, tanned and barnacled. Some in uniform, some not. All deemed nomadic parasites as his revulsion grew and, as destined, all themselves invaded. Where they'd once lain to receive his tinctures and suppositories, to hummed and whistled harmonies of the Middle Ages, rows of students now sat for a year's duration, lethargically learning the intricacies of the German tongue. But when such opportunity had arisen, for both him and his sister, quick ears and a greedy desire to please had yielded much more rapid results.

*

Clement bought some salad rolls on his way out of town and stopped at the first garage on the Perpignan road. Thereafter he took the wide valley route north through vine-covered slopes bordered by the Corbières, to Quillan and on to Limoux. Her car was running well in the warmth, under the dappling leaf shadows, between boulder-strewn, sanguineous hills, and the swirling river Aude. Snatches of her songs came maddeningly to mind - that is, until the cyclists caught his eye. A line of neat, tight young men, in black, elasticated shorts, tempted outdoors by the fresh summer day. His eyes were fixed on their small, polished buttocks snugly moulded against the thin, hard saddles.

He slowed down behind them to admire at leisure the pummelling strength of their bulbous, muscled legs, and those handsome, boyish profiles straining full ahead. Clement tooted discreetly, hoping to elicit a smile as he finally over-took, and was rewarded by a warm, collective wave. Thus buoyed up, the journey to *La Récompense* became a joy, taking him through yet more bright green vineyards, this time, those of the *Blanquette de Limoux* - light and sparkling - and a must for the return journey.

Through rolling hectares of young yellowing sunflowers, undiminished before the browning, blistering summer heat, the road to the hamlet led sharply upwards in a series of tortuous bends. These ended in a cul-de-sac of old houses clustered around a church. Below, the vast counterpane landscape once trampled by Simon de Montfort and his followers and then by the purging royal commissioners of Philip IV, spread out as far as the eye could see towards Carcassonne.

Clement noticed the circular chapel, newly rendered, abutting from the church's end wall, adorned with a large, occupied cross. He stopped the car in the shadow of what was a life-sized crucifixion, whose stigmata coursed red vermilion down the Christ's white marble body. The tortured, bearded head was bent his way as he gathered up his papers.

"*Monsieur?*" A woman's voice called from his left. Clement jumped, already nervous in the presence of such searing piety. A face he recognised peered out from an un-glazed lower window. His heart sank when he saw how the upper part of the building was quite derelict with the remnants of a roof silhouetted against the sky. "*Maisons du Soleil?*" She queried.

"*Oui. Je viens.* I'm coming." He wasn't keen at all, but nevertheless, in a business-like fashion, tucked his files under his arm and a slim-line camera in his pocket.

"Madame Vilalongue." The old woman extended a veiny hand through the rotting, unshuttered window frame. He'd recognised her voice immediately. "I think this is what you're looking for... " She ventured.

"We've struck lucky then." Clement muttered under his breath, surveying the dereliction with a practised eye and sinking heart, aware he was being watched.

"Pardon?"

"Nothing." He said, with an asking price already in his head.

"Many English are travelling this way." She stood in the empty doorway. Her well-worn clothes coated in a fine dust.

"I hope so." Clement compared the house with its pristine neighbour, and stepped back to compose the most flattering photographs he could. "Uninhabitable, obviously." He crouched in the road, clicking away.

She laughed. "It is for - how do you say - *le bricoleur*?"

"Ah! The do-it yourself enthusiast."

Madame Vilalongue smiled, gratified.

At least the sky made a pretty contrast to the wreck, and he was able to focus on a stone-carved detail over the lintel.

"Tell me, Madame, what does *La Récompense* mean?" asked Clement. "A reward of some sort?" The shutter clicked again as the vendor's expression changed. She quickly looked about her and signalled him into the dark hallway. Dampness seeped through his thin, cotton suit, and he shivered.

"I've no idea, but there was a big house here once, so they say. Built for the priest of the church over thare." She pointed in the direction of the Crucifixion. "Two Chevaliers were found hiding. If they'd been part of the Blanchefort Templars in Roussillon, they'd have been left alone... "

"Really? Why?"

"Apparently, to guard the exterminated Cathars' hidden treasure. Whatever and wherever that was. To this day, no-one knows."

She then frowned, as if still puzzled by all this after almost seven hundred years. "As for those two runaways, thanks to Guillaume de Nogaret, Councillor and Keeper of the Seal for Philippe *le Bel*, a small fortune rested on their heads, and the horse. Why they vanished into the night." Madame Vilalongue suddenly flung her arms in the air. "Phut! *Comme ça*! No wonder de Nogaret was called the king's '*advocatus diaboli*.' He hired many agents – local people – to round up these 'animals' while he kept his hands clean. By the way, his name originates from the word *nogarède*, meaning 'walnut.' A pity he wasn't as harmless."

"When exactly was all this?" Clement produced a notepad. Anything historical, however grim, was an added bonus.

"From 1307 until 1310. A long time ago, but... " Here she paused. A faraway look in her eyes.

"But what?"

"People sometimes say to the *curé* they've seen the ghost of that big, white horse, still free."

"A ghost?" When all Clement could visualise was the selling price rising. "How interesting." Nevertheless, he focussed his lens on that same glassless window, but that grisly crucifixion blocked the view. "Damn."

"Sometimes on a sunny day, it's said he gallops across the fields down there. But who knows?" Madame Vilalongue led the way through to the back room, open to the sky. Cobwebs festooned the walls and attached themselves to Clement's well-groomed head. "The floor is good. No?" Her booted feet stamped the boards to prove it. "And here Monsieur. Look at this!" She knelt down and pushed aside a huge concrete slab to reveal a man-sized hole. Clement immediately heard water. He bent closer, only a yard away from the lapping, blue-green sea below.

"Jesus!"

"It is without bottom." Madame Vilalongue stood back as he grinned. He'd liked the way she'd said that. "Very, very ancient. Possibly Roman." She clearly felt encouraged.

"OK. I'll get some more shots." He adjusted his light meter for the gloom. Afterwards, he snapped the case shut. "You certainly have something different here. Not for your usual punter... "

"Punter?" Madame Vilalongue looked confused.

"We'll do our best." Clement beamed, sweetening up before the stroke. "How about five thousand sterling. *Cinquante mille francs?*"

She was behind him, silently dismayed.

"It won't be easy, but as I say, leave it to me," he persevered. "You'll have our terms in writing, and if you agree, I'll bring a brand new *Maisons du Soleil* sign for you."

*

Afterwards, he sat in the hot Renault to gather his thoughts as the dominating Holy Martyr and a couple of neighbours stared in. No shops, no pool, not even any sign of *boules.*

"Last place your Papa made, I reckon." He murmured, reversing smartly away, little realising that this was the best he'd see that afternoon. The sun was now high and bright, with only thin cloud veiling the far Pyrénées, and as he manoeuvred the car back down the road, he subconsciously scoured the view for any sighting of that mysterious pale horse.

XV

'And when the seven thunders had uttered their voices, I was about to write: and I heard a voice from heaven saying unto me, Seal up those things which the seven thunders uttered and write them not.'
(Revelation.10.v.4.)

Long summer days at the St. Cernin *Commanderie* passed one into the other, suffused by the clear mountain light, the heat and heady scents of thyme and fennel that furnished the surrounding slopes.

The two travellers had been welcomed with undisguised curiosity, not only for having endured such a marathon through France, but also because no brother of the Temple abandoned the security of his base in such precarious times. Those too old or young for Louis' last crusade had clung to the ordered life, tending their olive groves, vines, and the peaceful armies of goats that swarmed over the foothills, filling the air with their gentle *sounnaions*.

"We hope you will commit yourselves here until the Lord finally claims you." Hugolin de Caudiès, the *chef des troupeaux* had not easily looked the albino in the eye, but he could tell when a man was strong and *doulz* in equal measure. "Our flocks have increased tenfold since the fall of Acre," he said. "We have need of shepherds who can endure both the May storms and the January snows, for summer's bounty is too short-lived in these parts. But with God's help, we shall prosper."

"It is our very calling." The newcomers knelt before him, heads bowed in grateful servility. "There is no danger we cannot face, and our horse is of the best, despite his journey."

"He eats double of our destriers." The tall, slightly stooped man gave a wry smile. "But that is no matter." On the days you will be guarding the pilgrim route over the *Roc Cornu*, they will doubtless find such a creature re-assuring."

"Indeed." Said Mordiern, timid no longer. "That has already been proved."

And while the first July of the new century slipped into August, so did the new goatherds fully discover that this earthly paradise was no dream. That nights reliably gave way to dawns warmed by the Mediterranean sun, soon to burn the mens' northern blood and inflame their yearning hearts.

*

At its noonday apogee with all sounds lulled to a dreaming sleep, Girard Corbichon and Mordiern Guyon lay together in the cooling shade of an old fig tree. It stood with others similarly untended, in a dry gulley set below the vineyard's edge, some ten hectares from the *Commanderie*. Even the cicadas were defeated, leaving only Druide draped in a summer blanket, picking desultorily at the ground, while lizards flickered unnoticed over the riders' recumbent bodies. Both were awake, lightly touching, staring up at the dancing blue between the leaves.

In disobedience, Mordiern had loosened his new, plain belt while Girard did the same with his. The Baal-faced clasp glistened against the earth while his hand, pinker than his cheeks, passed over the young man's waist, freed now, rising and falling with each quickening breath. He began to sing.

"*Amours me fait desirer... et amer, Mais c'est si folettement... que je ne puis esperer... Ne penser... N'ymaginer nullement... Que le dous viaire gent... Me doie joie donner...* "

They turned in unison like leverets doomed on a spit, lips brushing, close, then closer, fusing white on brown, as the bells from the plateau on the *Pic de la Vièrge*, summoned the other monks to Nones.

XVI

Léon Tavernier's wife was always glad to get her panatelas. A small gesture on his part, and the only price he paid for peace. After Marseilles, and the Riviera enterprise, he'd acquired the house on the Avenue Victor Hugo very cheaply, together with commercial premises and two apartments in the Rue des Templiers. But this attractive villa with its green shutters and tropical trees had become a prison of her own choosing. A repository of remorse. She had never ventured beyond its small, manicured garden and for the past ten years, had remained ensconced in her smoke-filled sanctum, unable even to look upon the various wartime perquisites that furnished every room, except hers, and lent the place a refined yet cosmopolitan ambience.

Her world was set apart. Cluttered with old photographs - moments in time on stained impermanence - curling and blurring a little more with each passing year. Estelle Bonbois as student of the cello; at social gatherings as a doctor's wife, mother of Agathe, whom she would never see again as long as her father was alive. Always her long, oval face and what some had said were clever, lively eyes dominating each memento, but never his life. Eyes that were tired now, turned towards the vineyards of the Albères, and the workers with their little white *camionettes* trundling back and forth between the rows where once the Troubadours and pilgrims had travelled into Spain. They were old men too, she could tell. Knarled as walnuts among the bright, new leaves.

Like them, there was no need to hurry. Time was on her side, and whilst they nurtured and watched for mealy bugs and honey fungus, so she must be vigilant and conserve herself for her moment.

Her revelations.

She would often say as much to the simple, dark-haired girl who came in to change the sheets, polish the Riviera silver and bring the secret mail. Today, her husband was late, so she opened yet again Agathe's most recent letter. Between readings, it was kept warmly hidden under her barren body, brought to birth by other surrogate agents over land and sea. Examined until she knew each word by heart. Bland-pap words, with no reassurance or clue as to any possible return. For she couldn't ask. At least they were of her hand, soft, once tiny, not touched for thirty years. At this, Estelle's eyes welled up with tears, and her lumpen body shook in violent grief.

Suddenly Léon Tavernier was in the room and she stuffed the letter away.

"*Voilà.*" He threw the packet on the bed. "Where's the Jew?"

"She's somewhere." Estelle kept her head lowered, which, for an unproductive burden was appropriate.

"Good. It can clean up my shoes."

With that, he left, and the room was immediately a lighter place. Then she knew that soon he'd be coaxing that same old tune from his harmonica. Some meaningless song of love...

*

After a late and hungry lunch, Clement consulted his map for the whereabouts of the hamlet Montlagarde. His light beige suit already felt travel-worn, and embarrassingly, a tomato pip stained the fly. He moved the driving mirror to smooth his hair, and followed directions back to Quillan, wondering idly what five hundred *livres* would be worth today.

The turning off the D117 narrowed abruptly so that its thick, dried grass banks brushed the car on either side, slowing it down. The prospect of an oncoming vehicle with nowhere to pull in, brought a high colour to his cheeks and an overpowering urge to relieve himself. However, the tarmac gradually widened bringing signs of habitation into view, albeit abandoned builders' yards and single-storey cabins, some with washing strung out alongside. Then a cemetery bristling with overblown memorials and miniature, marble houses complete with sloping, tiled roofs and ornamental doorways. More enduring than beach huts, and sparkling more brightly than homes for the living.

Clement stopped to urinate against the wall in readiness for his next transaction, when all at once, a figure in black appeared by the wrought iron gate. So startled was he that his penis stayed outside his trousers. She was a large woman, with hair severely scraped from her face, waxen in a land of dark, outdoor skins. She was sobbing a grief too profound for anger.

"Jesus Christ!" Clement quickly made himself decent. "You scared the shit out of me, you did!"

Crying all the more, she advanced towards him and grabbed his arm.

"*Mon fils! Il esst mort! Mort*!" The words almost unrecognizable in her Catalan patois, were launched on a sea of deep, reverberating sorrow and Clement had to think quickly.

"That's terrible. I'm sorry. How?" He really wanted to go, but her grip tightened, her eyes grew wilder.

"Le SIDA! Le SIDA! I can't live any more!"

AIDS...

He tried to edge away, and she stared at him contemptuously.

"All men are the same. They only love each other, not any girlfriend or wife!" She wailed, and her hot saliva fell on his hand. For the first time since leaving England, he felt uneasy. Made a dash for the car but she followed, beginning to run. Although big, she was quite agile. His jacket caught in the driver's side door...

"Men like you!" Her fists beat upon his window as he crashed the gears in his haste to get away.

"You'll be punished, too!" She shrieked, and through the mirror he could see her finally give up, to stand, a solitary figure in the middle of the road.

Still shaken, Clement accelerated hard to increase his distance until she'd finally disappeared out of sight. His spirits flagged. He felt like opting out of yet another dreary dwelling trapped in the back of beyond, in favour of the sanitised, printed words in the office. Yet he kept on, to terrain that was neither pasture nor terrace, only scrubby enclosures and makeshift shelters populated by brown goats and leggy sheep. Quite unlike the round-barrelled sort that grazed the coastal Home Counties and greeted the visitor from abroad.

*

The next ten kilometres seemed more like a hundred, with the mountains a distant backdrop and the sea only a memory. Past several *Chasse Privée* signs and isolated holdings down to a river and a junction signed Montlagarde over the bridge. Here the water had gelled to a stagnant scum littered with rubbish, and hens scattered in panic under his bumper where a narrow weedy track met the road. This led him up to a plateau bearing four whitewashed buildings set around an earthen courtyard. Sounds of sporadic gunfire came from a nearby wood and the smell of foul straw filled Clement's nostrils before he closed his window.

He spotted a crudely written *'À Vendre'* sign nailed to the furthest barn, so he touched the horn only to be answered by a cacophony of yelping, hunting dogs who frantically scrabbled at the ground beneath their cage door. Having straightened his tie and with his folders again under one arm, he advanced towards the hovel, noting in his trained way how there was a television aerial and mains electricity connected. The main feature was a large opening where normally a front door and lower windows should be, and he peered in.

A feral cat with a litter in a dung nest snarled at his feet, and further back in the dark stood six veal calves caked in excrement and tightly tied at the neck to iron rings set into the nearest wall. Their stench turned his stomach and drove him back. He banged in vain on a broken down-pipe.

Fuck this...

No-one was around. Certainly not the sculptor, Monsieur Martin who'd phoned the day before in search of a larger studio. Clement then made his way round to the rear plot - a small patch of land fenced round by scrap wire and littered with half-finished wood carvings, some of which were propped up against the wall. These included long, lean women, with huge, sagging breasts in sycamore and mahogany, half- rough, half-smooth, gouged out by a myriad, tiny cuts. Those other figures which had fallen, lay criss-crossed in bonfire-ready piles. None was complete. The smell that reached him this time was different. A lethal cocktail of rotting, organic matter coming from elsewhere. He went to the far edge of the plot and looked down.

There, heaped in a nettle-filled gulley, lay an animal graveyard, uncovered and open to the elements. Corpses made mongrel by decomposition. Cockerels, dogs, rabbits, other vermin; unrecognisable heads and other body parts detached. Clement clamped his hand over his nose and ran back to the Renault before anyone appeared. *La Récompense* was a palace compared to this, and soon he was back on the road and driving too fast.

"We'll have to raise our ceiling to twenty grand," he said out loud. "These dumps are just a waste of bloody time."

Past that cemetery again, with the mourner thankfully gone.

"No bloody history there," he added bitterly. "Are you listening, Greenbaum?"

So he sped onwards, tense and disillusioned, down towards the widening sea-sky through Estagel and Casès de Pène, past the former concentration camp at Rivesaltes, determined to telephone London first thing in the morning.

*

Catherine had passed most of the day in a fitful sleep, but when her husband returned, was sitting up at the table in her nightshirt, hair in turmoil falling between her fingers. She was reading aloud in French from a drab little book on World Sculptors that she'd found in a wardrobe drawer. Amongst Maillol, Brancusi and others, was a monochrome photo of a nude, muscular, Aryan male drawing his sword. 'Bereitschaft' - 'In Readiness' - cast in bronze by Hitler's favourite sculptor, Arno Dreker in 1939. Beneath it lay scribbled words of admiration and a stain at the corner.

"You'll like this, as well." She pushed the open book towards him. "He could be you."

Clement glanced at the image without comment. He wasn't going to be baited. Besides, other things were on his mind.

"Fritz Koppel... Vienna 1942... " Catherine read out the sculptor's name written in faded pencil, as Clement undressed slowly, automatically and walked naked and pre-occupied towards the bathroom.

"Oh, by the way, there's a letter for you. From London," she added as though an afterthought, for she'd planned never to speak to him again. Not even about him using her Renault. But the day had worn on too long, and as this was the first post they'd received, she was curious.

Clement re-appeared and stood over her, turning the square, white envelope with its typed address several times before inserting his finger and tearing open the edge. The letter inside had been folded as if anxiously into a tight square and she could hear his breath quicken as he unravelled it. Then he gave out an uneasy, ominous laugh.

"It's Dan. Dan Madox. Good God!" He'd forgotten his nakedness and his warm-woolled groin was so close that she could feel his penis give a sudden little jerk against her arm. Something it had never done for her.

"Please let me see," she urged him.

"It's addressed to me." Clement turned away, shielding himself with the closely written page.

"I've had more to do with him than you." Catherine reached out.

"Oh, have you now?" He smiled conspiratorially and returned to the shower, waving the note alongside. Her thoughts raced on, blurred by the rumours she'd heard before they'd left. What did they mean, and what did he want? Her Hermes in his close-fitting jumper and springing curls? How his eyes came alight whenever he sang the only real possessions she still had.

"Has he got problems then?" She tried again, sweetly this time, watching as Clement got dressed. But he was immune now to such feminine whiles. She could wheedle all she liked. His stomach rumbled loudly and with the lunge of a hunting man, his head was inside the fridge. Empty and bright.

Unsatisfied, he slammed the door.

"For Chrissakes! What's a man got to do round here?" He stood up, his hair a dark, clinging skull cap. "I'm bloody starving, and bloody pissed off... Greenbaum's going to get a mouthful tomorrow, you'll see."

"I bet his marriage has finished." She persevered, referring to the conductor, ignoring his demands and complaints. "I mean, Daniel. Just another statistic now is he?" Was as detached as she could be.

"Nothing to do with you. It's my affair." Clement checked his wallet.

"I see." She was on dangerous ground again. Watching his hands.

"He wants to come down here. That's all."

A shiver of excitement passed through her. Invisible, unbetraying.

"Says he can help me run the business." Clement pulled a clean tee shirt over his head and it felt good. "Not such a crazy idea if you think about it. Could have done with someone today mind you... "

He was mellow now, soon to be maudlin. Catherine knew the score, knew exactly when to interpose.

"Can I please see the letter?"

And obediently, Clement reached deep in his new trouser pocket, and passed it over without demur. She read of the mess, of a life unfulfilled, all the while seeing the rapt expression of that faraway rehearsal face.

"I'll write then." Catherine said, handing it back. After all he was still more hers than his. He who had coaxed those words from her body... those heady words of love...

"No. *I* will." Clement countered, suddenly tense.

"OK. No problem."

*

Léon Tavernier's days were now full, and meaningfully so, thanks to the English couple. In between monitoring the apartment in the Rue des

Templiers and perusing the latest *Maisons du Soleil* properties on display at least twice daily, there was little time to spare for his other more established routines.

His 'butterfly' seemed sadly withdrawn whenever she emerged. Enough people noticed her, how could they not? But no one engaged her in conversation, and it was only through severe self-restraint that he didn't fling himself at her feet. She was loosening his mind from its safe moorings, and as day turned to even longer night, nothing apart from her and her husband's interests mattered. His home was now on the street, pacing the narrow boulevards, crossing at different places for variety, knowing without looking where tarmac changed to gravel or tiles to pebble.

Wednesday was still too far away. He'd even calculated the seconds but they moved so slowly, and all the while she contrived to look like an iridescent angel - always in white, with tiny, fabric creases below her breasts and at the junction of her thighs. His hands from the shadows could barely desist from reaching out to caress and pull her close, while his eyes, lustre-glazed, reflected an unshared Heaven.

The three porticos set into the façade of M. Philippe Ferand, *Notaire*, provided a useful venue for observing the young estate agent's comings and goings. A concrete bench had been thoughtfully provided, set into the wall. Welcome warmth for his old spine, and if the seagulls had fouled it, he would sit precisely on a handkerchief square. Every so often he consulted his watch or made discreet jottings behind the day's '*Indépendant*', for the Englishman kept him busy. He was always telephoning or being telephoned, and sometimes, suddenly without warning he would leap to the window to re-arrange his photographs.

More passers-by were stopping now. The simply curious; Dutch,

Scandinavian, local couples whose children spilled from prams and pushchairs and who couldn't afford to build new. Hard-working low-income families looking inland away from the spread of immigrant ghettoes. Away from the livid, black faces that swarmed the bright, supine beaches by day and prowled by night. Looking to Jean-Marie Le Pen and indifferent to news of the vandalised Carpentras graves. He could tell their sort, for he was one of them.

But it was Mr. Ash, whose clothes and demeanour disturbed him far more. A man for other men to be sure. Vain and audacious with his body. He'd seen it all before. A veritable octopus, sinuously trawling, multi-legged, poised for prey and never sated. Never. For viewing trips it wore the lightweight suit, tightfitting of course around the pubis and anal crease. For internal operations he'd don even more revealing items, probably with no underpants, and usually in combination with a skinny top showing his nipples. This would be topped by a spotted kerchief round his throat.

The sailors he himself had treated in the Boulevard Montricher house had been no different. There, he'd seen kiss burns on the neck and other wounds, not of war but from themselves. Tissue tears nail-drawn, lesions in the anal mucosa; passion lines that altered with each muscle movement like a military map. How he had loathed and despised them, but they had kept his cupboards full in hard times. Now this *Anglais* had come to swell the ranks of the other *lusus naturae* that populated the coast. Worse than raw sewage that passed out to sea, only to return on certain tides, and bind exploring fingers and paddling toes. These were more permanent pollutants infiltrating every walk of life, and he, in his rôle, had been but a straw in the wind.

Such a pity that Monsieur Ash had landed unhindered in his place of retreat and unthinkable that he was somehow part of Madame Ash, bound by a mere band of thin gold. The old man folded his newspaper and went unobserved for his usual cup of chocolate to re-warm his blood and think things through.

It was then that the estate agent dialled his London office only to be told that there were too many problems with unsold Docklands real estate for Greenbaum to concern himself with the small Mediterranean offshoot. Dammit, he had the sun, the sea and his wife. It was up to him. Clement slapped down the phone and paced the office, mindful of other eyes outside.

"Yes sir, no sir, three bloody bags full sir!" He snarled. "I will not from now on be taking on animal graveyards or insanitary derelicts. I'm going up market and... up yours!" His V-signs caused some merriment amongst a group of students resting their rucksacks against his wall. "And" He shouted, "I'm getting some bloody help!"

Ten minutes later, having taken details of a villa in Amélie les Bains that had once housed escapees from Vernet's internment camp, and asked André Gelat of *Immobilier du Sud* if he had any properties of historical interest he wished to offload, Clement began his fervent reply to Daniel Madox and signed it solely from himself.

XVII

'Behold I come as a thief. Blessed is he that watcheth and keepeth his garments, lest he walk naked and they see his shame.'
(Revelation.16.v.15.)

Noon, October 13th 1307. Four years after Guillaume de Nogaret's arrest of Pope Boniface at Agnani and the Pontiff's death in Rome. Twelve months since Philippe *le Bel* had turned on the Jews, stealing their money, selling their goods and herding them into prison. Three weeks since the *vendange*. Two nights without sleep, for brother Girard was possessed with a presentiment of doom, unable to influence the mood of celebration that always followed the harvest at the *Commanderie*.

"Anger and sadness have entered my heart, so that I hardly dare remain alive... " He sang Olivier the Templar's words to a wistful tune as he rested with Mordiern and the goats near Rasiguères. The day was strangely warm, heavy with disquietude despite the pleasant sun barely clear of the distant peaks and the gentle, tinkling bells. Suddenly, Druide threw up his grazing head. Ears alert at the sound of hoof-beats drumming ever closer and a sharp, repeating human cry, shattering the peace.

Mordiern sprang up, his pulse too fast as he ran alongside until the intruder stopped. The youth aboard a sweating, chestnut horse was breathlessly incoherent. Something was terribly wrong.

"The Archevêque of Elne is in Trouillas questioning our brothers!" he shouted. "You will be next! Escape while you can. The arrests have already begun! Everywhere!"

His words fell like seeds from Hell in that giddy, pastoral paradise. He then spoke of the traitor Floyran of Béziers; of Guillaume de Nogaret, the king's chief minister, 'that viper in the grass' and his closing net. Of the crimes they must confess... Filthy things; the issue of an evil mind.

He reined his mount round and was gone in a cloud of dust that still lingered as the two brothers without speaking, urged their pale Boulonnais into a gallop.

*

There followed several cold, watchful hours at *La Récompense* on meagre, soiled straw, before setting out under the starry heavens, galloping unshod through hectares of cultivated fields with no sheltering trees, towards Carcassonne.

Thereafter, distant flares kept the fugitives to copse and forest, bruised and stung by warring branches. Then, on to Moissac, tired and weak, disguised as Santiago pilgrims in stolen clothes.

Next, three nights wide-awake in the town's Abbey Church. Under its tympanum of Christ, adorned in the multitudinous company of elders, seraphs and the four evangelists as animals, clasping books. All in cold, chiselled stone, hostile to man's nature.

"What faith now?" Each asked the other, deliriously unholy. Numb from hunger, with nothing left to give.

*

December in the Agenais on a horse lame in the left foreleg. A laborious journey, forgetting all joys in the present pain. Over the frozen river Garonne and the snowy vastness of blanketed hills, to St. Just, the hamlet farm, once part of Girard's long-ago childhood. A girl, Élise, there now, where his mother had been. They denied him the truth of her end of course, but warned he must in future hide his alien face lest he bring them greater misfortune.

"We are old." Said Marthe and Hilaire Roland, so Mordiern kept the flocks, taking the smooth-skinned girl for company, while Girard could only watch with red-filled eyes, and pen his longing verses to the younger man whom he loved.

XVIII

The atmosphere in the flat above the *boucherie* was now quite changed, charged with the expectancy of the choirmaster's arrival. Subtle alterations had been made to the genteel dinginess, including a new cotton cover for the double bed and a pot plant whose one tropical bloom had lasted just an hour. Tired of Agathe Tavernier's simpering smile, and not a little jealous, Catherine had interred the photograph in a drawer.

Clement meanwhile, had taken it upon himself to ask Rosa Tavernier if their friend could stay for the short term and, after quickly calculating that the added rent would be the equivalent of twenty kilos of *saucisses* per week, *La Propriétaire* had agreed. With one proviso, and a curious stare from her hard, berry-like eyes.

"He must have the right papers of course, after three months." She had always been adept and co-operative with rules and regulations, and at this stage of her life, nothing was to be out of order. "Then we look again... By the way Monsieur Ash, has your friend... how shall I say... much of hair on the body... like so... ?" She ran both hands over her fat-stained chest and groin in one rapid movement.

"No... not that I know of... " Clement was caught off guard. Before the man's curly nape and covered arms came to mind

"*Bien*. That is all."

And despite her brother who seemed to have already found himself some amusement, she would be especially privy to the *ménage à trois des Anglais*, with all the implications that would bring her bare, cadaverous life.

*

"Two weeks today." Clement snapped his briefcase shut, and reshaped an eyebrow with a wet finger. "And not a moment too soon as far as I'm concerned." He then checked his tie, and Catherine could tell it was one of his reconnaissance days but gave him no comfort.

"It's still my car you know," she reminded him. "I may need it."

"Why? What business have you got?" Her reflection was behind him.

"Never you mind," he teased, for today was Wednesday. Besides, unsettling him just before work was a new game and a precarious one. Clement's wide, brown eyes glowered. The *bandillera* was in his shoulder and like the Abanto bull, he swerved away with a flourish of his tail.

Her victory. Then silence.

Catherine glanced up to where the absent photograph had left a grimy oblong on the wallpaper. Was her *rendez-vous* with Paradise for the morning or the afternoon? In the cool or the heat? She couldn't recall, as her new acquaintance's words had come too quickly on that busy street and now the faithless Daniel Madox had interposed.

She gingerly opened the shutters allowing first a slender strip of light to intrude then, enough to reveal dark bulbous clouds threatening the tip of the *Pic Martineau*. That decided her. She studied herself in the mirror in her tee-shirt nightdress populated by colourful birds on branches. She lifted it over her head and stared like a man might stare; like the butcher next door had once stared, missing no detail.

One breast was as bruised and mottled as the sky - livid against her other whiteness. She carefully smeared on a pale foundation which only deepened the blemish. Then in a panic, talcum powder. Better, but only temporary, with the friction of clothes. And of course there were still the others. She pulled up her hair into a high, bobbing ponytail. Sweet sixteen and never been kissed - or lovingly touched. It was a more youthful Mrs.

Ash that the choirmaster had never seen, who slipped on an ivory-coloured polyester shift over nothing at all underneath, and glossed her lips with Mulberry Madness.

He'd said to bring a basket, but hers had long gone with other childhood things to jumble sales and Barnardo's. No matter. There'd be no more shopping from now on. She had other things to do. Like going out to play. She snatched one of Clement's jumpers from the chair, knotted it casually around her throat and ran unencumbered by any mother's call of caution down to the street.

*

The air outside seemed heavy, hemmed in by the lowering clouds, and the roads leading to the Mediterranean coast were unusually quiet. No-one lingered before a storm in those parts, but the London girl paid no heed to such portents, as she walked, sometimes skipped up the hill. One or two people sat on the dingy shingle nearby whilst further out on the flat sea, a black windsurfing figure pulled and stretched at his sluggish sail. Arms also reached out from upper windows to secure the shutters, for without any wind there was no telling which way the rain would fall.

Already Catherine was warm and she untied the borrowed sweater. The *Musée de la Pyrène* was opening its doors on the few Picasso pots and rapid sketches by a Matisse who'd been passing through. She was momentarily tempted to cross into the coolness, but suddenly realised Clement had left her no money. At the end of the lane, the gate marked L. T. was half-open. So perhaps after all, his surname was also Tavernier. As she approached, the first drop of rain fell on her cheek, and faraway, a deep, melancholy thunder rolled.

"Bienvenue, Madame Ash. Welcome to *le Jardin d'Eden*!" A man's voice called out. She realised it was too late to turn back as the wooden door was being pulled wide open then quietly closed behind her. "Come," Léon Tavernier said, brushing past. "I will show you everything."

And Catherine, as the first Eve, stood transfixed by such a panorama of abundance. Green upon green, so many hues, so many shapes. Everywhere fruits and berries hung warm and limpid, ripe for the picking in colours of the sun. As she followed him down to the far end, dark spots of rain began to mark the dry fawn earth. They came finally to a thick curtain of reeds that blocked the view beyond.

"I won't need to irrigate today." He said, his leathery head turned to the sky, and so light were his eyes she could scarcely tell the pupils from their corneas. He prodded the hard soil with his favourite old stick, probing and parting the foliage on either side, all the while hissing a tune she recognised between his teeth.

"Good Lord! I've sung that!" She cried. "With the Early Music Balladeers. In London. What a small world... "

"Indeed." But all the while, he was busy. "Look." The gardener suddenly presented her with a wide, red strawberry plucked from its hiding place. "For you. First kiss it, then eat. My orders. *La première bise d'été*."

Catherine drew back, but those unusual eyes were on her.

He pressed the fruit against her lips and as she opened her teeth too late, the juice trickled down her chin to fall on her dress. He let his stick drop to the ground as he plucked another.

"*Encore*," he smiled, and in that moment she felt his hand rest on her undamaged breast. He was close now, keeping the rain from her and circling her nipple with his finger. "Now see, you have your own little fruit... May I?"

Catherine felt her stomach tighten as his dry lips fastened on the stain. She should push him away. Make a run for it. Report him - to whom?

To Clement? Instead, she was naked and he saw the bruise she tried to hide.

"Who has done this?" He frowned. "Mr. Ash?"

"My fault. As always."

"How can that be?" His voice was meltingly soft as he studied the blemish, and because he was expert at soothing and healing, making tissue grow, so her buds grew big inside his mouth, and he passed from one to the other, letting his palm touch her left thigh.

She should move now, show her revulsion at this adventurous stranger, but she was now his butterfly fixed to the spot. Pierced by pleasure. So she closed her eyes. The former doctor's skilled hand felt the thigh's smooth slenderness from back to front, then around again, circling higher until it lay between both. She gasped, hearing him laugh as he played unhindered. Stroking, tweaking, and gently dilating where no other man had ever been. Then with a strange noise, he discovered his prize.

"*Quel Schatz!*" he exclaimed. "You're a virgin."

Another German word...

Here was no man from long ago on the run from Froissy. This wasn't a dream. This was real. Happening now. She stood blind in his power as he stiffened against her and heat from somewhere burned into her neck. The thunder's moan from the north met hers and the rain glanced off her skin, flattening her loosened hair, conspiring to weld one player to the other, glistening and soaking.

"Now, see what I have." He said, pulling something from his pocket. A long, slightly curving courgette. "For you, Madame. A true fruit of the earth... "

It didn't matter that what was nudging her was merely vegetable, without blood or nervous tissue. She closed her eyes again.

"Feel it." The doctor breathed his old thin breath on her cheek and, obediently, in her trance, she stroked its full length. Tentatively at first, and then with more assurance, clasping its width in her fist, moving her hand from end to end. "Good," he whispered, lowering it to be near his fly. Then he opened his trousers. "Now *meine Schmetterling*... time for some pleasure... " He urged, beginning to sway. "Which do you prefer? Me or our other friend?"

By now, his forefinger had slipped inside her again and teased her secret spot to a tumulus then a mountain far bigger it seemed than those rearing up behind the reeds. They trembled as she trembled...

"I don't care!" She cried, so first of all he drew the cool, pulpy courgette, then his own hot, veinous flesh along her wet cleft. She took both in her hands and with each stroke, one grew in length and hardness to match the other. He groaned, rubbing the heavier, purple head to ecstasy before entering. Such sweetness and pain combined, devouring her dreamlike encounter in *L'Hotel du Coq Rouge's* room 28, reaching the reverberating sky, as drops of fire-blood fell to his shoes.

In the aftermath, with him weakened and drained, she'd asked his name, and realised it was he in that old photograph in the apartment, taken in happier times.

"Léon Tavernier."

"And that young girl?"

"I can truthfully say, I don't know," before another roll of thunder filled the sky.

*

Clement was now making a habit of skipping lunch. Anticipation of Daniel's arrival coupled with recent interest in properties near Thuir had played havoc with his stomach. Where his day was once structured around a midday meal and a glass of *Corbières*, now his emotions bore him hither and thither, like the flimsy *Tricolore* above the bank. He even blushed like a girl at the very thought of the new man in the apartment, and thus destabilised, found it increasingly difficult to function. At the same time he was anxious to impress, and show off a thriving business to the new arrival.

His visit to the *Mairie*'s public foyer had been useful, where he'd helped himself to details of various properties, some derelict, some '*habitable*'. After all, Philippe Ferand, *Notaire*, who was handling those sales, had not so far passed him over anything as promised. Historical or otherwise.

"You have no ethics." M. Ferand had then shouted at him down the 'phone. His French deep and strangely guttural. Perhaps not French after all, Clement had wondered at the time. "And maybe no qualifications either. Who knows? We don't want any dirty London tricks down here... "

And Clement, misjudging the mood of Doctor Pierre Arnajon's erstwhile associate, amicably informed his rival that he had a current *Carte Professionnelle*, and suggested therefore, he mind his own business.

"But it is not just my business that you hinder." The *Notaire* had threatened. "And may I remind you I have been here many years, a respectable figure with my wife and three children. I am as you would say, a decent family man."

"Indeed." Although finding the last rejoinder quite incongruous, Clement suggested he pay *Maisons du Soleil* a visit once his business partner Mr. Daniel Madox was installed. "Anyhow, all's fair in love and war," he'd joked. "And as the war's over, that just leaves love, *n'est-ce-pas*?" He'd laughed as though slightly drunk, forgetting his wife in the equation.

Philippe Ferand had scowled as he'd slapped down the receiver. "Why there's no vetting of such *Menschen,* I cannot understand, We shall soon be overrun with a different enemy if we lose our guard." His young secretary had looked up puzzled for a moment, then continued with her typing.

*

Simultaneously, at mid-morning, two thousand miles away on America's Eastern seaboard, Agathe Tavernier, formerly Arnajon steeled herself for the second time to write to her mother. Her letters were now more frequent but harder to compose, coming as they did, closer to the core. Yet still her words were the un-ripened fruit of an ever-present nightmare that no circumstance, no mood change, no drug pedalled by Doctor Henry Dainton, her 'trick-cyclist', could alleviate.

In fact the burden of the oppressed and broken was added daily to the one she already bore, by constant gorging of news from every part of the globe. Even as she wrote, the air letter was framed by a sea of magazines and newsprint starkly, vicariously exposing other tortures and tyrannies, racial cleansing, fever and famine, forever pressing her conscience and her purse. Her desk lay across the tall window that looked out over Boston's Bush Street Park, bordered on her side by a wide main thoroughfare.

"It's all fantasy". Henry had said, holding her shoulders less than an hour ago at the clinic.

"So how can you feel responsible?"

"But it's in me, through him!" Was all Agathe ever said. Her mantra resisting the sage-like armour plating. Impenetrable. And he was becoming fearful, perilously close to defeat.

Besides, she was even more fat now, grown from plumpness by

indifference to what she ate. Terror, coconut cookies, Mengele twins, syrup buns, survivors' stories, all devoured not to nourish but destroy. Colourful, oversize tracksuits gave her a casual flamboyance, but slowly, year by year the spinster of Bush Street West, and part-time tutor in Adult French Studies, was becoming poor. Service charges on her second floor apartment, modestly furnished and badly insulated against the severe winters, were now more than the original rent.

One third of her salary passed by Direct Debit to Joseph Weiss's *'Chasseurs des Diables,'* while Amnesty International claimed another portion. All discreetly, osmotically, bleeding her dry. Agathe expected more from her mother in every sense, but the confused, circuitous messages smuggled from number 56, Avenue Victor Hugo in Collioure, said nothing new other than that she was waiting. And the waiting was easy. No begging for her only child's return, for she knew that while *he* breathed, the Atlantic stayed between them. No pleading for her company or memories shared. Rootless, loveless, Agathe again studied the photographs of Saturday morning visitors on tour in Drancy's memorial gardens. How many times had she stared through a magnifying glass to bring each dot of horror to her understanding.

The cattle truck - rusted, motionless where railway lines meet, leading nowhere. Children play nearby around the neat hedges, while two dogs copulate vociferously in the tidy distance.

Agathe sighed and turned Fauré's *Requiem* to Side 2, before beginning her letter to her mother with the usual term of endearment.

XIX

'And the kings of the earth who have committed fornication and lived deliciously with her, shall bewail her, and lament for her, when they shall see the smoke of her burning.'
(Revelation.18.v.9.)

At harvest's end on the feast day of Sainte Fleur, Girard Louis Corbichon left the little farm at Froissy, taking only the huge, pale horse. As he he'd arrived the world, so he would leave it. Unencumbered. His songs, together with those of the *minnesinger* Holz were left by Mordiern's sleeping head, in a sapling box fashioned when words had finally deserted him. And he had kissed first those lips that were now only for the girl, Élise Roland. Then softly uncovered his manhood and stroked so sweetly as it swayed and lengthened as if the younger man was deep in another dream. Moaning, thrusting, as he entered him, out of sight behind the sheepfold.

"*Je vous aour, nompourquant m'estuet fenir. Vostres demour...* "The monk had sung as he'd pulled away, glistening newly white, bathed in fecundity. The end of bliss. *Paradis perdu*. Then a farewell touch before darkness with its cold early frost claimed him. The same bitter chill as the night of his birth. The same bleached moon as his escaping face.

*

Mordiern could not follow. Guilt at his old pleasures weighed more heavily than for the new, and he stayed on as grateful help to meet his recent lover's ageing parents. Even that collection of ardent songs couldn't lure him away in pursuit. Instead, he sewed them with coarse thread under his jerkin, out of sight, out of mind until she should next place her supple, young body upon him. With this first woman he forgot his faith and his dead father, and as the days shortened into nights, so too the man who'd loved him.

In place of the lance, he now had another weapon, *'Mon ostil en plaisir'* that had pierced no Saracen but the gentle virgin, and when, amidst the hay banks in the barn, she toyed with it solicitously, it could cunningly do all manner of things. Thus, instead of the Divine Service six times daily, other more human joys were rendered. Secretly muffled under the innocent puzzled gaze of Hilaire Roland's twenty veal calves. Her long hair, the colour of summer ermine, was more in his thoughts than either the albino's or the unshod, pale horse. Her little breasts, mere teasing buds, unprepared as yet for infant sucking. Her in-between, the most delicious place on earth, and one he pledged never to leave.

*

However, jus two days later, Marthe Roland and her daughter returned from the market at Froissy, ashen with fear, for John de Havering and his men were abroad, searching every dark corner, raiding the local *Commanderies* for brothers of the *Milice du Temple*. Prisons such as Chinon on the Loire were already full, and more talk promised torture and flames for these degenerate soldiers of sin, scratching their last words into the castle's sandstone pillars.

"We have already known terrible things. You must be away from here!" Marthe pleaded, her rough, old hand trembling like a moth on Mordiern's arm. Élise's face distraught and stung by tears, burned into his shoulder.

"But I left the Order almost a twelve month ago!" he protested. "You only need to swear I have since been a free man... " But his plea was to no avail. Their generous hearth was his no longer. Instead, only the sun and moon, the stars and the wild wind. So he gave his love the beautiful songs, carefully erased of the other man's name. For that was all he had left to give. And by evening he was gone.

XX

The quiet hours between morning and afternoon seemed to pass in suspended animation. Shutters had closed tight in the thunderous heat and huge raindrops fell without cooling the air. The broiling wrath of a greater force held the town in thrall, and even Clement felt moved to turn his door sign to *Fermé* and switch off the computer. He then went to sit at his desk to await the storm's passing.

Marks from past deals and deliberations scarred its hard, lignum surface, and underneath his blotter lay more doodles of a loitering mind. Aimless scratches, and coffee cup rings. But it was the swastika that was the most incisive and clear. Gouged deep, obviously with feeling. He'd never noticed it before, beneath his new, green plastic organiser replete with shiny paper clips and all the other paraphernalia of a busy modern office.

Clement followed its angles with his fingernail, speculating idly on the desk's origins, for surely such an item was not of these parts? He had no time for puzzles and immediately covered it over. Out of sight, out of mind. Then, as lightning ripped through the sky and rain battered the window glass, he pulled some hairs from his head and tied them together. Detached from their source, they looked strangely vulnerable, greying at the base, a meagre sample of what had filled the sacks for Ernst Heiden, rope-maker of Breslau. But Clement knew nothing of that, and wanted only to disguise this creeping anarchy by buying some matching colourant. The two-tone strands snapped between his teeth as the telephone rang, and caught in his mouth as he answered in French..

"*Maisons du Soleil.* Can I help you?"

"Clement? Clement Ash?" The voice seemed really close and out of breath.

"That's right."

"It's Dan here. Dan Madox... Look here this is terribly short notice I know but... "

Shit...

"My God!" Clement's face suddenly coloured. He grabbed a pen. "Where are you?"

"Gatwick. Taking off in an hour. Been some air traffic control cock-up..."

I like it...

"When do you get in?"

"Twenty one twenty. Is that O.K.?"

"Great!" Clement tried to contain his pleasure. In fact, this was more than great. Wonderful, in fact, now his brother Knight - his fellow warrior-at-arms - was on his way... "I'll be there. No problem."

"Love to Catherine. How is she, by the way?" Asked the other. but suddenly the line was dead merging the surly silence into space, while outside in the aftermath of fearsome thunder and celestial flashes, the whole of darkened Collioure was shaken to its ancient core.

*

Catherine let herself in to the apartment just as the first onslaught struck the *boucherie's* awning into sagging submission. Gravel flung up by the deluge resolutely stuck to her legs while the wetness bound her shift dress into a second skin. She still held the courgette, and Rosa Tavernier also noticed the bloodstains around the hem and how flushed was that usually pale, northern face. The leggy veal calf had been pierced, had she not?

The old woman withdrew from her carcasses to listen at the wall as her *locataire* went upstairs. She knew exactly all the sounds of doors and floor coverings, and the bathroom - whose plumbing was connected to hers - was Mrs. Ash's immediate port of call. Rosa Tavernier's well-tuned ear could tell she was now astride the bidet, sluicing away the same garlic-smelling giver of life as her other women had received from the *Kapos*. Then it was the shower, and using too much water as careless people always do.

In her block though, there'd been none, not from any shortage but because it was a clever game of make-believe where the silver sprinklers stayed dry. God knew they were needed when the filth piled up... The death panics always gave her more work. They didn't all take their cloakroom tickets either, those who knew, but the confusion hadn't lasted long. Considering. Anyway, there were compensations. She'd seen the rings and other bits and pieces sliced from their secretly tailored places, and those she'd fancied were quietly slipped deep between her breasts. Sometimes later, as befitted the owner of a prosperous business, she'd shown them off at local functions, fêtes and concerts in the days when she did such things. Sapphires from Salonika, garnets from Grenoble, the spoils of a war of plenty that had come her way.

But the war in the heavens was only just beginning with a sudden and obliterating darkness. A numbing void which, after each flash, erupted into a savage, celestial rage. The purring power for her freezers and refrigerators was cut too, and soon those hunks and chunks, huge parcels of meat and mounds of chicken with dangling, penile heads would soften and smell of what they really were, while the banks of mince would slowly swell to life. Unlike those who'd lain strewn in the black wet graves, whom she'd long forgotten.

*

Catherine felt her way through to the main room and lay sprawled on the divan, dazed and replete. Only that incredible garden stayed in her mind as one darkness enveloped another... She saw berries, leaves, hanging fruit. His fruit, his hands old and skilled. Master-craftsmen of pain and pleasure. And his unusual, yellowed eyes that never altered, were on hers before she slept.

"He's coming! Tonight!" Clement lit one of Rosa Tavernier's stubby candles with the lit wick of another. The small flames flickered nervously under his breath exuding a smell that wasn't entirely tallow. "Nine twenty. Perpignan airport. Hey, is that bed aired? And I expect he'll need something to eat as well."

"Yes, sir." Catherine was vague and slurred, at odds with his tenseness.

"Christ, you've been in all day! Wise up, woman!"

The first time he'd ever called her that. And indeed she was a woman now - sated and stupefied, part of another world. The flickering lights blew towards her and although the thunder had passed over to the north, the rain still fell, its power spent. His wife's head was wrapped in a towel turban, her eyes only on Eden.

"I mean, how much more must I do round here?" Clement prowled restlessly around the room. But she was unreachable, and hitting her would be pointless. Moreover, time was running out.

"He's *your* friend." Catherine smiled wearily.

"Well that's bloody charming, I must say. Oh, sod this fucking power cut." Clement whined, using the window glass as a mirror to preen himself. "I wanted to wash my hair. Hey, what's it like? Tell me." He wheedled, flattening his fringe.

"It'll do." She obliged, although not looking.

And in her car, through the rain-soaked streets, Clement had time to think. Time to recall how Daniel Madox's grip in greeting had lingered beyond the introductions after the choir's last concert. Time to re-imagine the six feet tall, lean man whose crisp, dried curls grew down his neck and threatened to swamp his whole body. To wonder whether his chest was as soft and warm as a bear rug, his back the same... This spurred him on through confusing new road works and scattered cones, past the glare of foreign headlights under a vast, black sky.

Catherine meanwhile stirred herself into life, and in that irregular, golden glow eking in between the shutters' shabby, wooden slats, she suddenly became aware that someone must have previously closed them and returned Léon Tavernier's photograph to the wall.

*

Moments later, the electricity returned as suddenly as it had cut out, and the doctor stood at the foot of his wife's bed and told her puffed, sullen face that he'd left some produce in the kitchen for *'das Stubenmadchen'* to deal with. Cooking didn't interest him, or her, and all too often the fruits of his garden just festered and shrivelled in their own juices, attracting flies. He didn't need to flaunt his things like the other *cultivateurs en chômage* - he had money enough. Instead they'd invariably be rolled up in old newspapers to clog the only *poubelle* in the Avenue with their rotten weight.

"There's surely no more water left in the sky." Estelle observed, looking out at the lightning as it retreated over the range of nearby peaks. Its act spent, ending yet another fleeting diversion that enlivened her waiting. "I hear there are new people in the town." She announced to his back as he was leaving. "English I believe."

He stopped. His hair, his suit, his scented hands detained.

"I'm told the young woman is quite attractive. She's turned a few heads already." Estelle blew out a stream of cigar smoke. "And her husband too." She smiled weakly.

"Who says?" The doctor snapped.

"Héléne."

"That Jew's wrong!" His face was suddenly changed. He struck his fist on the bed end with a terrible force. This eager official who'd helped fill the trucks for Drancy - that insatiable well of misery - now shared the very air she breathed. There was no forgiveness in her stare. Only hatred.

"Get out!"

✝

Then, washed and changed, he stood in the fussy dining room watching the maid set the only place at the table. How he despised her moon-like face, her wide, unwieldy legs.

"I employ you for your labour not your opinions," he snapped.

She looked up, uncomprehending.

"You are to discuss nothing with my wife. NOTHING! Do you understand?"

In fear, she nodded, then made her exit. He sat down, absently fingering the modelled knife handle engraved with the name, Benjamin Luberg, jeweller from Villefranche and lover of fine things.

Just like him.

The doctor helped himself to the red wine from Libourne. Unlike his sister, he'd eschewed the more common floor tiling for carpets. The woven luxury of carmine, copper and ultramarine. From Qum to Kiev to Vienna, these intricate patterns had come, and still glowed in the careful, half light, untouched by time. A fair reward, he felt, as was his porcelain collection, although he'd turned down the Kändler harlequin. These creations from Meissen and Limoges, fired hard to a glistening vanity included his favourite item. Female angels clustered around a celestial Ormolu clock. All mementoes of deeds well done.

He savoured it all as a steak was set before him, barely touched by the flames for its ripe blood to replenish his own. Then, when the licked-clean plate was removed, he saw close-up how the maid's calves bristled with razor-grown hairs, and called her back again for no reason.

More wine and a drowsy contemplation of the piano. Ebony shining, and big as a bed, it had filled Joachim Kreisler's small apartment with a joy he had no part of. Now the keys lay yellow and un-tuned but as neither he nor the butcher were pianists, it mattered not. This was, he mused, his greatest prize. Even greater than the pearl he'd found, or the Englishwoman's crazed desire, he mused, reclining.

Indeed, he smiled to himself, and on his way up to bed, once the girl had gone home, the tormentor flung his old harmonica deep into the garbage bin.

*

Daniel Madox indeed looked wonderful, Clement thought as the choirmaster strode bag-swinging towards him. More like a carefree student than a man whose marriage had failed, with curls rown quite lustrous under the bright, foyer lights. His crisp white shirt was open at the throat under a casual, brown jacket.

"Good to see you." Clement warmly took his hand.

"And you." The other's eyes showed visible relief. "Bloody cheek, all this... I'm awfully sorry... "

Clement responded by picking up the travellers various holdalls with impressive aplomb and leading the taller man to the exit. Euphoria had blunted the reality of what actually awaited in the Rue des Templiers' flat. Until that moment.

"Fancy a drink?" He suddenly asked. "There's quite a decent little bar here."

"Fine. Excellent." Daniel was alongside him on the stairs up from the Arrivals area. Long legs, straight thighs, close. In unison. "Flight was a bit iffy if you must know."

"Well we've just had a stinker of a storm. But then June is notorious." Was said with the authority of one who has lived in the South for many years. They found a small table that overlooked the quiet, dark runway. "Travelling a bit light, aren't we?" Clement set the bags down.

"Only essentials, except for Geraldine of course... " Daniel turned his head away as tears began to gather. "Look here, chum, I can never repay you... "

Clement comforted his shoulder and in perfect French, ordered drinks.

"Bottoms up." He moved his wine glass to intimately nudge the other, coinciding with a reciprocated smile of welcome.

The choirmaster despite his recent, matrimonial ordeal, was not in a state of neglect. Far from it. His teeth were clean and straight, his skin a good colour, and those hands that had guided The Earl Music Balladeers through a litany of love and longing, were lightly tanned and smooth.

"How's the lovely Catherine then?" He suddenly asked, breaking the silence. "We were cut off the last time I asked."

"She's fine. Just fine." Clement answered, with no mention of bruising her in hidden places, bullying and indifference. Days of solitude and nights of nothing.

"That's good." Daniel Madox seemed genuinely pleased. "The choir wasn't the same when she left. Anyhow, it never compensated for a lot of bad things... " He gazed out at the activity beyond the large window, now normal again.

"All's well that ends well." Clement gave one of his six-teeth smiles, and laid his hand firmly on the other man's arm. "We're going to be busy you know. Things are really picking up and I'm seriously into things historical... "

Daniel's faraway look became more focussed as he drained his glass.

"Sounds great."

"Well, I hope my dear wife has risen to the occasion of your visit." Clement escorted him out, wondering all the while if she'd even got herself dressed, never mind put a meal in the oven.

*

Indeed, his wife had changed from stained to spotless, and the most concealing clothes she had. However, it was her subtly bronzed, bare feet beneath the hem of a long, cotton skirt that were the first things Daniel Madox saw at the top of the stairs.

"My God, Catherine, you look terrific! Doesn't she, Clement! It's doing you both good here that's for sure." His embrace was warm and prolonged. She was thinner than he'd remembered and smelt of a sweetness he couldn't quite place. Then he touched her hair. "I had visions all this would have been chopped off because of the heat."

"One has to hang on to something," she smiled. Clement, meanwhile, rested the conductor's bags impatiently on the step behind them and sighed too loudly to be merely tired. "And what about yourself?" She asked, taking her time, as innocently golden as a sun-ripened nectarine.

Daniel felt his own luggage against his buttocks, pushing him forward.

"We'll talk about that later. I say... not a bad little *pied à terre*," he lied, looking around. "You've made it very nice. Even got a... "

"I'll put these in our room." Clement interrupted, pushing past in irritation. "Anything for dinner, Catherine?" He asked in a lightly threatening tone. "Or are we to be unlucky?"

"I'm not hungry." Daniel had already sensed tension. "Really."

"Catherine!" Clement persisted noisily in the kitchen. But she stayed silent.

"A bit of bread and cheese will be fine. Honestly." The visitor sat down uneasily and Clement putting their only two wine glasses on the table, saw how the choirmaster's strong, corduroy-clad legs were apart...

"Who's that man?" Daniel asked, for something to say, catching sight of the photograph.

God knows, but it keeps re-appearing." Clement dispensed a red Corbières none too carefully. He felt better now, ready to enjoy his new companion.

"How's business, anyhow?" Daniel ventured. "Is Europe opening up for you?"

"Yep." Clement positioned himself opposite, and rapidly drained his glass. His upper lip rimmed red. "The more idiots we get down here the better. The natives won't touch the derelicts, you see... "

"That's very cynical of you!" His friend laughed indulgently and looked over to where Catherine was studiously doing her nails.

"Well, I've got a smart office to pull in the punters. I'm my own boss. Can't be bad eh? Bit of hassle from our fat, local *Notaire* - but nothing I can't handle." He refilled Daniel's glass, and met his eyes.

"Be a love and get us a little meal, eh?" Clement then called over to Catherine in a voice more pubescent than baby. "So we can talk."

"That would be nice." Daniel conspired, winking. So, unsmilingly she zipped up her manicure set and proceeded to the kitchen.

*

"Mmm. Looks superb." Daniel grinned, bread in his mouth.

"*Ratatouille des légumes.*" As Catherine served him first. The coloured strips hung steaming from the ladle, including the courgette that had recently been inside her. "From the garden," she said, moving on to Clement.

"Whose?" Anger and politeness were hard to combine.

"Ah ha." She tapped her nose. Secure with a third person present. "A secret." Then came a coquettish grin which made his colour deepen.

"Well *I* don't care where they've been." Daniel enthused. "They're just delicious. Clever girl." The guest devoured and spoke at the same time. "This is more than Geraldine would ever have done, I tell you. It's been all purée this and purée that, with the baby of course." He stopped for a moment, his eyes as if fixed on his child far away.

"I can't have children. Did you know?" Catherine announced suddenly, and in the silence that followed, the dying thunder returned to the skies. Clement snatched the pepper mill and furiously twisted the top, back and forth, raining a black plague on his food.

Daniel coughed and diplomatically dabbed his mouth.

"At least I was in the right place," added the married, calm and caring Mrs. Ash. "Doing *in-vitros* for a thousand pounds a pop. Sending them off with hope in their hearts. But those women weren't stupid, you know. They could tell... "

"Could tell what?" Daniel had recovered. "Go on."

Catherine threw back her head and gave out a grotesque laugh.

"That I was a *virgo intacta*!" Like artillery fire in that small room, those two words tore them apart, and let Léon Tavernier's warm slivers go cold on their forks. "Imagine my shame. Fat women, scraggy women, every ugliness you can imagine, all getting poked at least twice a week, and me just having to pretend... "

Clement scraped his chair back and stood over her, very close. Close enough for her to see the hairs up his nose, to feel his trembling hand on her shoulder.

"So how could I stay? I have *some* pride. So here I am. Cheers!" She raised her mug of wine anarchically to just under his chin.

"I think, Catherine, that Dan has come here with enough problems without wanting to be burdened with ours." Was his pompous, schoolmasterly tone saved for wayward clients.

"Yours. Not 'ours,'" she said, lips hardly moving.

"... Er... I think we're all tired." Their visitor pressed his paper napkin into a tight, tense square. "It's been one hell of a day actually." Then he brightened. "Tell you what, mate, I can't wait to go and suss out some of those bargain dumps of yours... Be good to get right away. Got anything lined up for tomorrow?"

"Two places near Soulatges." Was thin and expressionless.

"Great! Will you be coming, Catherine?" He asked, watching her move swiftly from table to kitchen in that same leonine way he remembered - her mane swinging from side to side.

"I might, or I might not. It depends." This man was a false flatterer, and had turned too quickly to Clement.

She plunged the plates into the soapy sink while the two men got themselves organised.

"Bathroom's through there." Clement pointed. "Steps and a hole, sorry. Grooves for toes and a handrail though... Oh, and a bidet."

"Gosh, they think of everything. Thanks... Goodnight Catherine!" Daniel called out, collecting up the best towel Clement had left for him on the bed.

*

Rosa Tavernier knew it was the newcomer who was showering as the other two never washed at night. That would have to be extra on the rent next time. She grew tired of pressing her old, flat ear to the wall, and the smell of herb sausages that seemed to cling too long. Instead, she went to her body-hollowed bed and its human-hair mattress, where her restorative cup of urine awaited. Where dreams of the butchering past had never troubled her snoring sleep.

But Clement persevered and was rewarded with a good view, for Daniel Madox had left the plastic shower curtain to one side and stood trance-like under the water's soothing flow. His was a firm-muscled body luxuriantly hirsute, with dark whorls nestling where his white buttocks conjoined. But more importantly, the man was playing with himself - absently pulling on his penis as might a child who has found comfort.

His host felt himself quicken. It had been a long time since the Chute Street gymnasium - too long since he'd touched another man and held him close... His past and his future were bound in that very moment, and he therefore heard nothing of his wife finally clearing up and firmly shutting the small spare bedroom door behind her.

*

The storm had cleared the southern heavens to an electrifying blue, and the morning breeze that replaced the Mistral gently nudged along the few, thin clouds above. Clement and Daniel stepped out smartly together, dodging Collioure's slower shoppers and lingering sightseers. Neither man mentioned the revelations of the night before, for them, this was a new beginning under a new sky. They had decided to have lunch out, as Catherine couldn't be relied upon, and then take her car to the vineyard district of Soulatges.

In public, Daniel's greetings echoed Clement's - his smile enlarged, his handshake warm and sincere, freed for a while from other cares. The butcher however had been more restrained, for broad daylight had revealed the extent of this new Englishman's carpeted body. She'd extended her hand to him, but in revulsion, and wouldn't hesitate to inform her brother on their obvious close relationship.

"*Mon bel-ami, Monsieur Madox.*" Was how Clement unwittingly introduced him to all and sundry, and also the ears of the old man taking his early morning chocolate. He could see for himself how things were between them, and had no need of his sister's observations. The two men seemed inseparable. If this was in the street, what did they do in private? He spared himself the answer. Instead, his claw-like fingers tightened on his cup's china handle; flint-hard knuckles straining hatred on his old flesh as they passed. The hand that had given the English woman the only pleasure she'd known. The hand now needed for other tasks.

They glanced his way. His little butterfly's husband - shorter, more slim than the other with still the reddish stain on his tight fly. Large, brown eyes that would have looked prettier on a woman and skin quite dark against the other. The doctor got up quickly, paid his bill and followed the pair at a discreet distance until they reached the estate agency's door. He had a full schedule ahead, and hadn't felt such pleasure for a long time.

The silver Renault stood dulled by the convenient shade of the apartment in the *Rue des Templiers*. Under less scrutiny now after almost a month, hardly anyone paused now to read that Supadeal of Leyton was the supplier. For it had become part of the street furniture. Only the doctor showed any interest. His darting search noted property sheets scattered on the rear seat together with various items of men's clothing and a can of insect spray. The mileage was high already for a new car, but there were no scratches, no marks of contact - unlike his own latest acquisition. Wheel nuts clean, wiper rubbers unworn... This was a quite obviously a good, reliable car.

The meat purveyor from her empty shop could see he was busy. She saw him check his watch, and the street, but never once did he look skywards to those narrow, shuttered windows above.

"She's up there." His sister then said to him, once he'd stepped inside her shop. "I've heard her."

"That's of no interest to me now." The doctor knocked a fly off his hand, and pointed to a portion of horse, divided by a fatty furrow.

"For you or Estelle Bonbois?" She slowly but meticulously smothered it in a coloured section of *France Soir*.

"She pleases herself." He answered absently staring out of her window. "*Gott in der Himmel.* Hello, they're coming!" His face lit up, and sure enough, both men advanced towards the car, unaware of those four eyes upon them. The taller man now sported a new Panama hat and sunglasses, and they seemed to be debating who should drive, with smiles and pats all round. Finally, Mr. Ash took the wheel and revved his manhood full throttle into the traffic as the mournful little shop bell broke the silence.

*

Catherine spent the morning half asleep, half awake, unable to lose her memory of that special garden and its abundance. Of that light and growing heat which had made her open like the flowers, and like a summer's morning, she was still moist with his dew... Then, in her drowsiness, he was there, her hierophant, seeming taller than before, with his arm around her waist, guiding her down towards his stream, *'le ruisseau de desir'* ... but first he stopped and picked from its bushy bank, a purply-velvet aubergine...

*

She had yesterday's strawberry-stained shift dress to soak, and wanted her hair to be held this time by only the lightest of accessories. Two tiny clips were set aside to support the sidepieces below the parting. These would then fall at a touch to cover her shoulders and breasts... Thus began her preparations for the afternoon. She painted her nails pearlescent pink and her toes to match. He'd like that. She knew. Then her clothes - something other than white for the Nymph of Eden. Catherine chose black. Black for the woman who had known love. Black for the sky that had borne witness.

*

The car was hot, so Daniel Madox helpfully improvised a sunblind with his jacket, and rested his bare, lower arm on the open window ledge to catch what cool air there was.

"Fantastic!" He said, taking everything in. "I still can't believe it."

Clement grunted in concentration as the D117 narrowed past a feldspar factory and a succession of container lorries approached on the other side. White-dusted trees tossed to confusion by the traffic's flow blocked the view either side before the landscape opened out, revealing high limestone ranges to both left and right, harbouring their mounded vineyards in a warm embrace. The heat haze muted the scrubby colours on the slopes, but lower down, the undulating carpet of vibrant green dazzled the eye.

"I say, this is superb!" The choirmaster smile widened below his sunglasses and Clement suddenly felt good that this man was beside him.

"Just smell the earth!" Daniel breathed in deep. "God, I could live here!"

"Well, it's not so difficult to sell a barn for conversion, but some of these little village places aren't shifting at all." Clement was in the know and enjoying his superiority.

"What's your publicity like?" The other asked. "I've not seen any Clement Ash signs yet."

"You wouldn't. We're *Maisons du Soleil*. Greenbaum thought it best not to use either of our names."

"Oh?"

"Besides, I found a swastika carved into my desk the other day. Not very nice. Thought all that sort of thing was well over."

"Nothing's ever over." Daniel said idly, waving to some children picnicking in a lay-by. This seemed to silence his companion as they left Maury and climbed up a poorly made road towards a gap in the rocks and a view beyond. Daniel Madox kept a long finger poised on the map, and Clement smiling, half-squinting, could pretend it was his member.

His hand reached out, touched it and withdrew.

"Sorry mate." He laughed, embarrassed. "Don't know what came over me."

"It's alright. O.K, now take the next left... Christ! Look at that! Up there!"

Clement braked and both men stared out at the ruined Cathar tower of Quéribus rearing skyward from its craggy base. Daniel's eyes couldn't leave it alone as the car moved down towards Cucugnan amongst more vineyards and itinerant back-packers broiling in the heat.

"Left again... difficult to turn round if we miss it... " The co-pilot was again back to earth.

But there was no going back for Clement, who let his hand fall to the other's thigh. It felt strong and lean under the cotton twill, as arched and muscular as the very hills which fell away as the road again ascended. He couldn't leave it, not for a moment, not even to change gear. The turning for Ruffiac came and went.

"Damn!" Clement looked straight ahead, gripping hard now and Daniel Madox covered his hand with his own.

"Not to worry... God, I've got so much to tell you." Then eyes a sudden, frantic blue met the brown. "The last six months have been hell... " He returned to the map, ashamed. "Let's get to this place of yours first. There's a layby coming up."

*

They reached Soulatges, decked in posters, layered with the newest on the old. The past bleached and tattered under forthcoming attractions for *dégustations*, *vente directe* and all the other paraphernalia of a small village summer. Daniel was glad to read anything rather than open his can of worms.

Clement wound down his window to interrupt a wizened, little woman beating her doormat in the narrow, shaded street.

"There's a large barn for sale here, near an inn," he said in his best French. "Can you please help us find it?"

Her answer, although in rapid Catalan, was at least precise.

"*Merci*," he smiled afterwards.

"I got most of that." Daniel then proudly relayed the directions.

"Clever boy." Clement grinned, steering the silver Renault along a track whose high, grassy central ridge brushed the chassis underneath. "Lot of Spanish round here, mind. Doesn't do much for one's text book French I'm afraid."

He still felt good. In control.

Meanwhile, the sun was high and the sky now quite clear. The cacophony of roadside crickets filled the car as they reached the barn. It was half hidden, barricaded by broken wire fencing with jungle-sized weeds suffocating its crumbling walls. The roof bore an unruly landscape of displaced tiles that heaped in a pile round a small chimney.

"Mmm." Daniel Madox stalked its periphery. "What price this little gem?"

"Eight thousand francs. *Prix à debattre*, but not too much, mind." Clement was busy attaching an agency notice to the hot, grey stones. *A VENDRE. MAISONS DU SOLEIL* together with the Collioure phone number screamed for attention. When he finally pushed open the only wood-wormed door, the blackness seized him, and something struck his foot.

"Christ almighty!"

The smell was indescribable, and the open door's light revealed an iron snare stuffed with rabbits, weasels, other smaller rodents - all decapitated. All rotting. "Watch out!" He flung the whole gory, contraption outside, and a rotting head hit the choirmaster on the knee.

"Thanks." Daniel said wryly, entering the gloom.

"Got the tape measure?"

"Yep."

By torchlight, they began taking measurements, negotiating uneven, stone slabs and musty straw. An old bicycle lay twisted in the far corner, changed by mould and rust. A torn wicker basket hung from its handlebars. Daniel tripped on a pile of coats that could have been sacks, riddled with holes.

"Strange," muttered Clement, helping him to his feet.

"God, who'd want all this?"

"You wait. There's one born every minute... ah... there's electricity." Clement was jotting things down. "That'll keep the price up. Good."

"Any water, taps, etcetera?" Daniel was catching on fast.

"Dunno. Madame just said *'pas habitable'*."

"The answer is no." Daniel was keenly on all fours, sacrificing his clean trousers in the search, and suddenly Clement was on him. Astride, like a rider, gripping with his legs.

"Gosh, you scared the shit out of me!" His mount shouted, making no attempt to dislodge the incubus. And soon Clement's soiled hands, not so careful now, not so reticent in the dark, were passing under and over, clasping and stroking. Releasing and taking again. Horse and rider breathing as one.

"Now see what you've done." He murmured, moving his hips to and fro, while the other man arched his strong back and began to fake a trot. "Faster! Faster!" They neighed, they bellowed, rubbed and rocked together, while those pale, almost colourless eyes which had followed them to the door, gradually grew accustomed to the lack of light.

XXI

'And the dragon was wroth with the woman, and went to make
war with the remnant of her seed, which keep the commandments
of God, and have the testimony of Jesus Christ.'
(Revelation.12.v.17.)

On the stroke of four, as Mordiern Guyon fell into a troubled asleep in the Fontcouverte woods outside Saintes, Girard Louis Corbichon's blindfolded head rolled from his body to rest at the feet of two priests still in prayer for his soul's safe passing. The crowd's roar from the scaffold and nearby windows filled the *Place des Oies* and lifted over the town of La Baume to taint the Autumn countryside.

A tall, black hat thrown from an upper room, lay alongside the dead knight's body, while another, stiffened and softened in turn by winter frosts and summer suns, landed on his horse. The aged *Boulonnais* with only a simple noose for slaughter around its massive head, reared up and charged through the rabble, dragging the executioner's old servant behind him. In the stunned aftermath, those whom The Whiteface's huge destrier had bruised and trampled, were helped to safety, whilst the remaining, unscathed revellers having quickly crossed themselves, drifted down the narrow street towards the church of St. Jean du Pouce for refreshment. But in the fast-fading light, the watchers at the windows remained transfixed by the unfolding scene near the Arche de St. Paul.

Meanwhile, the three men who'd travelled from Beaupréau, stood together drinking. Strangers to the town, they'd walked most of the way for the spectacle in La Baume. Robert Sagan, the eldest was also the heaviest, and his creased girdle was added to by a length of rope. Since his farming days in the Cotentin, he'd lost most of his hair, and both ears curled purple in the cold. But what he'd lost in hair, he'd made up in other ways and, like his two companions, had grown prosperous.

"'Tis a bad sign," he said, passing round the cup of wine. "To lose a horse ready for the fire."

"Did you see how he took Aymeric Forgue's old servant?" Noë Roche, black as a Moor and sometimes mistaken for one, belched loudly. "As though he were light as a fart."

"That is the nature of the breed." Was all Sagan dared say, hoping Druide, now twenty-one by his calculations, would have the wit to find shelter.

"What about those two bitches?" Othon Lamaire suddenly remembered, grinning lasciviously. In the commotion they'd forgotten that Hilaire Roland's widow and daughter still stood bound together at on corner of the makeshift dais. "Let's have some sport!"

The rich wine of Libourne flowed in their veins, bearing them smartly back to the square. Three men, hardened and slightly stooped from a life on the land, stumbled to where the expectant crowd had re-formed. Where those who'd stood at the rear were now rewarded with a place so close they could reach out and pull the captives' rags. An emaciated dog circled nimbly between their legs. 'Bézu' had followed from the farm and would not desert them. His ragged, arched loins pushing in and out of the stakes tied to his owners' bodies.

"We'll have him as well!" Someone kicked him sharply in the ribs, and his cry mingled with Marthe and Élise Roland's pleas for mercy, as their eyes already burned in terror at the approaching populace.

XXII

"From now on, *mon papillon blanc* must be gold all over." The expert gardener had ordered Catherine in the most winsome post-coital tones he could muster before *le petit mort* had claimed him in the heart of Wednesday's storm. Then after the tempest, the gentle rain, and slumber, had come the awakening. In his shed, in the Garden of Eden, where he'd prepared a flowering bougainvillea seed bed of cotton lawn, together with a bottle of warm *Contrexéville* water nearby.

"If you turn golden, I will love you all the more." He'd promised, letting his mouth stray where she thought mouths shouldn't go... and he'd stirred again, just as the rain renewed its bombardment on the roof.

*

So his creature had obeyed, and willingly. Anything to be what he wanted, and in his strengthening arms again. But not before she'd spent the morning combing Collioure's streets for him as soon as the two Englishmen had left the flat. Under the pretext of shopping, she'd left stone had been left unturned, but still remained empty-handed. The market, the cafés, the poets on the beach. Ignoring the catcalls and whistles that followed her dispiriting progress.

The town seemed empty without him, and tempting though it was to prove her potent memories were real, his 'white butterfly' hadn't the courage to re-visit its garden.

*

Dejected, but nevertheless determined to improve herself, Catherine lay across the first, tiny balcony which jutted out from the lounge, smeared only with the remains of some old olive oil. Gradually she'd peeled off her clothes, and slept on through the day, above the busy street with only her heels visible to the butcher below. Daniel Madox was quite out of her thoughts now, replaced by things she could never reveal. She clung to the vision of the *le Jardin d'Eden*, fearful of it fading, fearful of yet another loss.

*

Nothing had ever harmed her so. The sun knew a victim when it saw one. That equatorial burner, that child's drawn yellow ball, harmless in books and on brochures for the honeymoon she'd never had.

And when the carillon pealed from the church by the shore at six o'clock and woke her, she could barely crawl back into the cool linoleum shade. It was then that she must have passed out.

*

Rosa Tavernier slapped Catherine's tender cheeks as though forcing paté into a pot, all the while casting disapproving glances in the taller Englishman's direction. If she'd known he was so grossly hirsute she'd never have given him house room. As it was, Mr. Ash had been less than truthful.

"No need for a doctor." She turned specifically to Clement who, on impulse had called her upstairs, and was now regretting it.

"... golden all over... He wants me golden all over... " Catherine moaned, motionless. Her swollen eyelids still closed like those of newborn mice.

"Does he now?" Rosa Tavernier laid a cold hand on her forehead. Daniel stared.

"Too much sun, silly girl!" He admonished publicly lest this ugly woman in black should penetrate his real thoughts.

Meanwhile the butcher's stolen glances at the young woman's body didn't go unrewarded. She had never seen such skin, burnt though it was, with nipples bristling like dice and a stomach un-stretched by any birth. But red, so red... he wouldn't want her now...

"Will she be alright?" Daniel then ventured, keeping his distance.

"All will be well if you keep her in your sight. I have some little goats' livers. Rub them like so... " She demonstrated the procedure with those huge hands attached to speckled arms of hanging skin, armatured by massive bone. Still strong enough for her present work, after the endlessly busy *Himmelfahrtblock*. The chamber to Heaven...

"Thank you." Clement said, as they followed her down to the shop. He noticed at the same time how hair that settled in the nape of her neck was quite black. Unlike the roots at the top. In her cool, empty morgue, the only customers were a few industrious flies, and Daniel, not especially fond of meat, who felt he was going to be sick.

*

"Christ. Never again!" He raced back upstairs with indecent haste. "Doesn't smell like a normal butchers to me, and I keep getting the evil eye. What's she really like?"

"I don't see much of her actually." Clement made light of it, setting out the frozen livers in the sun. He then turned to Catherine. "You're a stupid cow! Actually, a *veal* cow." Without caring if Daniel heard. This was a bloody nuisance. He roughly arranged a wet cloth on her forehead and her big, grey eyes opened.

"I really have to be golden all over. You know that?" Her dry lips mumbled, sealed by sleep dribble.

"Try this." Daniel had fetched some water and passed it to her, trying not to look at the nearby purple offal beginning to melt. Catherine drank as though it was the last water on earth. Like the captives in those steaming trucks who'd drawn in precious air at Neuberg when the doors were briefly opened for the change of guard...

"Interesting place tomorrow." Clement tried to change the subject. "An old olive mill. Lots of history. Bags of potential."

Catherine gripped the glass in case it was taken away, gleaning every drop.

"I'll fetch you some more." Daniel offered, and duly returned. She took a full draught then, unable to stop herself, coughed a sudden spray in his face.

"There's bloody gratitude for you!" Her husband gave a sour laugh, as Daniel wiped his cheek and solicitously began to work those pulpy, purple organs into the worst of the sun's damage. "Who needs bloody women?"

Clement meanwhile, had emptied his briefcase on to the table, carefully setting aside papers relating to that property's registry details. Plans and more plans for conversions never attempted. "It's quite a find." He said to Daniel's back. "Apparently, there was a Templar community nearby, once upon a time. Ideal really, with the river and grazing... "

"Oh."

"One tends to think they all buggered off on the Crusades, but that wasn't the whole story apparently. Must look into it. Definitely a good selling ploy." He walked over to the window, ignoring his still-prone wife.

"Just think, for the price of a British Leyland family saloon you could have a stake in the land of the Templars. Get it? A stake? Good, eh? 'Cos you do know what happened to them, don't you?"

"No."

"Hardly McDonalds. More the slow-cook... "

He missed how the choirmaster, with vomit rising in his throat, had rushed off to wash the calves' blood from his hands.

"We'll try and get some decent shots of the place. Make it irresistible. What do you think?"

"Fine. Great." But Daniel had returned looking pale, still smelling his fingers.

"I've been thinking." Clement continued to address the street outside. "Obviously we've got to go and check it over, but... well, just a thought, spur of the moment kind of thing... how would you like a permanent base down here?" He turned suddenly, his white teeth bared in a smile. "I could run my own business and finally crawl out from under Greenbaum's fat belly, and you... well, there's always demand for a choir..." Tentatively were his ideas given birth, and quietly were they received with small, polite noises.

Clement was encouraged.

"Let me see now." Returning to his papers. "It must be just off that road we took yesterday... Here, look!" He rested his body weight on firm, brown wrists - a primate pose with legs apart. Daniel stood nearby.

"No harm in looking I suppose. Nothing ventured and all that... "

The other man's lithe power had delivered a sudden tremor of fear and elation. Yet also the faintest warning - confused and ambiguous - of dangerous possibilities lying along those straight, tree-dappled highways.

Clement then tidied things away. He was hungry.

"Better rustle something up for the old *diner*, then." He snapped his case shut. "Got to keep our strength up. Places to go, people to see... " He glanced over at Catherine who was beginning to stir.

"Give us a hand, hey, Dan?" He almost pranced into the kitchen.

"OK." Yet from the back of him, it was obvious Clement wasn't wearing underpants. In a moment of panic he wondered if they'd been left at that barn for anyone to see, but was unable to ask.

Men hunting, Catherine thought bleakly, watching them scrabble and slam about for what little food there was. Everywhere she touched, hurt.

"Oh, bugger this!" Clement snatched away his apron. "Let's have a pizza instead." And because he suddenly envisaged olives and anchovies sunk in a melted sea of cheese, and because the musician was so in thrall to his smooth masculinity, Catherine was left alone where she was.

*

Meanwhile, the doctor found himself suddenly busy, with not enough hours in the day or night to fulfil the demands of his detailed lists. Being a creature of habit, such things had always structured his days, and now with such convoluted affairs to deal with, they were invaluable. He was a man with a purpose, unlike the hordes of idly meandering tourists drifting under the palm trees towards the loud, crude ethnic music and booths where instant portraits and slickly airbrushed images of fishing boats could be bought for greedy sums.

He'd even eschewed his regular *chocolat chaud* and stroll around the *Palais Royal* for more important things. Even his Garden of Eden could grow on its own, unattended because he had his car to see to. His first trip yesterday had exposed battery and alternator problems. After years of confinement under a blanket in the garage, the old Citroën needed an overhaul. Like him, it was out of practice.

*

He waited impatiently in the shade of a peeling plane tree outside Ets. Davide's servicing workshop in the *Rue d'Argile*. It would soon be lunchtime, and then nothing for three hours. Small wonder such people never moved from square one. Unlike him, who had grasped life's many opportunities. He tapped his watch in obvious annoyance.

"*Salut!*" A heavy hand suddenly clamped his shoulder. Philippe Ferand, *Notaire*, briefcase under one arm had just been in the *Bar des Frères* and now breathed *pastis* into his old friend's face. "How goes it with *mon copain*? My friend?"

"*Ganz gut*. Can't complain. And you?"

"I'm having problems. Got a moment? How about a drink?" The official wiped his red, rippled forehead on his sleeve.

"They're doing my car at the moment. I'd better wait here," replied the other, glad to have an excuse, for this was not a man to cross. Especially when drunk. "Why? What's the matter?"

"It's him. That piece of scum!" Philippe Ferand knocked the side of his case hard. "*Der Abschaum* Englishman!"

"He seems harmless enough, the little I've seen... " The doctor chose his words carefully.

"Don't you believe it. He's up to dirty tricks alright." Ferand raised his voice and the Citroën's mechanic peered out in surprise from under the boot. "And I mean, dirty."

The old man restrained himself. He knew nothing.

"*Einigen Idioten* thinks he can shift their junk heaps better than I! It's preposterous!" The *Notaire* bellowed, sweating profusely in the sun. "But only I can make things legal. Only I can sign any *Compromis de Vente*." He broke wind, unawares. Kept talking. "Have no fear, old *collaborateur*, he will not thrive."

Collaborateur? Merde...

His voice was still far too loud, and the doctor nervously looked around.

"Never use that 'c' word!" He hissed. "Never!"

"But such a sweet sound my friend, is it not? And of course it bought us both great things, you more than me perhaps, but that's all in the past... " He touched the older man's arm confidentially. Philippe Ferand, friend of the *Milice* and responsible for 'Internal Enemies' had been thorough enough when sober, but since then, in his new profession, had never shown the same zeal or determination. Now the English usurper, his 'deportable element' was abroad with a lover. On active duty.

"Ever seen the wife?" The official suddenly asked lasciviously, and the one who had pierced her coloured under his leathered tan.

"No... I don't think so."

"You've missed a real treat. Nice bit of pussy there I should think."

"Oh." The former doctor eyed his car with some urgency hoping the mechanic would soon re-appear.

"They say she leads a very, very solitary life. The life of a virgin nun... "

"Who says?"

"Your sister's customers. All the latest news, wrapped up with their *chevaline*."

The doctor studied him closely. The man had spittle at the corner of his mouth. Thinking of Mrs. Ash had plainly excited him, and he surreptitiously checked the other's crotch.

"*Plus ça change...* " He said cryptically, recalling how Ferand had often lured the prettiest of the young *Juives* into the freight sheds at Nice station, with promises of little comforts. Then returned his weeping, even more dishevelled conquests to the convoy.

"Monsieur Tavernier?" The man in oily, blue overalls suddenly called out. "Your car's ready."

"I have to go." The doctor moved away from Philippe Ferand rather too eagerly...

"But I've hardly started... " the other protested, grabbing his wrist. "She has *the* most amazing legs... and as for that arse... "

"I'll leave you to your dreams, my friend. À *bientôt*." He left the official, still shouting and swaying in the sun, while he entered the garage's cool office to pay.

"Time he retired, don't you think?" The young man signed the service sheet, staining it with a greasy smear. "Making a fool of himself like that."

"We are all fools." The doctor checked the details carefully and folded it away in his top pocket, where his harmonica used to be.

"You'll find your car will go like a bomb now, sir. Remember to give it plenty of choke to start with." He shook his hand, satisfied with a job well done. "Could do with a bit more mileage, mind, a car of that age…"

"I'll do my best." The doctor smiled, then suddenly remembered that he'd left Mr. Ash's less than clean, yellow underpants in his glove box.

*

The remains of the *Moulin des Olives*, identified as C8560 on the Cadastre with some fifty hectares of land, was barely visible from the road. Its old walls camouflaged by crooked box elders and limes forced to lean by the wind. Rusted sections of a galvanised roof sat askew and incongruous to its other history, while further afield, smooth pastures swelled and hollowed, bearing narrow tracks into the hazy distance. Although no flocks or herds of anything were in evidence, Daniel swore he could hear the tinkle of bells.

"This is Heaven." He scoured the surrounding hills, to where scrubby, accessible slopes became sheer, glancing rock that edged the cloudless blue. Clement's camera meanwhile clicked shots that would lie, creating a greater perspective, soft-focussing the imperfections...

"Good job I didn't have to wait for S.A.F.E.R. to approve." He clicked again, crouching on his haunches. "Something like this shouldn't be hanging around too long." Then he was inside, stepping proprietorially over piles of rubble littering the huge entrance hall. Rooms without doors led off from either side, and at the far end, a dilapidated stairway staggered up to an open landing whose boards were pitted with large holes. Daniel was meanwhile still down at the main door singing snatches of a late Guyon *virelai*, and marvelling at the southerly aspect, towards the sea. Its echo carried upwards, hauntingly rich and clear, but to Clement it meant Catherine.

"Very nice," was tinged with sarcasm as he sniffed the dung beetle air like a *chien de la chasse*, and like such a creature, relieved himself in a dark corner. He came down the stairs, zipping up his fly and strutted over the more even flags to peer through a tall, unglazed window.

"What did I say?" He asked teasingly, for attention.

"What *did* you say?" Daniel was still with his choir and his best soprano had the verse to herself with her light, seamless voice...

"This will do perfectly for us. Can't you feel it?" Clement shouted, possessing the dark and trying to possess the man. "Main road access, water nearby... and the land... Christ! We could sell that off, no sweat." But his new lover had meanwhile wandered off and found other things unlikely to be listed in any particulars.

Syringes and condoms lay strewn in the dirt behind the stairs with old calendar pages crumpled and smeared with human faeces. Here a shoe, there a woman's brassière...

"Anyone can come in here." He said ruefully. "And anyone has."

"No problem." Clement preferred not to look. "Next time, we bring hammers and nails." He felt uncomfortable that the other man had seen such things, and wished to protect him.

"Hey!"

"What?"

"Come and look at these!" Daniel had disappeared but his voice was close. Urgent. "Right at the end here... it's a sort of cupboard. How strange... " Then he tried to read the stencilled names on the sides of several old tea chests that had avalanched to the floor. All flimsy, rotting, accompanied by the faint sounds of fleeing rodent feet... "Ephraim Fischer from Beaulieu: Nathan Dwork, Menton. And who's this? Joachim Kreisler, Cavalaire... "

Straw and dead beetles had also fallen out, and he stamped them underfoot. The faded, indigo words were barely legible.

"All men, " Daniel observed. "All from October 1943."

"Jews." Clement said, coming over.

"Were there Jews in Provence, then?"

"Dunno. Must have been. They're everywhere. Look at Greenbaum. What the hell" he shrugged. "Makes no difference to me."

"But the south was unoccupied, surely?" The conductor, although puzzled, recalled his 'A' Level history. His finger traced over Samuel Finkelstein's name. A doctor from Venice, gentle and clever, expert in allergies and now a table lamp near the *Notaire*'s bedside. "Not too keen on all this actually." He pushed a heavy curl from his forehead. That Greek-lookalike face a mask of consternation.

"Soon shift them if they're getting to you. No problem." Clement dragged two tea chests outside and returned for more. Daniel began to help.

"Shit!" His thumb had caught one of the sharp, tin linings, and wine-dark blood welled up from a small, jagged wound.

"Let me make it better." Clement sucked softly, relishing the intimate, almost metallic warmth.

"Thanks." Daniel said absently. "I'll be alright. These obviously weren't meant to be seen, stuffed away like that... But why not burnt?" The taller man spoke slowly, trying to understand something beyond his comprehension.

"Does it matter?" Clement held one aloft and kicked another as he went. "Probably only junk, anyway. There's so much crap in the world. Now what I'd like is somewhere really spacious, no mess, no clutter... " He'd forgotten the cool greys of Chute Street where Jasmine Khan had a well-ordered schedule of visitors. In fact, he'd forgotten everything. There'd just be him and Daniel, playing horses and jockeys forever in a horizonless hinterland of pleasure...

He let the chest crash on to the stones outside as sharply as rifle shots. And splinters fell just as the flinty, white bodies had fallen, backwards in perpetual motion. Bleached ninepins into the black earth, like a slow, dead rain…

"What say you, Danny boy?" Clement stood silhouetted against the daylight. "Could all be rather fun, don't you think?"

But it wasn't so simple for the deserter who'd left his wife and child in a tree-lined suburban street. Who'd known the other man's body next to his, and suddenly felt a terrible past locked into those very walls.

"Not sure old chap." He ignored the annoying nickname. "It's a big decision. Anyhow, there's Catherine..." That gave him breathing space. He soothed his cut thumb in his mouth.

"Who's she?" Clement laughed.

"God, Clement. Life isn't that simple."

"It can be. Look, do you want me or not?" The white suit came nearer and stood close by. So close behind that Daniel could smell the combination of sweat and aftershave. So close he could feel the man's thighs and a certain lump press against his buttocks. Two clamps on his arms. Hot, firm hands cutting off his blood flow... "Well?"

"I just need time"... The musician's breath was tight and shallow as the other's fingers twisted on his curly nape and held his collar fast.

"We'll have time". Clement pushed again, his body hard now and insistent. "In fact, all the time in the world... " He unclasped the belt in front of him and eased his other hand down, below the tucked-in shirt and the boxer shorts' wide, ruched band. Smoothly he ventured over the flattened mound of pubic hair and grasped what lurched and lengthened in his palm.

"Oh God Clement!" Daniel suddenly spun round and they stood fused, face-to-face, as one. Tongue on tongue, lips on lips, stubble-grazing teeth, and tears, while from the cobwebbed ceiling high above, a huge arachnid abseiled down into the taller, tousled head, and outside, a giveaway, plywood fragment snapped under careless feet.

XXIII

"And as it were a great mountain burning with fire was cast
into the sea: and the third part of the sea became blood."
(Revelation.8.v.8.)

In the Place des Oies, yet more men and women smiled sores, emitted foul breath, and gesticulated at Marthe and Élise Roland with their accusing, soiled fingers. Even the tattered children laughed at the fear on those two women's faces, but Aymerigot Forgue's thick, woollen cowl shut out all such distractions, leaving only his blue, buried eyes exposed. He cared not that Bérengier, his faithful, servant had gone. Too feeble now to properly earn his keep in the busy months ahead.

He slowly returned his sword to its *'estuiel'* and tidied the wood pile, hoping it wouldn't smoke unproductively to delay the moment. Then he pulled out a branch. One that almost touched the tied, quivering hands. Its bark peeled away easily, exposing a length of stripped, green ash as smooth and vulnerable as the young girl's body. He flung it back at their feet, and the little dog bared his teeth. Another kick, this time bringing blood. His four, stringy legs still in motion as though running in a dream, were suddenly still. Someone cheered. But Élise could feel the dead weight against her feet
and could contain her grief no longer.

"Have a care for your own skin," Aymerigot Forgue smilingly said to her, and slowly re-adjusted his hood. "While you have time."

These two, sly colluders from St. Just had taken long enough to confess to sheltering both Girard Corbichon and Mordiern Guyon for nine whole months. Now the gestation was over it was his turn to prolong their wait. He reached for another stick, but this time, Noë Roche suddenly snatched it from him, using the forked end to prod where he knew their private places to be.

"Open your legs, you dirty she-dogs!" Roche shouted, jabbing again, before the executioner pushed him aside and beat him soundly round the thighs.

"'Tis *my* business, you ape. Not yours!"

The two former labourers and farmer whom fate had previously denied any wealth or position, withdrew to the edge of the crowd, while in the cool dusk, people were impatient to see the spectacle of fire and smell traitors burning.

"You!" The tall, disguised man had changed his mind. Wanton with power, he beckoned the trio whom Guillaume de Nogaret had also hired, to come forward, himself leaping nimbly on to the dais. They were flattered into action.

"Take The Whiteface not where he can poison the soil, but to a deep, watery grave. I know such a place in Fanjeaux." He kicked the dead man's shoulder and peered down to where the severed, bloodless head had rolled free, but since vanished. Where only blood remained.

"Who has it?" Aymerigot Forgue scoured the surrounding cobbles, more crowded by the growing throng, well wrapped against the frost, which in those parts heralds the bitter *ivernage*. "The King's Councillor will surely offer a substantial reward."

But other conversations engrossed the onlookers. Some remembered Marguerite Corbichion, the 'witch from Alençon,' disposed of seventeen summers before. Now her son, the work of the Devil masquerading as a soldier of Christ, had by his demise, left their air a little cleaner.

XXIV

Catherine was surprised to see that the new man in her life owned a car. To her, he was distinctly of the earth, a foot traveller, *un piéton* in shining shoes. She peered down through the apartment's barely-opened shutters, undressed, unmade-up, not wanting to be seen, yet watching his every move as he returned with shopping and what looked like new binoculars hanging round his neck. Certainly her wooer seemed ill at ease as he placed himself in the long, black Citroën's driving seat and awkwardly fumbled with the controls, without once looking up.

The saloon occupied almost two parking spaces alongside the *boucherie*. Its dark bulk aligned upwards at the rear like a streamlined hearse. She watched it move away from the kerb in the wrong gear and someone hooted from behind. A brown hand emerged apologetically from its nearside front window. *Her* hand, and it was strange to see it so. She suddenly felt excluded and alone. Burned where the sun's warm kiss had turned to rage, and nothing soothed the fire.

Her crazy desire to please had rendered her untouchable. Red valleys and crimson plains were now disfigured by acres of dead, parchment skin, still attached. Nothing like the brown and even slopes he'd hoped for. The car slipped away amongst other traffic, leaving more than just an empty gap in the road. With nothing, not even coffee in the cupboard, and a long, house-bound afternoon ahead, she prepared to go out, wrapping a cotton sheet around her shoulders, carefully and loosely to create a hood, then round again to cover her chin. For the rest, she spun a gentle fabric spiral held by safety pins.

Thus did the chrysalis emerge into the early sun, and crept along the *Rue des Templiers* to the small, untidy *Supermarché*. Stares accompanied her strange progress for although a *musulman* wasn't unusual in those parts, her eyes were of a northern light, and her nose a rare vermilion. Such a shame, they said, that the Englishwoman, Mrs. Ash was '*malade*.' Perhaps the butcher from her useful vantage point, would be able to enlighten them further.

*

An hour later, Catherine had positioned her chair by the spare bedroom window to keep watch. The sun never touched that corner, and was slipping now behind the Albères mountains. Its fire spent. Then, she saw him. Léon Tavernier, her lover, who seemed to share a knowledge of German with his sister, standing as he used to do, amidst the brushing crowds. She began to wave and was about to call out, when suddenly she noticed her silver Renault return, sliding into its space below.

Damn...

It was all spoilt.

Instead of getting out, both men stayed put, deep in conversation, with Clement reassuringly stroking Daniel's cheek.

"Selfish pricks!" She shouted, unheard, as the gardener stepped seemingly unthinking from the kerb. He was hit like a dog by a passing truck .

His sudden cry filled the shocked silence. Then came sounds of a gathering crowd and car doors slamming. Catherine turned away. Numb and void as if her world was falling apart. The butcher meanwhile had abandoned her sausage machine to run across and press her gristle fingers under the head that had shared their same womb.

"*Au secours! Au secours!*" She shrieked at the surrounding wall of legs as Clement and Daniel joined her with the hapless tile truck driver. "Help! Help!"

"I'll phone," said Daniel racing to the shop. "Get a blanket!" He yelled, and Clement, under sufferance, made it to the flat. Fresh bloodstains on his shirt.

"Oh God," Catherine moaned as he dragged off the bedspread. "Will he be alright?"

"Dunno. Silly old fucker wasn't looking... " Then he was gone and the front door slammed her into oblivion.

*

Under the dying sun, the doctor's eyes, drained of what little colour they'd had, rolled around on their yellow orbs. His mouth that had given her life, lay open, edged by cracked, brittle lips. The butcher meanwhile, searched for his slippery tongue and pulled it forwards, while the truck driver kept his dirty chamois leather under the nose to staunch the bleeding.

"He didn't give me a chance!" The man pleaded. "He was just there!" He began crying pitifully, and Madame Valauris, the florist, encouraged him to sit on the small chair she'd brought outside, while Daniel took over. "Business was just picking up," the driver went on. "I've a wife and three kids... " His sobs increased as a wailing siren drew near and the crowd pulled back. One or two leaning forwards to take photographs.

"Was he following anyone?" The SAMU ambulance driver asked innocently, making a quick examination of the victim. But the butcher turned her bleached, hostile face towards him.

"He's my brother. He has a name, Léon Tavernier."

The man signalled two other medics to bring the stretcher.

"Nothing broken," he said finally. "But his head's taken the worst..." He helped ease the body from the road with the utmost care and supervised the fragile loading into the large, estate car. The butcher squeezed in behind him and the doors were closed just as the Police arrived to draw the yellow outline of corpse on the tarmac, and begin making enquiries of those in attendance.

"I'll look after her shop," the florist called out. "You never know."

"Rather you than me," said Daniel, not quite recovered from his last visit, as one of the police officers advanced, notebook and pen poised.

"English?" He asked him. "How long are you here for?"
Daniel looked nervously at Clement. He didn't want too many questions. Besides, his thumb was hurting.

"Our *cartes de séjour* gives us three months here. Also, our *cartes de commerçant*." Clement was impressively official.

"Did either of you know Monsieur Tavernier by any chance?"

"Never seen him before in my life." Clement took the initiative. "Could have made a real mess of my new car though... "

The officer smiled wryly and moved away to other onlookers who'd stayed to extract the last moment of drama. Catherine, on the other hand, had closed the shutters, weary of the lies. Knowing there'd be no more light. For clearly, her saviour was gone.

*

The next morning, as his wife's melancholy became more of an irritation, and as there were no clients to escort into the wilderness, Clement and Daniel went to celebrate at the office. Clement had brought in giant-sized, iced Cokes, and thus ensconced side by side at the desk, he made the first telephone call to Philippe Ferand.

"Monsieur Ash? You need me? Aha... " The lawyer sneered.

"Indeed I do, Monsieur. About the *Moulins des Olives* in St. Cernin. Number C8650."

"Well?"

"Madame Duval has approached me directly with this old mill. She needs the money to improve her present property, and I wish to buy." Clement spoke as crisply and concisely as he could, and in the face of such belligerence he was not a novice.

The other man snorted as though he was blowing his nose without a handkerchief.

"You do, do you? Well I'm not so sure about that."

"Naturally I have to see Monsieur Gallin at Crédit Lyonnais, to clear my deposit, then I'll be with you." Clement continued brightly, winking at Daniel. "Say eleven thirty? Madame Duval has agreed to that, and I'd appreciate it if its deeds were available for us then. *À bientôt*." He clapped the receiver down and beamed a vivid, lightning smile.

"Bloody marvellous!" Daniel thumped him on the back.

"It's meant to be, that's for sure." Clement seeing already the clean, white spaciousness and old stonework restored. "Don't worry about the money side of things by the way. It's all on me."

"I can't expect you to take everything on." Daniel appealed to his new master.

"Why not? It's my decision. You just stay being wonderful." He placed his hand quickly and accurately on the other's corduroy groin as another siren pierced the busy morning and faded at speed. Daniel closed his eyes contentedly...

"That reminds me," he mused. "Wonder how old Joe's getting on?"

"You mean Léon." Clement sniggered, clattering ice cubes noisily around in his mouth.

*

Jules Lefêbvre, the tall, white-haired Senior Registrar didn't like the look of Monsieur Tavernier's injuries at all, and telephoned the *Curé* from his office in the *Hôpital St. Vincent*.

"Mercifully, it may not be long." He'd added, before striding back along the blue-tiled corridor towards Intensive Care. He didn't recognise the fat man slumped on a chair by the wall, but as he passed, Philippe Ferand whose suit seemed to have been slept in, jumped up from his seat and pulled on the doctor's immaculate, white sleeve.

"That Monsieur Tavernier," he began, flushed and frantic. Newly intoxicated. "The one you've got in there... don't listen to him! Do you understand? He'll say things he doesn't mean."

"Don't we all?" Lefêbvre disengaged himself good-humouredly from the man who held the deeds to his house, and moved on.

"He has these dreams. Is convinced he's someone else!" The official raved on in frustrated isolation, saving his own skin while busy hospital traffic gave him a wide berth.

The small, stuffy ward the Registrar entered was lined by a bank of winking terminals, recording the remains of life. After various tests and brain scans, the patient now lay like a dead catch, but bandaged, with a masked nurse in attendance at either side. They tensed visibly as Lefêbvre came in.

"We'll keep going on this one." He looked into the old man's unfocussing eyes. "And try and exclude his sister if you can. She's not very hygienic, and that's an understatement."

"She's being impossible!" One of the nurses looked over to the ante-room door where the butcher's angry face filled the small glass panel.

"Well, that's tough." He ignored her stares. "I make the rules round here. By the way, Father Duran will be calling, but we can't risk him giving the Sacrament. Not now."

Then he was gone, and the nurses looked at each other bleakly.

One picked up the doctor's heavy hand.

"Who is he?"

"Léon Tavernier, I believe. 56, Avenue Victor Hugo, although I've never seen him around." She fiddled with the collar of his hospital nightdress, aware of the sister's black eyes boring through into the room.

"Any family, apart from her?"

"She said no."

Suddenly those bleached, ochre eyes rested on the girl with his hand.

"Jesus Christ! He gives me the creeps," she hissed. Can't we change places?"

"No thanks."

"Who needs enemies?" Before letting go.

Suddenly a small noise like crackling paper rose above the monitors. The old mouth was trying to speak... Words they didn't know... names hard to distinguish. Then a slight convulsion brought his head up and down on the pillow-less bed.

"He's getting frisky."

The drip was re-adjusted as the butcher banged again on the door. She had to stop him talking too much. Instead, *une auxiliare* asked her to strip inside a curtained cubicle. Privately, with some dignity. Unlike her women, and without their fear. Their ignorance. A coat hanger, not a stick for her convenience. But no ticket of receipt. That at least was something to be thankful for.

"Look!" said the nurse who'd released the old man's hand.

The nearby electrocardiogram showed a stronger rhythm. Fluorescent green peaks of equal height processed across the horizontal.

"That's better," said the other, before Rosa Tavernier was ushered in, naked under a stiff, cotton shift. Hands gloved in latex. She made straight for the bed.

"No, no. Too close I'm afraid." The nearest nurse firmly drew her away to the visitors' bench as those coal-black eyes burned resentment. "We have to be careful."

The door then opened and Doctor Lefêbvre appeared carrying a set of still-wet prints. He pinned each on the wall in turn.

"Fortunately we have a phenomenally thick skull." He scrutinised the first image of black and, grey, blurred and mottled, revealing a sudden whiteness - the eighty year-old head revealed, but not revealing. Abstracted, and mysteriously so. A landscape of subterranean depths stared out at everyone. Eyeless. Picked clean by the Rontgen rays.

Father Duran was then shown in, and the Registrar whispered briefly in his ear. The *curé* nervously made the sign of the cross over the bed, then retreated two paces.

"I cannot offer you the body and blood of Christ," he began. "But I can absolve you... have you anything to confess?"

The butcher tried to leave her seat, but was restrained.

"Our Lord is waiting... " The young priest strained for even the faintest murmur from the patient.

"... Kreisler... Joachim Kreisler... Joseph Weiss... Nathan... " The invalid began...

"Stop, Léon! Stop!" Shrieked the old woman. "He's delirious! Can't you see!"

"Who's he talking about? Are they relatives?" The priest turned round, puzzled.

"... Müller... Simon... Max Bernstein... " The old wheels rolled on, unstoppable... the rubbly track unending... "*los... los... heraus und einreihen...* " *Herr Doktor Käfer* ordered, breathless, for there was much, much more to deal with. Then he subsided into sleep.

"Yes, yes!" Cried his sister. "Of course! He means our cousins in Bavaria... I remember many, many of them." Rosa Tavernier's membranous hands flailed the air as other pairs of eyes exchanged uncomprehending glances.

"I think we can continue now." Father Duran knelt down, resting his protected arms on the coverlet. A position favoured by the *Marschunfahig* after the *Doktor's* first few sessions and before *der Stock*...

"*In nomine patrem...* " the priest began in rapid Latin mingled with the tinny chorus of space-age voices supporting life. Then came his final blessing, *sotto voce* and melodious as the old man's bowels silently moved beneath the blanket.

"It seems we have a miracle." Father Duran stood up and smiled. "God is not yet ready to claim Monsieur Tavernier as his own. But we must still pray. We must not lose our guard. Remember the foolish virgins... "

"He needs rest now." Jules Lefêbvre signalled the butcher to leave, and she obeyed, unsteady on her feet. Those, ringless hands still trembling as a strange smell lingered around the bed.

Once outside, the priest removed his clinical mask with some relief.

"I just couldn't kiss him." He confessed to the senior doctor. "I'm not used to this sort of thing... just yet."

"There's no risk." The Registrar shuffled his notes into a tidy pile. "With S.I.D.A., it's the body fluids we've got to watch. Don't worry now."

"Thank God."

So they parted. One to Haematology to check on the truck driver and the ambulance men, the other towards the bright glass foyer where Catherine Ash, inhibited by her appearance, agonised as to whether or not she should complete her mission.

*

Clement waited impatiently in a shaft of bright sunlight for the *Notaire*'s return while his young secretary, obviously new, struggled with an unfamiliar keyboard. An errant fly on its deranged journey around the small airless office, collided with his forehead.

"I haven't got all day," Clement snapped, even more irritated.

"Monsier Ferand's still at the hospital." The typist finally looked up from her problems, little more than a schoolgirl with a sun-bleached ponytail and an irksome holiday job that kept her from the beach. "Goes there every day now... Said he'd be back by noon."

Suddenly Clement heard an animated conversation beyond the door and Philippe Ferand entered, none too steadily, immediately filling the room. His tiny, weevil eyes alighted on the estate agent who stood, hand extended. The lawyer avoided him, and instead made straight for his desk where he began hunting for his glasses amongst the clutter.

"I'll tell you this before Madame Duval arrives, I don't like dealing with queers. Never have. But I'll take your money. Now that *does* interest me, so long as it's sterilised, of course!" He laughed, banging his hand down on the desk in a mirthful beat.

Clement moved towards him and leant over the disordered paper landscape, causing some sheets to fall to the floor. He grabbed the German's tie and pulled the frightened, red face closer. *'Ein Lebewesen'* for certain slaughter. The girl made a hasty excuse and left. Her skirt still caught up around her thighs. "And *I'm* only interested in getting that bloody place, d'you hear? Not in your dirty little problems!"

The official was gasping for air, eyes extruded, when Madame Duval walked in, unannounced. A slim, elegant woman of uncertain age wearing backless mules. Clement still held him fast. A rhinoceros of a man. Twice his size.

"Now that we have Madame's company, I think she should witness a boor when she sees one," he said. "Someone patently unfit to represent either of his two honourable professions. In fact," he tightened his grip." I may pursue this with my lawyer in London." Gradually he let go, calmly shook the woman's hand, then sat down, detached, as though nothing had happened.

Philippe Ferand adjusted his tie and grunted a few words into the intercom, whereupon his assistant appeared to the accompaniment of loud rock music in the background. Clement pulled out his money, laying the notes down carefully overlapping so that none was missed.

"Two hundred thousand francs." He said. "I've been waiting one and a half hours for this privilege." He surveyed the room with disdain. No competition here with its faded photographs of various other *Maisons des Maîtres* abandoned to old ghosts; overpriced studios on the Côte Vermeille and a slinky-girl calendar two years out of date.

An embarrassed Madame Duval searched in vain for something in her bag, while preliminaries were completed on the form, identifying the *bien* – the empty property - and he, the Englishman as sole purchaser.

"And your lovely wife?" The *Notaire*'s tongue licked the sweat from under his nose.

"None of your business." Clement coloured, as the widow from Tuchan eagerly signed. Committing and binding. She would now have her patio and balustraded walls, not to mention a cultivable plot and orchard. She let out a sigh of relief and smiled her happiness. The Mill had proved a risky burden for too long.

Philippe Ferand loathed such confraternity. He wanted the foreigner isolated. To fail. Deviant interloper that he was. Such a pity the 'Deportable Element' category no longer applied. In anger, he slammed his desk drawer shut.

"I have so many plans." The woman shook Clement's hands warmly, thinking of nothing else.

"So have I." He turned to the overweight man with bad skin. "And I want this conveyance returned from the Land Registry by the end of the month so you'd better not keep me waiting. As you know, I'm not over impressed with your establishment. And," Clement grinned mischievously, "isn't it strange how busy things are for the *Maisons du Soleil* despite your so-called assistance?" He placed a copy of the document in his briefcase. "By the way, just for your information, all my properties will in future, be dealt with by Monsieur Siguera in Perpignan. Deeds can be transferred, remember."

Before the other could conjure up a reply, Clement was out of the building and on his way to give Dan the good news.

*

"Did you manage to find out any more about those intriguing tea chests?" The choirmaster asked after the euphoria had passed.

"For Christ's sake, Danny Boy, don't you think I'd better things to do?"

XXV

'For without are dogs, and sorcerers, and whoremongers, and murderers, and idolaters, and whosoever loveth and maketh a lie.'
(Revelation.22.v.15.)

"Who has the head of The Whiteface?" Aymerigot Forgue bellowed again, striding from one side of the platform to the other as the Templar's corpse was lifted over the wooden barrier and dropped on to a hessian pile. As if hypnotised like hares to the hunter's torch, no-one dared murmur, lest the man from Moncoutant alight on their ignorance. "Very well. I give one hundred *livres* for that which connived at sodomy and enjoyed such base kissing, and fifty for his horse that bore so willingly both evil fundaments." He paused, smelling fear. "Who speaks?"

The following silence strangled every breath. Only the Roland women's quiet sobbing escaped into the gloom.

"I'll find the *Boulonnais*," volunteered the godless Robert Sagan. Eagerness shining in his hard, black eyes. "He knows me. Will surely eat out of my hand."

"Only *I* can find him and the head, sir," boasted Othon Lamaire, also quick to impress and find more favour with de Nogaret, as he knelt to tie the foot of the shroud in a clumsy knot. "Though I have to say my hands be loathe to touch it." He'd whispered that afterword under his breath, helping the other man throw the long, heavy bundle into the waiting cart. Aymerigot Forgue leaned over its wooden ledge to exclude other listening ears. Another whose eyes were crystal sharp and clear of purpose.

"I have a half-brother in *La Récompense*," he hissed at Lamaire. "Further south, near Fanjeaux, as already mentioned. He is a priest. That horse near severed both his legs, so he will certainly oblige. He owns a Roman well whose depths no-one has yet plumbed. It is a long journey, but you and your filthy cargo will be made most welcome."

Robert Sagan meanwhile, coloured at his exclusion, but knew it safer to stay a friend than a rival.

"You come with me," Lamaire finally offered. But the once full-time farmer from Beaupréau was not to be so easily coerced. For he remembered how Corbichon's lover, Guyon, whom he had to his shame, first delivered to the Order, still evaded capture.

XXVI

Those visitors to the Languedoc Roussillon coast, expecting to find late summer by the sea more conducive to exercise, would find the days and nights still too hot, between the clearing storms. Not so Catherine Vitello Ash, oblivious to the time and type of day, beset by violent, unsummoned bilious attacks. Unlike Bernissende, the other Clement's illicit lover, she'd never been the recipient of any exalted dedication whether *'trobar clus'* or *'trobar leu,'* least of all from his modern namesake living life in the fast lane. Instead, she was a prisoner of number 8, Rue des Templiers; her endless hours bringing snatches of songs once sung. Of lives lived and lost...

"Tu es plus belle que le jour.
La neige n'est pas plus blanche
Pour traverser le ruisseau d'amour.
Je ne voudrais pas d'autre barque..."

Secretive words of love whispered then died, like those of the white, brother monk who'd suffered that very Pope's treachery and the taunting, torturing sword.

Even the harmonica in the Avenue Victor Hugo was silent.

Her body burned and shivered in turn, while the estate agent spent the day in shirtsleeves, full of boundless energy. Something had certainly revived him and, with the choirmaster habitually now in tow, they both went out early and returned late. So late that when his key rasped in the lock, she noticed how the huge, black sky beyond the shutters also bore yolky streams of dawn. Even then it wasn't her room he came to with its sickly pillows, and their door would shut with a sly finality.

*

Daniel sometimes called in early while his partner washed. He'd sit close by and touch her face, no longer the lovely creation he remembered but different. Terribly different. But she had a favour to ask, with big, pleading eyes.

"Enquire after her brother," Catherine began. "See how he's getting on… "

"Who?"

She lowered her voice. Walls had ears. Particularly there.

"The butcher, of course."

"Why?"

"He's only an old man, but he's helped me settle in. He might feel awkward if I did it."

"Do I have to? I hate that place." His gaze moved downwards in the direction of her shop.

"Just for me... please."

"He didn't seem too bad when they got to him. Only a nosebleed." Daniel reached for her hand.

"Please," she insisted. "I'm asking as a friend. And also, can you find out his first name?" She wanted to be sure, but then resisted pushing her luck. Why both siblings seemed to know German was for her to find out.

"Well, alright," he smiled. "You're putting up with me I suppose. You know I'd do anything for you, poor Catherine… "

"I'm not poor Catherine." Then she suddenly kissed his mouth. Its fervour caught him unawares, leaving the faintest taste of bile, and the following morning before leaving to accompany clients to Elne, Hermes duly returned from the Land of the Dead with a portion of paté and the good news that Monsieur Tavernier was out of danger. Also, that his Christian name was Léon.

So, he hadn't lied.

*

For the first time in almost a month, she ventured out on a suitably overcast day. The southerly Mistral that whipped up the harbour waves caught her hair and lashed it to her cheeks, impairing her vision. It would surely be impossible to find him in that elemental tumult, amongst that morass of tourists driven in from the blowing beaches. Woollens had replaced tee shirts, and trousers, shorts. People irritated by the loss of their heliacal drug, shuffled aimlessly up and down to the Palais Royal devouring *frites* and pizza slices. Shoulder to shoulder, hip to hip. This impossibility decided her to concentrate instead on finding his black car.

But the Citroën was under wraps in the dusty garage behind the house, until such time that the headaches eased and his stamina improved. Léon Tavernier now wore a dimpled hat of pale, flattened straw, *de rigueur* amongst the army of retired professionals and bureaucrats who spent their days patrolling the gritty sand in unseasonal clothes.

*

From below its rim, protected from the glare, he could see her. Safely anonymous on his perch - a low, stone wall set round a dusty palm tree's base - behind a leather goods stall. Glossy, liver-coloured handbags and belts with large, gold buckles. Beads and trinkets as well as soft-soled moccasins and dung-smelling slippers tumbled down the leathery slopes, new and unworn. Unlike those that had been banked high, reeking of train-soiled feet. Stinking pickings parcelled up for use elsewhere.

The butterfly was changed indeed. Neither smooth and delicately white as before, nor the all-over brown he'd ordered. Just another scorched and peeling sacrifice to the sun, like the hosts of campers, hitchhikers, those on the fringe of prosperity attempting glamour on a budget. Was this what he had dreamed of? *Die Scham!* He saw how she picked at this and that, with no intention of buying. Sunglasses, a hat, then a necklace. Mules perhaps, with her eyes restlessly searching. A tripper like all the rest, with red, raw flamingo legs and a traffic-light nose...

He got up, careful not to show his face, and took a slow, meandering route between the various stalls. Too late. Catherine recognised the familiar walk, slightly stooped, and the same quizzical tilt of the head. She began to run, nudging and bumping passers-by as she drew nearer.

"Bonjour!" She shouted, tapping him on the shoulder, and an unknown old man turned round.

"I... I'm so sorry... I thought you were Monsieur Tavernier." She was too loud, and people stared. "He... he's my... " But she couldn't finish. Couldn't even begin to say.

She then dropped back, disconsolate, to lose herself in the human sea that watched transfixed as a crystal glass salesman re-started his clockwork banter in English, with the odd French word thrown in.

"Hey! You!" He caught sight of her from his elevated position. Her obvious dejectedness set her apart. "I know the weather's not much, but it's not *that* bad." This caused a ripple of laughter. Attention focussed on her. "What do you do then, darling?"

"I make love."

Uproar followed. Even children with ice creams wedged in their mouths, giggled. Then a piercing wolf whistle called order as the salesman pulled another glistening *carafe* from the box and set it on the ledge in front of him.

"Ooooh!" He cooed, eyeing her. "Where do you like doing that then?" A pregnant silence.

Catherine turned her grey, steady gaze to the road that snaked upwards out of town, and saw again the curtain of reeds, the overflowing beds of beautiful things, then *his* things...

"When you walk in the garden, the Garden of Eden... " she began to sing to herself before being suddenly overwhelmed by all the close-up faces, freckles, pock-marks, wrinkles, troughs and hollows, retching with laughter. Garlic and anchovy breaths choking hers.

Eight horses. Forty men. More often fifty on the run...

She too, ducked and ran, blindly, madly, through the cobbled walkways, over the footbridge by open- air restaurants packed with early diners, then onwards and up to the moribund bulk of the town's fortifications. She threw herself down on the dry scrub that bristled like glass paper on her new skin. Her heaving sobs pumping a rain of hot tears into the ground.

*

The telephone at the *Maisons du Soleil* office rang just as a middle-aged couple with a large, apricot-coloured poodle came in to study the 'NOUVELLES PROPRIÉTÉS' board. Clement picked up the receiver, waving a welcome to his visitors. It was Harold Greenbaum. Unexpectedly.

His employee greeted him with forced *bonhomie.*

"Fine. Everything's just fine," Clement said in reply to the first question. "Did you get my last report?"

"Indeed. Most impressed." The other man seemed uncannily to be in the next room.

"Yep. We're showing up well here. Good footfall so far. See, I'm not just a pretty face." He tickled Daniel's adjacent thigh, but quickly stopped when the two clients hovered too near. Clement flashed the woman a disarming smile.

"Do you need any help? Why I'm phoning."

"Do I need any help?" Clement repeated, grimacing acrobatically. Quick-change expressions were essential in his line of business. "Heavens, no. Better to be a one-man band, that's what I say, Harold. Life's complicated enough. Anyhow, who've you got in mind?"

"Me."

Clement glanced at Daniel and gave a thumbs down sign. "Oh God, no. Look, really, I'm fine." But under his breath, he muttered, "It'll cock things up totally."

Daniel also sensing the French couple's disorientation, stroked their dog's woolly head and enquired if there was a property that had caught their interest.

"You're coming down here?" Clement queried into the receiver, giving Daniel another despairing look. "When?"

"Early next month... Oh, and Mrs. Greenbaum too. A change is as good as a rest, as they say."

Clement swore silently.

"Well, that's up to you of course. You've had the photos, seen how smart it is here... There's no real need... "

"I'm curious. So keep me updated, won't you? "

Shit...

All the while, his pen was creating heavy, doom-laden blobs on the blotter as the situation worsened. Daniel signalled to him to start crawling, while the Frenchwoman stared in amazement.

"Er... yes," Clement conceded. "Of course, and our records will be ready, no problem. And by the way," thinking of his boss's gross, bare bulk on show half-in, half-out of the sea. "Bring your bathing costumes. The water here's so warm... "

He covered the mouthpiece and laughed, making a rounded belly shape with his free hand.

"Fine... You'll be in touch," he repeated, at which point, the man in Holborn rang off, and Clement swivelled round and stood up to face his visitors.

"*Monsieur 'dame*, my apologies. What can I do for you?"

The couple hesitated, wary now.

"We're looking for something with a past... a little history... " Almost in unison, and physically identical too, with well-groomed, grey heads and neutral-coloured clothes. The dog's pink nose meanwhile was busy around Daniel' crotch. "We heard the old Moulin des Olives was for sale near St. Cernin... "

"Aha!" Clement was quick to intercept. "I'm afraid that's just gone. However," he plucked one of his other clever photographs from the board. "We do have this. A truly beautiful barn in that very same area... Ripe for the personal touch, and on the old pilgrim route to Santiago de Compostela don't forget... Would snap it up myself if I could." He handed over the photocopied details and an agency card. "By the way, we also do escorted visits. Saves a lot of aggro. Five hundred francs per half day for anything over five kilometres away. Can't go wrong."

The couple seemed unimpressed and their mouths tightened. The man harshly reined in his dog.

"I don't know if my wife told you on the 'phone, but we're particularly interested in the Templars. That olive mill was once part of Jean de Montjoie's preceptory, and Hugolin de Caudiès was in charge of flocks there. Would have been perfect." The Frenchman looked Clement straight in the eye. "Who is buying?" He asked. Grey eyebrows raised.

"That has to be confidential."

"Is it a Frenchman?"

"I'm afraid that's confidential, too."

The man sighed.

"I can soon find out. Monsieur Ferand will know."

At that, Clement, who was well used to thinking on his feet, moved smartly to the filing cabinet.

"Hang on!" He burrowed deep in the section marked 'Special Interest' which to date held only the one property now bandied in the air. "This surpasses *Le Moulin des Olives*, and I'll tell you why. It's *'La Récompense.'* Two Templars on the run hid there during The Purge, apparently. Even more up your street I'd have thought... Have a think about it anyhow, Monsieur... ?"

"Lejeune... Émile... "

"Well, Monsieur Lejeune," he indicated Daniel. "Both of us are here each morning, ready and waiting... "

"That's right." Daniel beamed. "We're a great little team. Try us." Clement's nurturing confidence was catching. But like the old man at the window, Monsieur and Madame Lejeune found his keen schoolboy face too eager, and the other's smile too threateningly intense. Besides, that place would need gutting and re-building.

"I think we'll leave it for the time being." The man pulled up his collar against the wind, shortened the dog's lead, and left alongside his wife. Their gabardines almost welded at the shoulder.

Meanwhile, the details of Madame Vilalongue's house lay abandoned on the desk. Its bright blue sky winking between the ancient rafters.

"They'll be back." Clement began to tidy up the desk. "I think, personally, they were very interested. What do you think?"

"I think we had a nasty moment." Daniel smiled.

"Not to worry. That leaves the day free just for us." Clement put his arms round Daniel's shoulders and gave him an affectionate squeeze. "We could go and see a builder. Get a quote... " Then, as he went over to turn the door sign to *'Fermé,'* something caught his eye.

"Who's that?"

"Where?"

"At the window. Seems vaguely familiar," said Clement.

"I know. He's the old man who was knocked over... I dealt with his nose... "

"Right."

Clement was soon outside, meeting both the mistral and that bloodless face head on. He noticed too how the other's suit was shabby and un-ironed above the neat, bright brown shoes.

"Can we help you?" he asked.

"I'm just looking if you don't mind." And those strange, bleak eyes fixed directly, unblinking on the Englishman's face, like a reptile suddenly in the sun.

"Not at all. Feel free. Anything in particular?" Clement, unnerved by the stare, wished Daniel would come to the rescue.

"Ah yes!" With pale irises still focussed under the straw brim.

"Old? New? Urban or rural? What do you fancy?" Daniel was now helpfully in attendance, his tight curls lying flat against his forehead. "Your wish is our command. By the way," he ventured. "Are you better now, Monsieur Tavernier? After your accident?"

Those strange eyes blinked in surprise at hearing his name.

"I have to be careful," he said, "but I can't complain." His voice had the expressionless tone of a recorded message as if to deter small talk.

"Well, at least you're up and about." Clement grinned too briskly and dust filled his mouth.

"Needs must." The old man offered a thin, lop-sided smile.

"Ah! Let me see... We have a most interesting dwelling in a small, hilltop village, complete with Roman well, then there's a barn. Needs a lot of love mind you... "

"I know."

Clement, briefly puzzled, took his arm and led him through into the office, letting the door slam behind them. The doctor looked around, missing nothing. Then he noticed the lignum vitae desk. Its familiar, dark solidity. 'Wood of life,' some said. Also of death from all those years ago. Fritz Koppel would be very interested indeed...

"It's too far," he said absently. "Twenty kilometres is my limit these days. I am no longer young as you can see."

"No problem." Clement scoured the rest of his files. "How about Rougières? Nice little spot, isn't it, Dan?"

"Wonderful."

"Couple of recent villas there - for retirement. Good local builder. Lots of *carrelage* in every room for the long, hot summers." Not that the old man with such weathered skin seemed the sort to spend his life indoors.

"Good, then I would like to view."

"Great!"

Clement scribbled in his large appointment book. Then looked up. "May I have your full name please?"

"Docteur Arnajon... Pierre Arnajon."

Damn.

Too late, his past slipped forth, like an early birth, unguarded and unexpected. He suddenly seemed anxious to leave and made for the door. Daniel Madox frowned in puzzlement while Clement's flattering curiosity delayed the target.

"Ah, so you're a doctor?" Was against his better judgment, but two sales lost in one hour was not on...

"No, no, no," the old man protested. "I was confused. That's someone's book I've been reading. What a fool I am. Why the hell was I thinking of him? I am Tavernier. Léon Tavernier... " For a moment, he looked lost and confused amongst the glut of other lives set out in prints of six by four in that ordered brightness. Clement recalled what the signwriter had said.

"The butcher's brother?"

A nod, that was all, but enough for Clement to pass him the small, embossed *Maisons du Soleil* business card. So that sign-writer had been right.

"Well, Monsieur Tavernier, we can take you over there next Monday. Four p.m. *D'accord*? OK?"

Another nod before his uncoloured eyes passed from one to the other, absorbing as a trained mind will - despite injury and trauma - all their imperfections, while wondering where best to have placed their pink triangles.

"Seems serious enough." Clement said once he'd gone, then flicked the agency sign to FERMÉ and locked up.

"Very." Daniel's hand took advantage of the other's vulnerability, sliding his right hand smoothly down into the exposed pocket's cotton lining. "That feels nice."

"You're a naughty boy!"

*

"Nearly there. Not far now." Clement encouraged, this time a passenger in the Renault. He kept his window open to dispel the staleness of three weeks' dirty washing piled in the back. Travelling clothes and office casuals that couldn't be laundered in the flat since the butcher had complained. It was Daniel, in gratitude, who'd struggled to utilise the apartment's tiny, wrought-iron balconies, yet failing to keep wet-heavy garments from sticking to the wall. Not Catherine.

"Where's this builder, then?" He took the newly-surfaced road east from Elne, up into a wide vista of new vineyards, dotted with small hamlet clusters. Orange and ochre against the blowing sky.

"*Les Forges*... It should be here somewhere... "

Clement craned his head out of the window. "There's an opening on the left. Try that." Then he spotted a large billboard stuck in a barren, hedgeless plot. "Michel Villaine, *artisan maçon*... "

"Someone's greedy," observed his driver as tarmac became earth, rutted and dry. A group of new villas in varying stages of completion lay ahead.

"Just the job for our little old man, don't you think?" Clement mused out loud. "In fact, I could take this lot on, no problemo. Can't see any agency signs can you?"

"Nope."

In fact, very little was visible as the dust cloud obscured their view, including another car some way behind that stopped when they stopped at the grey, unprepossessing site office.

*

Léon Tavernier's driving had improved so much since his release from hospital that now, no destination was too far; no Pyrenean road too tortuous. It was only the clamping headaches that sometimes forced a modification of plans. Then he'd over-compensate the next day. For the Englishmen's lives were hardly ordered, as his had been, so a constant state of preparedness was essential. This meant a full tank of petrol from different garages, and enough foil-wrapped cold sausage for sustenance. Also, being on constant alert with his cold, trained eye.

*

During one day they'd find a valley, the next, a mountain. Either alone, or with clients. Mostly British in clothes that were an affront to any *savoir faire*. From hamlet to town, they'd go, from worker's cottage to pile of stones. Sometimes a miniscule plot, the last in any scheme of things and usually next to the local *'Decharge'*...

Then hurried visits to the other *Notaire*'s office near Perpignan station, usually a twosome, hands touching but not innocently. Eyes only for each other, but not in love. Wretched, feeble-minded men at the nadir of depravity, worse than any vagrant or pimp with their greased and willing sphincters.

And even more to the point, what were they planning, up at the mill?

It was time to return Philippe Ferand's visits and learn a little more. This twosome were always seen from behind. Heads close together between the restraints, noses in profile rubbing like a pair of camels. More dangerously, their car would suddenly heave over into a layby, forcing the curly-headed one to drive on and turn round. That sort of inconvenience angered him, increasing his determination, except on those days when his pains returned. He didn't have all the time in the world, and it was running out. This thought above all others focussed his mind, excluding the pierced imperfect Mrs. Ash and her ravaged skin. But why a builder? He wondered, jotting things down in the clever, efficient shorthand he'd learnt all those years ago in Nice, as the wind picked up and buffeted his car.

The shack door suddenly opened, and the pair emerged, escorting a small, deeply tanned man to their car. Michel Villaine, self-styled entrepreneur and lucky to be alive after his father's risky, wartime activities, walked with the swagger of one whose limbrous days are spent on scaffolding and ladders. Lean and fit. All muscle. Then smiles and promises lost in the swirling dust as they led the way on a journey the doctor was getting to know only too well.

*

The surplus *À Vendre* sign was soon torn down and left as litter to be scattered far afield by every whim of the wind. Clement replaced it with two huge *Vendu* and *Propriété Privée'* billboards attached to the dilapidated double gates. The old man followed, crouching low behind any cover he could find, mindful of his knees.

"Some job, this." The builder stood back, hands on hips, expert eyes everywhere. His French thick, slow. "When do you hope to move in?"

Clement and Daniel looked at each other, stunned by the suddenness of the question.

"Er... ideally I suppose we'd like the business up and running by next Spring. 1993 and all that..."

"I see... " Michel Villaine knocked the walls with a stone and the sharp hollow sound peppered the air where once gentle bells had nodded. "Needs restructuring. Badly." He led the way inside, away from the doctor's eavesdropping ears, as he gripped the ground lest he should fall.

So this was theirs. Yet another part of his country sullied. After all his purging, nothing had changed. And why hadn't his *Teilhaber* Ferand told him?

"Traitors!" His old throat shouted to the sighing trees. The world was full of them, making a mockery of his life, and the builder was probably no different - they always sniff out their own kind. He knew that. No matter if the rectovesical pouch and the *levator ani's* puborectalis fibres were ruptured and bleeding. Or the external anal sphincter torn and bruised. These boys liked to play rough. The rougher the better. Revulsion flooded all other sensibilities. The mill, the pastures, the summer scents contaminated as before. His fingers dug into the light soil as though to bury imagination and memory, but the grave was shallow, lined by stones. A strong smell of human excrement met his nose, and he edged away to a greater place of safety.

*

Three o'clock. His medicine slot. On the hour, every hour, buying him more time. He shook out two yellow capsules and swallowed them dry as Michel Villaine emerged. The former doctor saw him pick out things from the surrounding rubble. Items he recognised which Ferand should have already dealt with. His breath came in short, panicked bursts as other voices drew nearer.

"... my Papa was in the *Maquis*... Jesus they could fight!" The builder's sunburnt arms carrying the wooden splinters, attacked the air. "Ever heard of Vercors? He was shot there like a fucking dog... " He kicked a stone violently down the track. It ricocheted off the gatepost. "Anyhow." He strode out towards the road "I know someone who'd be very interested in these..." His lean, angular face caught the full sun, but there was no smile to greet it as the Englishmen followed behind, lightly holding hands. Their farewells were too close. The observer could almost smell their bodies, and when they were gone, extricated himself from his malodourous hideout.

Still stooping low, he crept along the densely-grown boundary reinforced by recent wire, and a walker looking down from his terraced hill buffeted by the wind, was surprised to see a hatted, suited man of advanced years clamber up and over the gate to land nimbly on the other side. But the Panama hat marked with another's name, was left behind, spinning away on its brim along a dusty furrow.

*

Today was different, he told himself. Today he would get closer. Doctor Pierre Arnajon – for that was who he would always be - spread shaving cream carefully over his jaw. For five hundred francs the debauched pair were taking him out to Rougières on reconnaissance. Just an old man, like all the rest, probably widowed, wanting something a little easier to maintain in his declining years, yet within reach of other company and basic amenities. For a change, it would be a passive, rather than an active day, but not a second would be wasted of this chance to bore and burrow like the Bilharzia into the couple's tawdry lives. Apart from the round-headed hermaphrodite, *Taenia Saginata*, he'd always admired the little liver fluke its persistence, once entrenched. And so it would be with his kind hosts, the obliging Mr. Ash and Mr. Madox.

Except that he was no parasite, and no amount of urination or antimony of lead would ever dislodge him. Their veins, portal and mesenteric, were now his viscous home; their vast intestinal and urinary tracts, his sumptuous feast. Yet the thought of such proximity, just even touching, made his razor slide too quickly on his throat and a blob of blood to balloon out against his collar.

"*Die Verdammung!*"

It welled up throughout the journey to Rougières as he sat with his window wide open next to their dirty washing now crammed into supermarket bags. By the time they arrived at the row of box-like villas outside the town, the blood-stained handkerchief around his neck resembled a battle bandage.

The settlement was loathsome, made up of little more than kennels, but he managed a weak smile as the brown-haired Englishman extolled the virtues of a quiet retirement amongst the vineyards in rooms smaller than the cloakroom in the Avenue Victor Hugo.

"Can I leave this somewhere?" Their client suddenly asked, unwrapping the sodden rag from his neck.

"I'll take it." The choirmaster offered, sensing a sale. But the blood that welded his fingers together felt strangely cold. Twice he had touched it, and twice felt revulsion. But no matter, he convinced himself. All in a good cause.

"I'm definitely interested." The old man lied, going through the motions of checking each meagre room's power sockets and air bricks. "Definitely." In addition, a few more eavesdropping trips out would be most useful, although so far there'd been few surprises. Their suit trousers had the same tautness across their groins, their hands restless as before, but never had those two pairs of ear lobes so raged with desire.

"You keen on gardening?" Daniel Madox asked, seeing Clement outside pacing the small plot.

"Once upon a time."

"Don't know why it's always assumed old folk want to spend their days growing things." Daniel opened the back door. "Anyhow, this patch shouldn't keep you too busy."

"Indeed." The doctor saw how the man's attention was suddenly taken by the sight of the estate agent bending down to retrieve his pen.

"How long have you known Mr. Ash?" The Frenchman demanded

in a tone that surprised himself, yet more courteous than that for the men in truck number 215941. No reply, for at that point, the man in question had returned, sensing tension.

"We can lower the asking price if that's the sticking point. Make it say, a hundred and twenty thousand?" He quipped, winking at the other man. The doctor saw that. He could play games too.

"I'd like to compare it with something else. Something slightly more... "

"Up-market?" Clement was quick. Eight years in Holborn hadn't been wasted.

"That's right. More space."

"I think we have just the very thing. New again, but with more lifestyle features."

"What sort of lifestyle?"

"You know, barbecue, sauna... you name it... " pattered from his lips.

But naming was easy. The doctor had seen the fierce, erupting flames on still-moving bodies and had choked on their fatty fumes escaping from the pit. He'd also felt the heat of the perspiring sprinkler room, and savoured the smell of bitter almonds...

*

Half an hour later, the threesome were back in the car and travelling south-east to Perpignan when Daniel felt a bruising draught on his neck from behind.

"Do you mind shutting your window a fraction?" He half-turned to the doctor who saw how his iris was lodged in the eye corner, just like those who'd submitted.

"I need fresh air," he argued. "There are too many odours... "

"Leave it." hissed Clement, and the choirmaster leaned towards him almost resting his head on the other man's cotton shoulder. The promise of unfinished business soon animated their close conversation, while the doctor who'd studied those bursting laundry bags on the outward journey, surreptitiously pulled out some striped underpants from the compressed *melée* of clothes.

Just as he thought. So it wasn't a fluke that the yellow pair already in his possession was also stiff with semen and bore a long, crudely cut opening along the central, rear seam. With a magician's dexterity he tucked the article into his pocket.

"And now for my next trick," he mused to himself as the car rejoined the weekend traffic north of Port-Vendres, travelling too fast against the wind.

*

"Monsieur, if you'd like to pay us now... " Daniel ventured, "it'll save time when we get back." The old man obliged, carefully extracting five one hundred franc notes from his thin wallet. They were new, tightly folded. Daniel counted each one, taking care lest they blew away and glad to avoid the dead, staring eyes he saw in the driver's mirror.

"Thanks," he said. "It's exact."

"I am always exact." Their passenger smiled.

"Sorry, but can you repeat your name, please?" Daniel balanced a notebook on his knee, and their passenger obliged yet again. Loud and clear.

"Léon Tavernier, with an *accent aigu* on the fierst 'e.'"

"OK. Got it."

"We'll show you the two-bedroomed property in Verbois as promised." Clement was also good with tricky-Dickies. "Half-price viewing. What do you say?"

"It's a deal." The old man looked over towards the thin, cobalt strip of sea just visible between the plane tree trunks tightly lining the road. He'd never made deals, and once word had got round to that effect, no-one had bothered him. He'd been above reproach; above the wiles of human weakness.

But this was different. There was no betrayal.

"How about Wednesday at ten o'clock?" Clement suggested as brightly as the full sunlight while parking in outside the Agency. "No point in hanging round, that's what I say."

"Excellent." Their client got out and was soon lost among the tourists, but Daniel, with the bloodied handkerchief still in his pocket, realised he'd forgotten to ask Monsieur Tavernier if there was a property to sell.

*

The weeks that had previously been without any form or structure, now assumed a more predictable pattern for the old man. Tuesdays were set aside for inspections of new acquisitions, while the rest of the week involved escorted visits and the occasional rushed trip to Antonio Siguera, *Notaire* of Perpignan. Thus Wednesdays in the Garden of Eden belonged to the past, and the *cultivateur*'s fruits had swollen and withered uncollected, while the damp, makeshift bed lay covered in a trapped and fearful lark's excrement. Its little, battered body lay where his 'butterfly's' auburn head had been on that day in the storm.

The Lord's Day was kept free for the *Moulin des Olives*, when both Englishmen were usually accompanied by some artisan or tradesman wearing carpet slippers. The doctor had never understood or approved such a sloppy, plebeian habit. He preferred a sturdy shine at the end of each leg.

Besides, a hard leather upper had always been better for kicking.

With company, their visits were short and instructional. Alone, they'd linger, fooling about in a variety of postures. One man more athletic and thrusting, the other passive yet playful. Grotesquely demeaning the animal kingdom. A slur on the land that nourished them, and the air that swelled their lungs and passed out polluted. Like their waste lying on the open ground, unfit for burial. There was no shame, and Philippe Ferand had much to answer for. The doctor sighed deeply in the quiet room below his wife, finally working things out.

But memory blurred by a headache intruded. How could it not? For his special stick stood upright in the corner amongst others topped by silver knobs and preserved pheasant heads. Easy to grip when walking. Easy to grip when striking. Or boring. The pink triangle captives had enjoyed that, or at least never complained. Then it was on to the unspectacular suburb of Drancy, caught in a web of wires so none could escape... He'd kept them separate so far, but *Obergruppenführer* Oberg had had other ideas... Even those trucks were too comfortable.

He'd let them sit on each others' faces as they'd done in private. If he'd had his way, they'd have been forced to kneel naked and show what less than beasts they were. Just for diversion, while in power, he'd made the music teacher and the jeweller give a special, extended performance between Nice and Lyon. Thereafter, both were invited to show off their talents, followed by the cooks from the Hôtel Mirador. A most rewarding journey, and one he'd never tired of repeating, courtesy of Hauptsturmführer Brunner, whose appreciation was always unfailingly generous. Lecturers, lawyers, artists, actors, biologists, research chemists, all had more than paid their way across the bleakly moving countryside. But the muscled Mr. Ash and the tall Mr. Madox were still deep in debt.

His tool kit was compact, packed with essentials. Just like his doctor's case, capable of both healing and killing. Pliers, spanners, mole wrenches of every size, ranged in parallel order inside the metal box, manufactured in Hamburg 1943. Of the best quality and hardly used. Another gift he'd accepted from the embarrassment of riches. Next, his gloves made from fine lamb's membrane which he'd always favoured, slightly numbing his fingers at first, on their diagnostic journeys into the labyrinths of the human body.

This would be easier. Cleaner, with no blood or bodily fluids to impede, because speed was of the essence. And then he reminded himself to curb his involuntary use of German, which had become too frequent. His sister, also.

XXVII

'But the fearful and unbelieving, and the abominable... and all liars, shall have their part in the lake which burneth with fire and brimstone: which is the second death.'
(Revelation.21.v.8.)

"We forget the other sinner is still free." Robert Sagan announced, expressing his earlier thought, looking Aymerigot Forgue in the eye. "I would rather set myself to that." He let out a soft, hissing sound, at odds with the bony harshness of his face. Thoughts of more rich pickings and an easy life with underlings to turn his soil and sow next year's fodder crops, made him clamber from the bloodied platform into the crowd. He was greeted by cheers and backslapping, for the parasitic Order was a scourge on the fine land of France. Far better that Mordiern Guyon be brought to swift justice than a horse whose burnt carcass would never even feed a pack of hungry hounds. As for the head of 'The Whiteface, it had probably been smashed to a mess and buried.

Under the *Arche de St. Paul*, the torch was finally lit. Aymeric Forgue''s dark form was bathed in its sudden golden power as he bent to ignite the lower branches. People pushed closer, taking the place of other women unable to witness the suffering of their own kind. Marthe clung to her daughter, the only fruit of her finished womb, and as the flames began their dreadful journey, she saw again that widowing, fatherless night when Hilaire had left the hearth forever. He had thrown on his cloak, lured by the howling of wolves near the sheepfold and the dull vibration of hoof-beats approaching, above the wind's sour, mysterious voice.

"Mordiern, save us!" Élise cried as the wind carried a spark to her throat, catching the carcanet of cornflowers he'd made for her. "Mordiern!" As she and his tiny, forming child succumbed to their fiercely crackling cradle...

XXVIII

Catherine felt well enough repaired and freed from the bouts of sickness to make an effort with her appearance. For the first time since her careless burning, she piled her hair upon her head and gave careful thought to what summery clothes would leave her legs bare. For they were smooth as before, and how nice it felt to rub in the brown tanning oil, giving a flattering bronze glow. She finished her 'look' with two patches of pale blue eye shadow and a smear of bright lipstick secured by a confident pursing of the lips. This completed the vision of someone who'd obviously had the good fortune to linger in the south of France longer than most.

Rosa Tavernier stared as she passed, despite receiving a tentative wave. The girl was quite back to normal. Not what she'd expected at all, and she also noticed how admiring looks came her way from men of all ages. At least her brother had seen sense and now left well alone, but he'd coupled with her, nevertheless. Nothing more than a tart and procuress. The *Kapos* would soon have taken her, passed her from one to the other, and maybe a little trinket or two would have come her way. But not enough to save her.

"*Poule!*" She shouted from behind her carcasses, seeing how like their dead flesh her own hands had become, and how the flies gave them a wide berth.

*

Now down near the shingle beach, Catherine inhaled the warm sea air which seemed purer without so many other tourists sharing it. She had to see him. Not least to ask some questions…

The flat in the Rue des Templiers was empty. Her life was empty. She could be the little smiling girl on his knee once more, looking up into that strong, clever face, fixed in time, forever and ever. Her tan under the short swathe of cotton lawn covering her hips, giving her courage. For he would like what he saw. *If* he saw her.

But the narrow lane to *les jardins* was empty save for its smells and a feral cat stretched out along the wall, twitching its tail in deep, carnivoral dreams. Weeds jammed his gate still marked with LT, and she had to push hard to squeeze through, ripping her short, seersucker skirt on the old wood. It hung limply out of shape like a damaged sail. She looked like some tramp...

Worse, what lay beyond was a memory gone terribly wrong. There was chaos in the Garden of Eden and Nature's rapid apocalypse almost barred her way.

Overblown leaves and giant unpicked brassicas repeated themselves to infinity up yellowing woody stems. A bristling army of growth unrestrained blocked out any view beyond with a sickly rotting smell. Massive melons and pumpkins still umbilically attached lay bruised and bloated, teeming with maggots and flies. Half-devoured strawberries lay bleeding under lettuce the size of shrubs, while the once beautiful courgettes now sprawled brown and pulpy, suppurating one on the other. The rows were in tumult. The ground hard as rock. He had deserted it all.

A trail of white feathers led to the shed consumed by its burdensome vine, and rampant knee-high grass. The door was held fast by weeds. Not the ordinary kind, but the steel wire variety that tears the hand when pulled. Impossible to uproot. Catherine held her breath. Listening. Her heartbeat audible as it had been then, but this time in fear. For inside his refuge was dark, but the gradual light revealed the mattress. Disembowelled, ripped apart, with the goose-down scattered like snow on ledges and cobwebs. Meanwhile, that tiny lark whose rigid, ringed legs had stretched up in sudden terror, escaped her, but not the *Contrexéville* bottle he'd drunk from before his *petit mort*. This had been stamped on and its water long since passed into the ochre soil.

She looked round, nervously, suddenly feeling sick. Again. The garden was choking her to death with no clear way out. She had to run like a hurdler to escape it. Higher and faster she leapt and slithered, gathering slime and burred fragments that incrementally weighed her down. While in the distance came quite a different sound above the brushing leaves and snapping stalks. The sound of loud, demonic laughter.

*

Léon Tavernier awoke early and alone to the massed sound of bells blown in from the sea front. From the *Chapelle St. Vincent* and the parish church came joy and melancholy, in contrapuntal discord as the sun rose up over the green Albères bringing another fine day. Warm yet fresh on the Englishwoman's morning skin, soon to be hot, but not hot enough to melt her altered womb flow and bring it forth.

Once more he chose the grey suit and gave a final rub to the shoes, before a silent exit from his wife who lay staring wide-awake at the fishing gulls cavorting in the sky. He'd never worn a beret before and endured the irritation. Mercifully, no-one recognised him as he drove down the Avenue Victor Hugo and parked his Citroën near the Crédit Agricole bank in the Rue des Templiers.

The two young men were leaving the rented apartment early, but as always, he was prepared. He was not, however, prepared for the shock of seeing the estate agent sporting his very own Panama hat.

Vious êtes un vrai idiot... Un voleur...

His headache threatened to return as they loaded up the car with paint cans and rollers, filling both the back seat and the boot with building tools. Still the laundry remained unlaundered, and even the clothes they wore looked stale and crumpled, a far cry from the crisp and clever co-ordinates usually favoured for such journeys. They seemed excited too, moving quickly so as not to waste a moment.

Unusually, the taller man got into the driver's seat, but neither gave the plain, sunless apartment on their right so much as a glance. Its shutters were firmly shut. Inert, unlike those of its neighbour. But his yellowing eyes weren't on them today as he bound his invalid scarf loosely round his jaw as car doors were slammed and the silver Renault's engine started. He followed at a discreet distance, and despite his anger, allowed various vineyard *camionettes* and holiday cars to interpose.

*

The Lord's Day once set aside for rest and contemplation, dawned deathly quiet near the inland mill. Still too soon for church traffic, or those intending to explore the fennel hills with guns and dogs at the ready. Too chill for the grasshopper chorus and the welcome of birds. Too easy to be casual and careless, which they were, by parking the Renault just inside the gates without even locking its doors.

The two Londoners galloped arm in arm up the rubble track, colliding, laughing open-mouthed in unearned freedom, their voices echoing in the ancient, vaulted hall. He let them settle into their usual intimate routines - no need to see all that again - which gave him time to walk in from the road and slither like a summer snake under their car. Simpler than opening the bonnet and far more private under the still-warm chassis. His mechanic from the Rue d'Argile had innocently given him clues, so he didn't take long, before finally smoothing things over where he'd lain. His back was dusty, his shoes out of order. Nothing that couldn't be put right as soon as he was clear.

In half an hour and overdue for the tablets he'd forgotten, the observer had left the rural tranquillity of St. Cernin for the main coastal highway into Spain. The black beret lay low and tight on his forehead as he passed a garage, then roadside stalls with fruit for sale. A timber yard and caravan park slipped by more slowly as a sudden numbness seized him. His hands gripped the wheel, devoid of feeling. His sickly eyes fixed unblinking on the road's central markings, and where he should have given way on a small roundabout, he kept moving. Locked into nothingness, with the same, blank stare that his chosen men had witnessed on the trains and under his waiting knife.

"Shouldn't be on the bloody road, morons like that." Another driver who'd had to brake gave him an obscene sign.

"Leave him alone. He's just an old man." The pig farmer's wife admonished, busy knitting a baby jacket. "I'd like to see you driving around when you're ninety five... "

This dizziness intensified as he returned to the familiar network of residential streets near the Avenue Victor Hugo. He ripped off his beret as the car lurched in gear against the end wall of the garage, and he sat for a few moments in the cool dark to recover and compose himself. The Girl, not normally employed on Sundays was in when he arrived, but was soon dispatched.

"What's it doing here?" He then bellowed at his waiting wife, who over the years had turned passivity into a fine art. "Doesn't it get enough out of me already! The greedy little Jew."

Estelle Arnajon *née* Bonbois winced, as she recognised that same, changed voice from the past. Half an octave higher and privately. Always, in the bosom of his family after each train departure. And so it was again.

She lay under a scattering of magazines that The Girl had brought in. Her bed a multi-coloured mountain with a mass of curlers encamped at the summit.

"What is *diese Schunde*?" He swept them all to the floor. She buried her face in the warm, stale pillow. "*Gebrechlich Hundin!*" He kicked the mattress. Then he left her, realising that the sooner he returned his tools to their hand-made resting places, cleaned and polished, the better.

*

Daniel and Clement never got round to emptying the Renault of all the gear they'd brought.

"Next time." They'd said, lying together on the butcher's plastic tablecloth, the Panama hat abandoned nearby.

So the afternoon passed into evening and the heady, burning sun sunk low behind the *Pic d'Estable*, bringing a chill in its wake. At nightfall, weary from love and endless talk of dreams, they left their future home for the relative comfort of the apartment.

It was Clement's turn to drive. That was how they liked to arrange it, and he turned the heater full on, misting up the windows in a whirlwind of warm air. The gradient down to Ansignan was negligible, and several well-lit cyclists were taking advantage of the empty roads to build up their speeds. He undid his seat belt to imitate them, jiggling and bouncing around without restraint. Alone again, with his fantasies, no longer tired, Daniel forgotten. It was the *Club du Cyclisme* from Baixas out for their final practise before a mid-week run to Barcelona. Clement put his foot down, denying them a wide berth and drawing shouts of abuse. He loved those limbs in motion. The muscle and brawn of hard, active legs and strong, wide arms. He parted his knees, rocking his groin backwards and forwards, as the adrenaline surged within, flooding everything, as if to destroy.

Then came a bend, suddenly darkened in the gloom by overhanging trees. The cyclists were well behind as he swerved out, misjudging the curve.

"Hey, I feel like another fuck." He laughed, wrestling with the steering and lurching all over the road. "And don't say I look like one!"

"For Christ's sake, Clement!" Daniel screamed, snatching at the steering wheel, but stronger, fitter hands rained down blows that hurt.

"I'll do it *my* way!" Clement roared, just as they hit the low, stone parapet of the River Agly bridge. Flung from side to side with increased momentum, the Renault rammed its huge, granite slabs and tilted up for a brief terrifying moment before a final shuddering stop.

*

Daniel felt cold air invade the empty windscreen, but nothing else. The seat beside him was empty, and warm rivulets of blood fell from his head to his hands. He moaned a prayer, seeing all the while his baby daughter, his wife, the little house in Poplar, in slow disappearing motion. Then he passed out.

People soon emerged from the apparently houseless hills, lured by the noise that had shattered their rural peace. They followed the paint trail and broken cement bags cluttering the road. Bright, glossy pools of moonlight spread down each camber, interspersed with the random scatter of dirty washing. The cyclists too, were there, leaning over the breached barrier, fervently crossing themselves.

"Holy Mary, Mother of God... " One clambered down through the broken gap and dropped to the slippery rocks below. His cries for help echoed above the river's own rumbustious journey between strewn boulders and other jettisoned debris that touched the Englishman's motionless, shoeless feet. Just as the night rain began to fall.

XXIX

'And the voice of harpers, and musicians, and of pipers
and trumpeters, shall be heard no more at all in thee...'
(Revelation.18.v.22.)

For Marthe and Élise Roland, the worst had passed. They were now at peace, rendered with their dog, as black and brittle as the kindling wood still smouldering, indistinguishable from their remains...

"On the report of persons worthy of trust, we have been informed that the brothers of the military Order of the Temple, hiding under the habit of the Order as wolves in sheep's clothing, insulting miserably the religion of our faith, have once more crucified in our time our Lord Jesus Christ and inflicted on him worse injuries than he suffered on the Cross. On entering their Order, they are presented with His image but deny him thrice and by a horrible cruelty, spit thrice on his face..."

So began the king's proclamation which together with the Papal bull *De Insolentia Templariorum* and the Hospitallers' claims of sodomy, accompanied the headless Brother Girard's journey back to the land of the Troubadour. But this time there was no singing to accompany his slow, tormented progress with six changes of horse through the bleak landscape of huddled hamlets tucked into the folds of empty fields.

Through this dead earth passed the small *cortège* of mercenary *'croque-morts,'* then upwards towards the large, stone dwelling set directly in front of the *Église de la Crucifixion*.

XXX

Once she'd reached the top of the apartment's stairs, Catherine was sick again, in an attack that seemed to wrench her very insides from their moorings. Her loosened hair fell like a weighted veil in lank, bilious strands. There was no more breath left, yet her heart still pumped its life, reverberating into her head.

She had escaped.

This was the fifth time the butcher had heard her 'problem' through her lightweight wall, and for the fifth time she hoped the tenant was using some sort of bowl to stop the solid bits lodging unhygienically between the floorboards. Unable to contain herself any longer, she rapped insistently with her gristle knuckles on the outer door. Then pressed the bell, knocking at the same time, without releasing the pressure of her thick, index finger.

"Madame Ash? Are you there"

"Go away!" Catherine murmured, the smell of bile trapped in her throat. She found the bathroom and knelt on the top step of its cold, white tiles. The hole lay beneath her, dark-stained and repellent, even though Daniel had only just cleaned it. He didn't seem to mind doing jobs like that, especially after Clement whose aim was always lazily askew.

The old woman's key was in the lock, working to and fro but impeded by the single bolt.

"Leave me alone!" Echoed down the toilet's abyss as Catherine gripped the raised blocks on either side of her and saw in that dark, constraining void, her life ahead. "Is this all I want?" She whispered. "Is this all?"

The retching stopped. There was no more to come, and downstairs was silent. She walked lightheaded into the small bedroom, monastic yet prayer-less. Remnant of nothing and no-one amidst all that Mediterranean history. The only identity - slight and fleeting - was provided by her suitcase which spilled half her life out over the floor.

*

The afternoon sun fell on the hills and valleys of clothes never worn and on the two photographs Clement had forbidden her to show. A black and white print of her mother and father on Southwold beach, and themselves, newly-weds, outside their Chute Street house the day they'd moved in. While she clung to that remembered smile, he was bounding unencumbered into a new future. Lance tilted south.

In an act of defiance she placed both photos on her bedside table. Then, having pulled the suitcase over to separate clean contents from soiled; useful from not,–began to re-pack, leaving room for those things still hanging damply in the bathroom. In went the fluffy, black mole given by friends at the clinic, together with a tiny Tower Bridge snow globe, with its constant winter. Then Serena's giant magnet 'to pull the punters in' was buried deep. In retrospect, a tasteless joke from someone who'd abandoned her.

After that, Catherine checked her passport which showed her looking more like a tipsy adolescent, and counted out what little money she had left. Eighty-two francs and twelve lightweight centimes. Although there was a joint account, Clement kept the cheque book and Visa cards. It had always been so, and she had never dared complain. Daniel would lend her the rest. She knew that.

There were no obstacles now and only two things remained. His necklace of wild strawberries ground to dry fragments in her hand. Next, she plucked the puzzling wartime picture from the wall, laid it face down on the unforgiving lino and jumped on to it. One, two, three, as if she was a hopscotch player, but child no more, landing heavily with both feet. Again and again until the glass fractured into splinters. Then she ripped out the photograph and dropped it down the lavatory hole to mingle with the contents of her stomach until only lightweight spittle remained. Her vengeance was complete, and the avalanche of foaming water bore the monochrome fragments away to join other waste, invisible to those late summer promenaders on the shore.

*

It was the rain against the shutters that woke her first, before the loud commotion around the street door. Catherine's little watch showed just after midnight and triggered a semi-conscious leap from her penance bed and a clumsy gallop downstairs as the banging and ringing increased. Clement had a key, so why all the fuss she thought, opening the door to blinding torchlight and men she didn't recognise. Except for one.

Daniel was upon her, enveloping her body with desperate, damp arms. A large lint pad covered his forehead and he smelt of blood. "Thank God!" His sobs burrowed into her hair. "I can't tell you! I can't tell you!"

"Tell me what? Where's Clement?"

"*Il est mort. Votre mari.*" A uniformed, tooled-up, gruff-voiced gendarme had edged inside to touch her arm. He signalled to the others to return to their van. "*Il est à l'hôpital...* you come now, please... " He placed the first of the jackets hanging up nearby over her shoulders. The light linen one that Clement had worn most often. "No other vehicle was involved," he added. "For that you must be thankful."

"Christ man, she's just lost her husband!" Daniel chose a jacket of his own. Thicker and warmer against the nightmare.

*

The lights were now on in all the neighbouring windows and Rosa Arnajon straight from her bed, stood close by with a none-too-clean jaw bandage - lest she die unattended in the night - framing her face. Under the nearby street lamp, her skin bore that same chalky ghostliness as what swayed from their rusted hooks.

She mused how there'd been more incidents in the *Rue des Templiers* in the past few months than in the last twenty years. Without doubt, the *Anglais* had brought *'la malchance'* some said, as front doors slammed and wheel spray finally settled in the quiet street.

*

Catherine kept her shaking hands in Daniel's lap all the way to the hospital. Occasionally, his heavy, curled head slipped from her shoulder, and those eyes that had once made her sing until her lungs were sore, had closed in pain.

"The gendarmerie weren't going to let me out," he said. "But I had to see you."

"It'll be alright." She whispered, suddenly free and soaring as their taxi sped along wet, straight roads. Nothing could harm her now. She released the musician's hands and crossed herself, at the same time murmuring what she remembered of the *Ave Maria*.

She did this again at the doorway to the morgue, cold, odourless and bright as a winter morning, where a white sheet covered the length of an occupied, wheeled trolley. A timid lift of the nearest corner showed long, black eyelashes fringing a face the colour of marzipan. A strand of equally dark hair caught on an eyebrow. No warmth, no breath, but at the same time, a strange sweetness. Her empty stomach heaved on nothing, for she was already cleansed. One of the gendarmes in attendance picked up a wall phone and turned away to speak.

"Route D308... *Pont de Cervera*." She heard him say. "Cause of death, severe internal injuries sustained upon impact. Time of death twenty two hundred hours... "

So the beautifully worked-out body had fallen, bruised and crushed under the arching moon. While she, victim of the sun, had survived. Catherine replaced the sheet and looked round nervously.

"Where's Mr. Madox?"

"Answering more questions," said the tall, white-coated Registrar, Jules Lefêbvre. He of the large, sleepless eyes who was silently at her side, easing her from the room, a hand under her elbow. "This way." He urged gently, wondering when her grief would come. "I have heard one or two things you know… "

"Oh?"

"That your husband's interests lay, how shall I say? Elsewhere." He pointed towards an anonymous door near the quiet foyer and ushered her in. "We may need to run a few extra tests, just to be sure, but that's nothing for you to worry about."

She looked far from worried. Far from anything in fact. He coughed, embarrassed. "I shall leave you now. Just remember, he would have felt nothing. He did not suffer."

"But *I* have. And my car."

The Registrar stared at her, seeing the face of a withered flower that harboured only dry, un-crying eyes.

"I must go." He said, and from his safe distance saw how absurd her thin, flamingo-legged figure looked, bulked out by an over-large, summer jacket.

*

There were four altogether in the interview room, in which coffee and cigarette smoke mingled like a late night bar. The younger of the two police officers occupied a chair in the corner, writing in a notebook while Daniel sat, head thrown back against the yellow wall. No songs, but keening sounds - *in extremis* - came from his throat. Catherine sat close, her arm around his shoulders.

"It's not your fault, Monsieur Madox." The other, older officer said. "The cyclists confirmed the Renault's driver was acting like a hoodlum. A danger to everyone."

She could see it. That sudden wildness. Too much muscle, too much of something she'd never shared...

"It's a miracle no-one else was badly harmed. Someone must be looking after you." He smiled, softening, and Catherine drew the choirmaster closer, feeling the heat of his tears against her cheek.

"We also have to ask some questions, and liaise with our gendarmerie colleagues."

"But you're separate organisations, surely?"

The smallest of pauses. An exchange of glances.

"Information sharing is vital. Now," he took a breath, "Is there any reason why Mr. Ash might have wanted to kill you?"

Cathrrine felt Daniel Madox's whole body stiffen.

"Jesus!"

"We have to consider homicide, Mr. Madox. It's only fair to warn you. Was there ever any demand for money? Any blackmail?" The interrogator then hesitated while the two foreigners looked stricken. Two shades of pale. The words 'one-upmanship' crept into Catherine's mind.

"You see, he had a business," the officer continued. "Things were going well. But maybe he had some, how shall I say, trouble?"

"This is madness!" Catherine shouted. "He loved Dan. He loved him more than me, if you must know. More than anything!"

Foolish, schoolgirl words. She bit her lips in shame.

"We know."

"Oh God!" Dan's head knocked the wall and a thin stream of blood seeped from beneath his bandage. The older, still unnamed officer passed him a coarse paper towel and stood over them, blocking out the light.

"We're asking you both to remain in Collioure until all investigations are complete and the Examining Magistrate has been alerted. Then, if the Post-Mortem also confirms accidental death, of course you can make the necessary arrangements."

*

Thus night had passed into morning, hazy with the befuddling smoke, innuendo and supposition, unremembered questions and half-truth answers which seemed for the moment to satisfy. Then, before the town was fully awake, they were taken back to the apartment under a leaden sky releasing hard glancing rain from the mountains.

"Georges Forestier," their taxi driver finally introduced himself, shaking only Catherine's hand, before they got out. "I'll be seeing you again. Try and get some rest."

Meanwhile, Rosa Arnajon's bound-up ears had picked up the voices outside, and her black eyes were quickly at the upstairs window. Abandoned on the pavement, the two *Anglais* moved silently, trance-like, almost floating... And where was Monsieur Ash of the tight trousers and smoothed-down hair? All this was very odd, but if she was as patient and observant as Alois Brunner had soon discovered, doubtless all would be revealed.

The apartment smelt damp as though all the rains that had assailed its ancient walls had finally penetrated. It was also as cold as the grave even though the electric fire's single bar glowed its vivid trickery. Catherine gathered up the pieces of scattered, broken glass before Dan had a chance to notice.

"Don't ask me to say anything." He subsided into the only chair with arms. "Please."

"There's nothing *to* say." Catherine left him for the bedroom. She couldn't make it easier, or harder. Words were only noises after all. She tidied the top layer of her suitcase and clicked it shut.

"What are you doing?" He sounded drunk.

"I'm going as soon as I can. I'm getting the hell out of Hell."

"You can't! We've got to stay for the P-M at least."

"So what? It's your problem, not mine. I wasn't there with you both, was I?" She was impatient now, sensing that same freedom that she'd felt in the car, and like the gulls which followed the tossing fishing boats taking their chance, she would now take hers.

"What about the funeral, then? And the mill?" His voice rose barely above the rain.

"What *mill*?" She stopped short, framed by the doorway. Frowning.

"Nothing. Nothing! This thing's got to me... " He roughed up his curls. Took care to avoid her face.

"I'll do a deal." Catherine's hands were on her hips. Legs apart. The ringmaster with the whip hand. "I phone Harold Greenbaum, and you sort the rest. There's got to be some money tied up in all this. Remember, you had a choice. I had none."

Silence followed as she went over to the window and pushed the old shutters out into the rain, securing the tall, inner windows. Each movement crisp, purposeful and alienating. Her mouth set hard, while his trembled. He took a deep breath.

"They want me for tests... "

She turned round.

"What tests?"

Again the tears came, but this time there was no comfort.

"I don't know... That Dr. Lefêbvre just said *'examens'*."

"Well, find out. Probably just routine." Catherine filled the kettle impatiently and banged it down on the cooker. "By the way, while we're at it, what about the car, Dan? *My* car?"

There was no space for his reply, besides she didn't want one, and kept speaking. "Just thought he could help himself whenever he felt like it, did my, or rather, *your* Clement. Mr. Easy Come Easy Go... don't mind if I do... Well I do bloody mind! The insurance company won't cough up for dangerous driving, will they?" She tossed her hair off her face and forgot about cups as the implications dawned, and hopes of an early escape faded. "God, I could kill him!" She shrieked, and the listening ears freed of their covering would later swear that the Englishwoman had said she was glad she'd killed him.

*

Outside, and despite the unseasonal weather, the Rue des Templiers resumed its normal business. One or two passers-by lingered to stare up at the Ash's apartment, but other needs, other errands soon took over. As distant bells chimed three o'clock, however, the sharp sound of the doorbell seared through the non-couple's uneasy sleep.

*

Léon Tavernier also slept late, with his brown head to one side and a stream of dried spittle etched in the groove to his chin. He had proceeded carefully, and everything that had been touched was wiped clean. Prints, fibres, smears, all erased before his black, aerodynamically-sloping car was once more draped in its shroud. His suit had been meticulously arranged on its hanger, shoes spotless and parallel; socks linked as one. His breathing came easily, his slumber, deep, for all was accomplished.

*

Fully restored but still restless after a light, late lunch at the *Café Régina*, he began a gentle reconnoître around the town. Although the rain had eased the air still bore a light dampening drizzle. From the other side of the road, he could see that *Maisons du Soleil* was closed. In spite of the extended awning and the new paint, the Agency looked drab in the unflattering greyness. Staring more closely, he noticed a man in police uniform hovering in the dark recess of the doorway. He caught his breath and hurried away, lowering the umbrella over his face. Something was up. He could wait no longer.

Aware that his back was still a little sore, he took the short cut past the *Palais Royale*, through the car park leading to half way down the *Rue Des Templiers*. An ideal vantage point, for he was close enough to the apartment, without being seen himself. The umbrella helped of course, but sometimes with a rare courtesy he had to lift and angle it out of harm's way. Then silently, unannounced, a police car drew up. That same *agent de police* he'd spotted earlier, pressed the bell long and hard while the doctor edged closer, tilting his leathery head.

So the Englishwoman clearly wasn't alone. His stomach turned seeing the other *Haeftlinger* emerge, hesitantly with a bandage on his brow. They'd obviously both slept in their clothes and stood pathetically dazed and crumpled.

"Madame Ash? Monsieur Madox? I'm afraid there are still more questions to be answered. Both the Coroner and the British Consul need full statements as soon as possible before the deceased's body can be released..."

The officer returned to the car to wait, while the elderly onlooker retraced his steps with legs suddenly rigid and his mind frozen in anger and fear. His face a chilling mask, muttering about useless bureaucracy. People idly turned his way, thinking he was just another lonely old man with only himself to talk to.

He made his way home, tempted to stop at the tall, portico'd building on the corner of the Boulevard Peyrefit to find out if Philippe Ferand had heard anything. He'd have to appear disinterested of course, asking for any news, but no. He must show rigorous restraint. Lie low. Get back to his garden, out of the way, and stop prowling around before somebody noticed. Like they always did.

The rain increased again, darkening his trousers and spotting his shoes. This was a botch up, but what to do now? That was the question. Like the vague, misted mountains that reared up on the right, devoid of any form and weight, he was confused and needed time to sort things out. The less digging there was, the better.

*

First on Catherine's list was Harold Greenbaum. Not her father, George Ash, alone and quietly disintegrating in Ilford. Nor Serena either. Not yet. She, who throughout the whole summer, had penned her friend only one, brief note, hastily scribbled between Green Park and South Kensington tube stations, deserved no more.

The police officer allowed her into the *Maison du Soleil's* darkened, blind-drawn office in the Rue d'Escabènes and switched on the wall lights studded around the room like illuminations. It took her some time to adjust in the full brightness, and to see how the place was transformed. Filth was now spotless. Damp stains and dingy patches glossed over green and hung with busy, pendulous plants. Two computers stood grey-faced on the long, well-ordered desk. Nothing was out of place or at random to the scheme of things where Clement had briefly reigned. Nevertheless, she chose not to sit in his chair.

The hurt that had left her, returned. He'd never treated her blemishes to such kindness, nor put a nice dress her way, like the quality awning that graced the window outside. Catherine kicked the waste paper basket into the far corner. It rolled and rattled away, emptied of secrets.

She then dialled Holborn.

"I think you'll be pleasantly surprised, Mr. Greenbaum." She said, having politely listened to his sympathy. "It's very impressive here... No, I'm not interested. Sorry... " She turned over a photo-file packed with properties... "I've got other plans."

Harold Greenbaum's voice then became louder and firmer.

"... Yes. I think so... I can do that... " She responded, picking up a biro to follow his instructions in good shorthand. Part of her old life was returning. "Business will resume on the first of October, under new management. Meanwhile, current transactions will be handled temporarily from this end, by Tim Harding."

She didn't recognise the man's name and it didn't matter anymore. That was Clement's past. Not hers. Then his tone changed.

"By the way, your local *Notaire* seems a touch unhelpful. Had Clement upset him by any chance?"

"I'm not sure. He never said much about work."

"Oh." He decided to spare her the news that the *Acte* to buy the mill had already been signed. "We'll have to look into that."

Harold Greenbaum then enquired about the funeral. He wanted to help in any way he could, but Catherine was caught unawares. That event was still a blur. Unformed, unthought of, like the embryo that now lived, and clung within her.

"Ilford," she began. "In two weeks... a week... I'm not sure... I'll be in touch."

Greenbaum, uncomprehending, decided not to pursue the matter, for the moment at least. Then, she told him about her new car that had been used for the business. How the assessors from Narbonne had called and shaken their heads. Now there were no lights, no windscreen, no driver's door, no chassis. Could he possibly help?

There followed a long pause. Greenbaum inhaled on a faraway cigar.

"Strange," he said. "We sent Clement money to get his own vehicle. Left hand drive and all that... What happened to it?"

Catherine was silent.

"Are you still there?"

"Not for long." She felt the same lurking nausea rise in her throat. "Look, it's not been easy, Mr. Greenbaum, as I'm sure you can appreciate..." She replaced the receiver before tears overwhelmed her.

The agency door opened and the young, uniformed officer looked in.

"Can I help?"

"I'm fine, thank you."

Dark, damp patches spread and joined on Clement's blotter like strange Rorschach **test** images, but the shallow, angular carving underneath it stayed dry. Catherine wiped her face on her sleeve, sniffed loudly and was left alone. She unfolded her checklist.to make order out of chaos. It was no good relying on Daniel. He was like a child, bereft and pathetic.

Besides, he was needed at the hospital for the rest of the week.

"Number two. *Crédit Lyonnais*." She snapped her bag shut, and left Greenbaum's hastily scribbled instructions under the 'In' tray. The officer smiled as she brushed past him in the strangest mourning clothes he'd ever seen. A creased, grey tee shirt with a black cartoon mole across her breasts, and chequered leggings tucked into boots. Those who knew she was now widowed, stared in consternation, and others who'd once cheerfully acknowledged the estate agent, also enjoying his adolescent good looks, ignored her. Thus she cut a silent swathe through the late summer crowds, her long legs scissor-striding towards the Bank in the Rue Valmy. Her eyes had dried under the new sun. It would only take one call to the Mile End branch to establish she could withdraw from their current joint account. Then the butcher could be paid her one-month's notice, with enough over for the journey home.

"My husband's belongings haven't yet been released." Catherine tried to explain why she had no chequebook, no nothing. She pressed her eager face to the glass as the cashier summoned a myriad balance sheets on to his computer. She spotted the name Ash above a long list of transactions. The screen suddenly stopped still.

"Two hundred pounds sterling please." She said. "Here, I have my driver's licence... " She produced it from her bag.

The man frowned.

"I'm afraid Madame, there is no money in the account. It was all withdrawn... I will check again... " He leant forward, as if doubting his eyesight.

Catherine felt as though she might fall. Her hands gripped the counter.

"What about the rent from our London house? That was paid in weekly, surely?" Her voice thin as a reed,

"I am sorry. There is nothing." He stared at the screen, shaking his head.

"And money from Harold Greenbaum?"

"Again, nothing."

"You stupid cow!" She suddenly kicked the partition. "You poor stupid bloody cow!"

People edged away. Then someone tapped her shoulder.

"Charles Gallin. *Directeur*. Come with me please." The older man had a neat moustache and a crisp, dark suit. Order and turmoil walked together to his spacious, palm-filled office, where, under a huge, spinning fan, he told her about the mill.

She steadied herself in a large, wicker chair. No longer of the dream world, the nightmare was with her. Now, in that room.

"What mill?" She heard herself asking.

"An ancient *moulin des olives*, near St. Cernin. Quite derelict. Your husband bought it in his own name only, deciding against the *Clause Tontine* as apparently he claimed, you could not... " Here, Monsieur Gallin cleared his throat... " there would be no children... " He moved away to his desk, and sifted through a slim, beige file. "Yes. It is all here, Madame. *Malheureusement*."

He went over to the door and unhooked a multi-coloured golf umbrella, for it was well past the start of his lunch break. "Monsieur Ferand has been more than helpful." He met her gaze. "I will spare you his feelings on the matter."

Words finally failed her. She stood up, gripping her little bag as though it was all she had to save herself from drowning.

"I suggest you contact the British Consulate in Montpelier. We can then liaise." Charles Gallin hastily wrote out the number, then escorted her outside, careful to keep a little distance between, as she looked like a woman of the streets, and already curious eyes were on them.

*

Catherine began to run across the crowded red carpet, and once outside she charged a two-legged gallop down the road till a brass band swelled by hangers-on, barred her way. Then up a side street. In flight, not gracefully lingering and dipping as the sea birds above, but noisily. Bumping into beach bags without apology. Screaming instead.

"You lousy stinking bastard!" Her red-amber hair blew into her mouth. "Rot in hell, and that's too good for you!... Burn!... Bloody burn!"

"He will." Said the old man to himself, sitting near the wall in the *Pizzeria* as he dabbed his lips after a plate of *crudités*. She ran past him, and he kept the napkin half covering his face. Women really shouldn't make such a spectacle of themselves - he'd seen enough of that sort of thing - shrill, hysterical hordes delaying, complicating, wheedling, clinging to their best furs even on those warm October days.

Mrs. Ash was no better. His friend Fritz Koppel had been quite right. She was just an 'easy lay'. Too easy, too willing, for a man who thrived on challenge. When *Hauptscharführer* Bilharz had asked for full trains, in 1943, he'd been able to oblige, but only after thorough groundwork ignoring lies and misinformation. His targets hadn't exactly grown on trees, ready for the plucking. Like the Englishmen...

Meanwhile, those legs he'd been between bore her down once more towards the dingy beach, accompanied by a barking dog. Instead of following or making an afternoon of wandering along the small, convoluted shore, *Herr Doktor 'Käfer'* decided to post his special parcel and buy the late edition of *France Aujourd'hui.*

*

Daniel Madox emerged from the hairdresser's shorn of his crinkle-curls like a summer sheep. His Praxitilean profile had rarely seemed so striking. Dark and light on bone and hollow under the late August sun while his surplus hair was swept up from the floor and left out with the rubbish. There being no call for such *Abfall* now.

This man of contrasts - even his collar, crisp and white - dazzled against a new Italian suit, silky on his back and shoulders. He blew his nose sharply, leaving it red and damp, while one eye welled up with surplus tears.

"This damned cold of mine," he muttered nasally. "D'y'know, I've never had one in my life. Never."

"Hospitals are crawling with germs. You've probably picked something up."

Catherine then looked instead along the length and breadth of the *Rue Des Templiers*. But what she searched for stood close by with only a sheet of plate glass between. He was there, in the shop.

"That Dr. Lefêbvre said I was in great shape. Considering... Not like... " Daniel began to sob quietly, cupping his head in his hands as the taxi arrived. "Oh God, I'm sorry Catherine."

"Bit late for that." Her words came as chill as the air round the butcher's freezer where the doctor kept watch.

Their belongings lay in a strange, isolated heap on the gravel pavement, dominated by two suitcases. Lives in transit, here today, gone tomorrow... The driver with large, damp patches in each armpit, helped load up his boot, and with only one solitary bag remaining, Rosa Arnajon quickly lumbered forth from her bestial morgue. Two minutes would make no difference. Things were always slow on Mondays which tended to be left-overs day. It wasn't until later in the week that serious meat eating resumed amongst the resident population. Besides, the one-month's notice rental paid by Monsieur Madox was safe in her pocket, and that was a bonus.

"*Adieu.*" Not '*au revoir.*' The same, ringless hand that had first greeted Clement and his lovely wife, now gripped a cold farewell, with dried blood lacing her white, ox-wrists. "Life is full of many sorrows." She smiled, seeing how oddly bare was the remaining Englishman's head. How red his eyes. "But now, you have each other. You have *Himmel*, no?" Joy lines formed a crevice on each side of that same, fake smile which had relaxed her many enemies to the furnace. Their scuffed shoes left behind, neatly tied together with a ticket.

Himmel?

"Why do you and your brother speak German? I've been meaning to ask."

Those lips pursed. That smile gone, as her eyes narrowed.

"We studied it at school. And excelled. One thing, mind, I want that photograph of him and his daughter returned to me immediately. It is part of my family and there is no copy."

"Daughter?"

A short snort followed.

"An irrelevance."

'*A stranger...* '

Then, having spotted the postman lean his bicycle against a nearby tree, the strange woman suddenly let go of Catherine's trembling hand. Her black bulk retreated noiselessly as the man approached.

"Madame Ash?"

"*Oui?*"

He placed a small, brown paper parcel in her hands, then after exchanging pleasantries with the taxi driver, swiftly remounted, as if relieved that there was nothing for that grim *boucherie*. Catherine stared at the handwriting in small block capitals, very precisely laid out. Postmarked Perpignan. She went over to the more private apartment doorway with Daniel following.

"What is it?" he asked.

"Don't know. I'm not expecting anything."

But deep in her core, knew she was...

She tore at the sturdy, folded paper, and a corner of yellow fabric appeared. Then red stripes...

"Oh Christ!" Daniel gasped. "This is so bloody sick!"

Two of Clements' underpants had been carefully folded, unlaundered, for they still exuded a stale sweet smell and were stiff to the touch. There was also something else. *'Schmutzingen Hunden!'* written on a little note attached. She flung everything at Daniel who ducked, as the items brushed his face.

"All yours."

And then she watched dispassionately from her distance, as he grovelled to reclaim them, scattered near the passing traffic. The taxi driver meanwhile, impatiently checked his watch.

"I have another client at eleven." He reminded her.

"Listen." She leaned in through his window, her mane of hair framing her face. "*La Méditerranée...* I just need to take one last look. Please."

"*D'Accord. OK,*" the man nodded, used to strange requests, but thinking them an odd couple nevertheless. "*Dix minutes.*" He then switched on his radio, while she took the shortest route past the giant fortress rearing up in the hazy sunlight over the cheerful line of restaurant umbrellas. Then down through the artists' easels and over the shingle between the tiny, bath time fishing boats, until she faced the sea. The same that Mordiern Guyon and Girard Corbichon had known on the big, pale stallion. The unchanging, lulling motion that had serenaded Joachim Kreisler with his adored and adoring pupil in the threatening air of the occupied Italian Zone. Until they'd put the placard *Urning*' round his neck. The sea, drawn in towards man from its destiny by the ways of the moon. In, out, in out... the rhythm of creation... foam flow... semen flow... Catherine rocked gently backwards and forwards to receive its valediction of wavelets passing under her feet.

Her bird was there too, looping and circling high above, higher than the tired sun that now hung heavily over the town. A child nearby squatted seriously on his haunches, digging a gulley. It subsided the moment his spade was lifted and he sat back defeated. Catherine suddenly grabbed his little shovel and plunged it deep into the damp, grey sand. Then its treasure was lifted out and flung, scattering stones shells and a popcorn carton. Again, this time faster and faster until the timid trough had become a deep trench, dark and wet below the pebble line.

The black hat, destined for the funeral in Ilford, immediately after their arrival at Gatwick, fell off. It skimmed along on the breeze out towards the sea as the new widow deepened the hole. By now, several people had gathered to watch. There was even a photograph being taken, for she could hear the camera's click.

"*Maman!*" The child shouted. "*Un tombeau! Regarde!*" His lisp noticeable. Then suddenly the performance stopped. Catherine had remembered something. Quickly she opened her purse, and there from its hiding place between a few old stamps and her blood group card, she extracted a coloured passport photograph. One she'd been told to keep for emergencies. A young man with smooth, dark hair filled the meagre frame, grinning a smugly muscular smile to himself, cocooned in a curtained booth. Like the lined coffin on wheels now boarding the plane, Clement landed face down and the little boy was on him, squealing with delight. Then another child joined in, and another - children he'd never made - naked and carefree soon filled the pit with laughter as the silent, creeping tide eased over its edge. She stood mesmerised, thinking of Leon Tavernier's 'irrelevant' daughter.

"Catherine!"

This time it was Daniel, hoarse, frantic. She picked up her new black shoes and ran up the beach, oblivious to the stones.

"He's gone!" She cried. "Gone! Gone!"

"Our taxi driver's almost bloody gone too! Come on!"

"Where's my hat?"

"Sod the hat, we'll get you another one."

They ran on over the coarse sand that harboured shell and mussel splinters, smooth-edged bottle glass and plastic ice cream spoons. Dried and withered condoms, half-written, buried letters from a summer drawing to its close. Daniel lagged behind, panting heavily, sweating under his suit.

"You go on," he wheezed. "At least he'll see you first."

And she did. Effortlessly. Free and weightless in flight at last.

"...Er... *Excusez-moi*." An olive-skinned man in blue overalls stepped out in front of her, by the *Tabac*. "*Pardonnez-moi*, but I have known your husband... "

Catherine simply stared. "You *are* privileged. I didn't."

He looked puzzled.

"Monsieur Ash gave to me all the work at the *moulin*. I am Michel

Villaine." He proffered his rough, square hand. "*Je suis désolé* – so sorry. It is a terrible thing that has happened to a man with so much to live for... " He caught sight of Daniel and tried to attract his attention, but the former choirmaster had crossed the road with laboured steps, too pre-occupied to notice.

"Thank you, but I have to go." Catherine saw him get in the Peugeot.

"Tell your friend over there I have discovered things about the boxes... "

"Boxes?" She looked bewildered. The car engine was already revving up.

"They belonged to men who were taken from Nice to Auschwitz in 1943. *Tous homosexuels*... Someone has been very careless... "

For a silent moment her heart stopped. Time stopped. She felt colour drain from her face and a sickness move her stomach.

"Monsieur Villaine, I... I... I'm not guilty... please!"

She must be crazy. Of that he was certain. The secular Jew saw her prettiness altered as though some artist on a whim, with clever sudden strokes of grey and purple, had rendered her tense and damaged. He took her arm as if to reassure her.

"Look, there is already how shall I say... *une enquête* – an enquiry. It will all take time, but it is now coming very near to home... You will see... "

"I don't know what you mean."

Then Daniel called out, and Catherine pulled away to run from the past, to sever its cord for good. But this bird was weighted now by lead shot, and would never again fly unburdened. Three pairs of eyes stared after her as the taxi door slammed and pulled away in an impatient cloud of exhaust. The butcher, grappling with a double handful of slippery kidneys. The doctor, who'd returned anonymously to the beginning, hidden once more by postcards in the *Tabac*. The builder, bemused but undeterred to find out more.

"Go, please." She tapped the driver on the shoulder, without so much as a glance up at the plain apartment walls and drab shutters that had imprisoned and excluded her. Like all the other traps of Hell...

As they passed the little beach and its fringe of heavy palms, Daniel again violently blew his nose and drew a little blood.

*

Flight 302 from Perpignan was delayed by forty minutes, so a drink in the bar was agreed upon, rather than exposure in the more public departure hall. They must have looked slightly unsettling, all in black like crows amongst the holiday casuals, An odd couple. His face as flushed as hers was pale, choked by a host of unspoken anxieties. Catherine placed a chilled beer in front of him.

"You came here with Clement didn't you?" She toyed with the glacé cherry on its stick. "Remember?"

"Of course I bloody remember." He sneezed, and she noticed how his hand shook on the glass.

"You're not well, are you, Dan?" There was no teasing this time.

"For Christ's sake, don't call me that!"

"*He* could." Her ice cubes rattled.

"He's dead!"

A few heads turned his way. It was too quiet with no taxying aircraft to distract, so Catherine bought a local newspaper. Heavy headlines coupled with a huge photograph dominated the front page... "**LES JUIFS SONT PUNIS ENCORE***!*'"

A synagogue in Toulouse had been bombed during the night, with the nearby graves of post-war inhabitants demolished and covered with placards. *'UNTERMENSCHEN!'* Vivid black on vivid white. Every letter clear despite the poor picture quality.

"Jews. Again." She sighed, starting her second drink.

"Oh."

"Clement saw me as a threat too, you know... hated me for it." Catherine angled her glass to catch the light.

"Come off it!" Another snort and blow. More blood.

"Why do you think I'm childless. Through choice? Did I want a little punch-drunk foetus to nurse for the rest of my life?" She then fiddled with her watch, moving the hands on one hour, keeping her own hands busy while her eyes filled with tears. "By the way, do you mind if I ask?" Catherine stood up, over him. Close. Slightly flushed. "I've been dying to know. Were you the man or the woman?"

Silence.

Daniel leant forward and banged his scar in a frenzy on the table. "You bitch!"

"Did you go like so?" She moved her hips backwards and forwards against his arm. "Or was it on all fours?"

He pushed her away at the barman's approach, sensing trouble. "It's alright," he said. "We're just leaving."

She smiled sweetly, helping the musician to his feet as the Tannoy called out various names to go immediately to the baggage check. Theirs too, which they didn't at first recognise. Daniel sulked behind her down the escalator, sneezing all the way.

"Your husband is in good hands, Madame." The official led them past the other waiting travellers. "All the clearance papers are in order, and we have a priest on board if you have need of one." He'd noticed the tiny crucifix around her neck, as he held the Exit door open. "*Père* Duran is *en route* to a seminar in London and I am sure he will oblige."

"We'll be fine, thank you."

They were out on the tarmac in a light drizzle, briskly walking towards where her husband lay.

"One other thing." Their guide turned round. "Do not be alarmed at the appearance of the *cercueil*. The coffin. It had to be reinforced as I am sure you understand. A Monsieur Harold Greenbaum has paid for everything and all is in order."

Catherine smiled politely and took Daniel's arm. They were now under the plane's huge belly, cast dark in its shadow. The engine's throb excluded all other sounds as their feet mounted the steps, leaving French soil.

"This way."

The English couple followed him to the end of the already half-filled cabin near the toilets, where a small area had been curtained off. A hostess in grey was busy distributing brochures.

"I hope, despite your unfortunate circumstances, that you have a pleasant flight," said the uniformed man leaving them to acclimatise to the close, stifling heat and the faint smell of urine. Neither, for different reasons, was able to look at the oblong, zinc box, secured to the floor by a set of restraining bolts, just like his apparatus in the bedroom at Chute Street. Redundant now, as his muscles sunk in repose, and functionless adrenogenital fluids lay bottled in, bloating his well-worked body. Chyle, mucus, enzymes, lymph, plasma, excrement, all to soon boil dry, to evaporate, be rendered harmless by fire.

Daniel on the other hand was awash with love, grief and a migrant virus undetected at the hospital that had saturated his only handkerchief. He stretched out, inert, staring at the low ceiling while the dull, ominous rumbling below almost drowned his half-remembered words.

"*Nous sommes cendres, et en cendres retournerons...* "

"What?"

"Nothing."

"It's bed when you get home. After the funeral." Catherine said in nanny-like tones, hearing the cabin behind fill up with more returning holidaymakers and those on school exchanges. German, Dutch, Spanish, Europe on the move, talking all at once, unaware of the sobering cargo behind the screen.

"What home?" He asked forlornly.

"Mine of course. Jasmine Khan will have left."

"How come?" The last consonant disappeared as the salt flow entered his mouth.

"There's a special clause following the decease of an absent spouse. Our solicitor's dealt with it."

"Oh." Even that was too taxing. "You said 'our'," he snivelled, searching her face with sad, wet puppy dog eyes.

"Did I? Well it's a bad habit. Anyhow, I don't fancy living on my own, for a while at least." She opened her handbag and for the first time in four months, applied powder to her nose. "Tell you what, Dan. Remind me to get flowers at the other end. At least that way they'll be fresh."

The little black case snapped shut on his feelings. Weak and vulnerable, he succumbed. He was in her hands now.

"We'll be off soon, thank God." She said, after the engines had suddenly throbbed into life, almost jerking Daniel from his precarious, slanting position. Their curtain suddenly parted and a young hostess poked her head between the regally red folds.

"Fasten your seat belts please, we're about to take off." She glanced at the tall Englishman uneasily. "Is everything alright, Madame?"

"Everything's fine." Catherine's mouth was full of hairgrips, then when the girl had gone, she leant over, arching her neck like a swan to gather her mane on top. Soon a prim bun with no escaping tendrils now replaced the softer, seducing, summer cascade. She picked invisible threads from her thighs, and stretched out her long legs as far as possible without touching the coffin. Her companion slumped forward as the plane lifted into the air.

"That's some temperature you've got." She kept a cool hand on his raging forehead, and felt the angry, disordered blood underneath. "We won't be long... I'll find you something to drink... "

At that moment, Daniel reared up, gripping her shoulders, eyes ablaze.

"He's getting at me, from in there! I know it! Can't you feel it?" His mouth trembled, nerveless, without control. "He wants me to die as well!" He kicked the metal casket so hard it jarred every bone in his body.

"Ssshh." Catherine held him against her. Fire on ice. And she was slowly warming. "Try to get some sleep now." She soothed, in command, with his head and its puckered bleached scar against hers. Another child. Another innocent. The man who had given her music and now forgotten the songs.

Meanwhile, in the main body of the aircraft, the film *'Platoon'* had just started and the first in-flight refreshment trays were being dispensed. They'd now soared above cloud, above peak and forest crossed by ancient walkways. Far from that genial sea edged by artists and poets, beyond the spoiled Garden and those hairless carcasses in the *boucherie*, concealing their vendor's offal eyes.

She, Catherine Vitello Ash was aboard her own huge bird of passage. Pointing north, not south as instinct would decree, and as she passed up its veloured gullet under the flickering screen, the old, suited man sitting next to the priest, hastily withdrew his worn, brown hand from its exposed arm rest.

XXVI

'Blessed are the dead which die in the Lord from henceforth:
Yea, saith the spirit, that they may rest from their labours:
and their works do follow them.'
(Apocalypse.14.v.3.)

"Divested of the clothes they wore in secular life, they are taken naked into the presence of him who receives them, and are kissed by him, according to the odious rite of their order, first on the fundament at the base of the spine, secondly on the navel, and finally on the mouth, to the shame of human dignity... " Aymerigot Forgue's half-brother, the priest, still limping, advanced with his church's accusations ringing out in the darkness.

He led the way by flickering candlelight along the cold narrow passageway to the rear of the kitchen, then knelt down, not in prayer but to slowly pull aside a sharpening stone. Then water beneath his feet, blue green and inviting as the *Mer Medi*, met his eyes. The man of God fumbled for a moment under his robe, and produced a bulky, bloodstained, linen parcel. All still now. Heavy and dead. Othon Lamaire had found it abandoned by some dog in La Baume. Without any blessing or consecration he let the severed, half-eaten head slip from his hands. The white, naked body followed, silently gliding like a finless fish. A mere shadow distorted for a moment, then borne away to a wider, calmer sea.

As his son's corpse finally nudged the rocks on the far Crusading shore, so the hermit Jean Corbichon's heavy, remorseful soul also passed wearily from that wicked *'paienime'* world.

XXXII

Catherine's happiness upon returning to Chute Street seemed complete, despite Daniel's absence at the London Hospital for further tests and the continued disruption to her monthly cycle. Even the Saturday street of greys and ochres, peopled by market shoppers seemed welcome-coloured, and she ran with elation from the taxi up towards the bright front door.

The Sotheby's buyer had left a surprisingly friendly note together with a small bundle of cards and letters of condolence from forgotten cousins - now no longer envious of two incomes - fellow gymnasts, and those in the estate agency trade. Their dismal commiserations were thrown straight in the bin. Even the padded *faux* lilies from George Ash in Ilford had outlived their function, and now took up too much room. She ripped them into rough quarters, only to find the filling under the velvet was merely shredded toilet paper. Rubbish flushed away, like the other memory from the *Rue des Templiers*.

She would confess it all later, but for the moment, needs must.

Everything was in it place, as she'd remembered. The soft, moleskin furnishings, cork tiles, and plants that had like her, grown and fructified, many sprouting rich, vermilion flowers. She paced around, feeling again the thick, white pile between her toes. All hers to enjoy in untainted freedom. Except for those body-stretching bands, assorted weights and other devices that cluttered the master bedroom, looking more than ever like abandoned modern art in some disused gallery. But unlike such obsolete icons, there'd be a ready market with the gym crowd, leaving her a normal room at last.

Catherine had left a message for Daniel at the hospital before discarding her ephemeral widow's weeds for the first proper bath in months. Her figure had undeniably filled out - now surely the Master from Cambrai would have invited her to lie amongst the oriental trappings of his flat interiors. She had arrived, no longer virgin, from the very place he'd chosen for his palette. South, where the sun had first flattered, then eroded, layer upon layer before its healing heat turned in penance, to her dull, viridian bruises...

She subsided into the scented foam, covering her heavier blue-veined breasts, with only the water-retentive stomach curve exposed. Things would return to normal once her cycle resumed. Like Estelle Arnajon, she could wait.

Meanwhile, countless other things imposed on her lassitude. The flickering flames that had beckoned her husband's coffin beyond the small curtains; cheap, piped music and his father's bewildered grief. The vicar who'd given his son's surname as Oak, instead of Ash, and Greenbaum, with his un-groomed nose offering Catherine a car and a clerical post at the Holborn branch. She'd been given a week to confirm. To try and re-organise her life as a singleton. But there was still the problem of the one-time conductor and lover of Mordiern Guyon's words – who'd soon be sharing her home.

*

Having amicably parted company from the friendly priest on the aeroplane, with a promise to meet up later in the week, *'Herr Doktor Käfer'* was relieved to be alone. After only forty-eight hours, the elderly native of Marseilles was already missing the southern warmth, and finding the British weather damp and disagreeable. Early Autumn in the metropolis had increased his aches and pains, while his habit of interspersing German with English was alienating and confusing to all, particularly his landlady. He'd found an unpretentious Bed and Breakfast, just off the Whitechapel

Road. A quiet street of Edwardian houses parallel to Chute Street and its new courtyard developments backing on to the lugubrious Limehouse Canal.

Accommodation was plentiful, with room-names recalling such faraway exotica as 'Shangri-La,' 'Arabian Nights, ' or 'Rainbow's End,' but after much deliberation, he'd chosen the newly-decorated 'Arcadia', whose white windowsills dazzled against the ochre brick façade, even in the murkiest light. Despite the lack of private bathroom facilities, the establishment, once a family house in better days, boasted a less than new television and an electric kettle in each of its bedrooms. Out-of-date magazines and car-boot sale paperbacks were also ubiquitously available, to make things more like home. Except that in reality, the likes of *'Herr Doktor Käfer'* had little time for such self-indulgence.

The inner entrance door boasted a colourful collage of acceptable credit cards, suggesting a lively, cosmopolitan trade. In fact, the Frenchman was the only guest, in the cream-upon-cream, anaglypta-covered rooms. Here, his shoes were never as clean as he wished, what with all the dirt on the streets, and even after a morning out, collars and cuffs would be edged with grime. Mrs. Daphne Robinson would have to oblige - for a little extra of course. He'd told her he had to look smart for his series of meetings at the British Museum, and in her simple yet practical way, she wondered why he was staying so far along the Central Line.

"Ours not to reason why," she confided in her neighbour, as she hung out the washing on a windless, unpromising day. "Cos there ain't much 'ere for tourists I can tell yer... To my mind 'e looks like 'es 'ad a bit of a life, know what I mean? But the funny fing abaht it is 'e don't never smile."

His shirts blocked her view, smelling of the floral conditioner she used on special occasions or when things were quiet. She thought it odd that their labels had been cut off.

"There's nowt so queer as folk. That's what I say." She summoned another dialect, to impress. Mrs. Robinson had him taped.

However she knew nothing of his impatience or that he was tempted to call on the *Untermensch* himself in the hospital ward, still-living proof of his failure. But no. The most *gründlich*, most thorough of them all must wait. He must find *der recht Augenblick* - the right moment.

*

Despite his earlier warning to himself, and the fact that the 'butterfly' had dared quizz his sister about their shared use of German, the language of that particular host country impinged more frequently on this other as his stay lengthened, with time to kill. And in that lull, from the deep, darkened land of Erebus, the Teuton tongue gave voice. But where was his audience? The erstwhile doctor was quite alone.

In the mornings, for an hour and a half, he would sit with the latest *Die Welt* in the small, peeling pavilion at the Hospital end of a little park. After an anonymous snack-bar lunch in Fitzgerald Lane, he would again resume his perambulations round the dog-dropping streets in the company of a few desultory skateboarders who wheeled and tilted close by. Too close sometimes, with the same hard, speculative stare as those persistent trinket traders on his beach, a thousand miles away.

"Watcha Mister!" Slanting on two wheels, hands tensed to balance. Then nudging, touching, brushing by so he could even smell their breath.

"*Gehenweg!*"

But too late. Three youths had him pinned against a damp and peeling billboard advertising holidays on the Rhine.

"Watcha got 'ere then!" Their faces close, two black, one white. They wore ugly, fluorescent clothes and he could tell they never washed. The smells of faeces and hair gel intermingled. Before he could react, his wallet was deftly pulled, and with a triumphant wave they clattered over the kerb and were gone. The old man gave chase; his kicking, torturer's knees suddenly weak and incapable.

"*Schwachsing!*" He panted. "Bastards!"

He found a bench and tried collecting his thoughts, the less calamitous first. Under normal circumstances, he'd be on his way to the Police, not sitting there, a passive victim, robbed and humiliated like all his '*Urningen*' had been. They'd have discovered a small photograph stamped R.MOREL. MARSEILLES showing a young Agathe pretending to play chess. So faint and rubbed, she'd almost disappeared. But no coins or notes. These he'd cleverly concealed in a sewn compartment inside his trousers, where the hip begins on the right. He'd learnt this from his Riviera tricksters, and once seen, never forgotten. Far better than having to draw attention to himself at a bank. He patted the hiding place, just to make sure, aware of his crippling headache returning.

The *Carte d'Identité* was another matter. It had gone and, bureaucrat that he was, this alarmed him more than the attack itself, for he would need it upon his return. Léon Tavernier, resident of 56, Avenue Victor Hugo. *Employé de bureau. En retraite.* What possible use to that scum? Besides, it had probably been jettisoned amongst the other litter when they'd realised there was no money.

Not so. It was of enormous interest. Sean Steiner had never owned such a thing before. Different from the usual Diner's Cards and American Express they collected, especially with that funny photo and all those words in French. Anyway, his mates weren't bothered, so he'd let them keep the wallet and the other thing while he had the prize to show off to his big buddy Martin down the pub that night.

*

Catherine eased Daniel's wheelchair from the hospital exit towards the specially-adapted ramp, but its unfamiliar weight pulled her along too fast down the slope.

"Brake!" He yelled helplessly, gripping both its thin, tubular sides, and she just managed to bring the whole cargo to an abrupt stop, inches before the kerb.

Suddenly, opposite, through the traffic, she caught sight of something familiar. An old man sitting motionless, his rolled up newspaper across his knees. Black hatted, head down, eyes averted.

"Look! Over there!" She cried, but the invalid was too concerned with re-arranging himself, and now that he was stationary, checking his eyesight with a series of squints. "I'm sure it's him!"

"Who?" Daniel's face was upturned upwards the sky, as if searching for somewhere else. For her part, to even utter the other man's name was too ridiculous. London was full of displaced, elderly men in cared-for shoes.

"Nothing." Catherine secured the rug around his shoulders instead. Thinner now, like his cheeks and fleshless legs shrunk inside their trousers.

The short walk was designed to do him good, but the traffic-stirred air brought on a succession of explosive sneezes, all the way down Gardiner's Road and over into Bush Street. Each like an earthquake wracking his system, and Catherine used all her strength to keep him in a pushable position.

Occasionally she looked behind, but that old man had vanished like a ghost amidst all the others that stalked unseen along those once commercial Dockland streets on that bleak empty afternoon.

Drancy was also chilled by the same dreary sky, the white-to-grey apartment blocks and stained, corrugated iron sheds of failed enterprise. But its doomed souls have long since fled, leaving their corral neatly and geometrically void. No chaos now around the solitary *Wagen* on display for tourists. No terrible tearing cries, or underground hands clawing, blockaded withing yards of freedom by the hard, stony soil. Two graveyards of ambition laid to unrest, each umbilically to the east of its great mother metropolis, and waiting for the first biting frost of winter.

*

There were very few signs of walking life near the Mile End Road, where Catherine paused and checked again before crossing. In the distance, groups of men and women collected children from a fortress-like school, while nearby, some Technical College students bantered and bartered noisily over a personal stereo. Then pensioners, close enough for her to see their delicately withered skins, drifted in pairs through the dried, blown leaves towards a cup of tea at the Day Centre.

"Nearly home."

And soon the soft, sheep-wool pile carpet was theirs. The underfloor warmth and open-armed chairs, barricaded by double brick against the sharpening river wind, bearing bulbous evening clouds in from the North Sea.

"Does Geraldine know you're here?" Catherine set a small tray on Daniel's lap and sat close by to help him.

"I've told her. I want to see Louisa. That's the only reason."

"D'you think they'll come?"

Daniel looked at her, stripped of his vigour, his desires, his future.

"Dunno."

"Well I don't mind if she wants to visit with her." Catherine held the cup to his lips. "Greenbaum's giving me flexi-time at his office to see how things work out, so feel free."

"Wish I did," he whispered. Noticeably hoarse. "Thanks." But his life-sentence had already begun. Then there'd been a letter from her asking for maintenance from his small invalidity benefit, with its terse postscript threatening a solicitor. His eyes, once brilliant clarions of energy that had moved a disparate company of City workers to sing their hearts out, had sunk without fire, and an unhealthy pallor replaced the outdoor tan.

Fortunately, Catherine had saved all Clement's tracksuits, and at least the heliotrope velour lent his lover some colour. Besides, they were comfortable for long-term sitting.

"Look, with this *thing*, you're going to get good days and bad days." She touched his arm. "So... what shall we do on the good days eh?"

He gave a quick, simple smile, then remembered something.

"Last night of the Proms."

"What?"

"I told the choir I had tickets, remember? You were there. It's on Saturday the twelfth I think... I'll have to check... "

"Sounds like fun. Are they in your wallet?" Catherine got up, eager for new memories to replace *'le temps perdu'* and highlight their murky and uncertain future. She found both in his bedroom. Two photographs, one showing Clement standing under blue sky in front of some derelict building. The other, a long shot of The Early Music Balladeers taken in concert, with her own head, mouth open, ringed in black ballpoint. She quickly replaced them between the collection of till and restaurant receipts, and returned instead with the four folded cards for the Royal Albert Hall.

Ten days to go.

"You didn't forget me, after all." She said, handing them over.

"What d'you mean?" Daniel was having difficulty clearing his nose.

"Nothing. Listen." Catherine switched on the stereo...

"*Ges pel maltraich qu'ieu soferi*

De ben amar no.m destoli

E si tot venta ill freid'aura

L'amours mi ten chaut on plus iverna... "

"My God, that's us!" He croaked.

"And that's me!" Her own voice above the chorus, soared high into the room.

"Happy days." Daniel tried to raise his cup, forgetting in that moment that he sat in Clement's clothes, in Clement's chair, in Clement's house.

"*El joi qu'ant perdut,*" as tea spilt down his chin, and the telephone rang.

It was Serena, feeling that after a decent interval, she could intrude. Orally and directly, with that over-painted mouth. After listening to several expressions of sorrow, and her opinion of the funeral, Catherine finally managed to ask her if she'd like an evening out in South Kensington on a spare ticket. It would be a time of joy and celebration. Something for them all to remember, especially Daniel with his serious and as yet, unidentified illness. Her friend laughed down the 'phone.

"*Mon Dieu*, Miss Veal. Is this a widow talking?"

"Indeed." She shielded the receiver as Daniel's rubber-coated wheels brought him closer. "I can't say much now. I'll phone from the office," was whispered carefully.

"Hang on a minute." Serena's voice became more urgent. "Did he leave a Will?"

"Who?"

"Mr. Clement Ash, for Christ's sake."

Daniel saw Catherine's face tighten, white and hard.

"I don't know what you mean. It's automatic isn't it? I get everything if I'm his wife?" As she spoke, the forming child leapt in her womb and pale, amphibious legs kicked an echo to the panic that shook its fluid sac. Two eyes with undeveloped lenses could only feel, not see yet another loss...

*

The next few days at 4a, Chute Street passed under a cloud of debilitating tension, and Catherine was glad to escape to work for at least a few hours each afternoon. Paul Rebone of Barker, Rebone and Hall, Solicitors of Chancery Lane, had formally written to inform Mrs. Catherine Vitello Ash of her late husband's re-worked Last Will And Testament, but was five miles away from its effect once she'd severed the innocuous brown manila envelope with a vegetable knife.

Daniel had stared dumbstruck at the terror in her eyes. An innocent, he'd been drawn like other countless unsatisfied lives towards not just the bright lights, but to passion and mystery. Immature, early lambs to the slaughter, and now he sat - for he could only sit - untended, unwanted, a wretched duplicitous pariah. To her rage, and true to his condition, he'd bleated like an abattoir sheep. Fear blocking its gullet.

"I never knew anything! Clement said nothing to me!" Not-so dumb animal that he was, with frightened eyes, locked in its steel and vinyl pen. And how she'd spat her goodwill in its unshielded face, glazed with mucus and saliva. And again, and again, as her firstborn inside threshed in its warm, private sea.

There would be no washing, no correspondence, no care, no nothing until things were sorted out to her advantage, and it was for that reason that she telephoned Harold Greenbaum with her problem and arranged to meet him early on Thursday morning.

*

"I'm also pregnant." Catherine concluded at the end, having shown the estate agent her lawyer's headed letter. "Dr. Prakesh confirmed it yesterday. So, all in all, a fine mess."

"Now then," the large, suited man swivelled round to face her. "We must think constructively. That is not a catastrophe, and survival is the name of the game. I have my tattoo to prove it," he added mysteriously. Ah!" As the second of the day's treacle-like coffee arrived, delivered by someone even newer than Catherine. Greenbaum re-focussed on her. "So, my congratulations are in order. What does one call a young Ash by the way?" He asked in mock puzzlement. "An Ashling? *Un petit frêne?*" He roared a cavernous laugh muffled by smoke and she felt a calming sense of reassurance as it trailed upwards towards the grimy ceiling.

"Now who are these so-called executors?" He began concentrating, frowning over the small print.

"Men from his Gym, I think, although I never met them."

"Surprise, surprise." He muttered. "This is dirty business. Naughty Clement. Kept you out of things down in Collioure, too. Not what I wanted at all... " He drained his cup in one long draught and pulled out a colourful paisley handkerchief to wipe his lips. "Now, leave this to me. You have enough to do, especially as you'll be needed to build things up in the commercial premises sector."

"What?"

"Oh indeed. Entrepreneurs are far more trusting if a woman is handling the deal, and these could be exciting times with greater developed access to Europe. Then, who knows?"

A substantial, mottled hand settled on her shoulder. Neither her father, nor God or her Guardian Angel, but a solid, barnacled anchor, keeping her fast as the uncertain swell increased threatening to swamp her life.

"By the way, what about the other chap, the invalid?" he asked. "Is he paying you rent?"

He'd noticed her hands, softened and bleached from wearing rubber gloves.

"Er, actually... no. I'm not sure how to... " She'd been caught unawares with no defence. Like the invalid's dangerously viral blood.

"Lose him."

She gasped. "How can I?"

"You have a door, surely?" Harold Greenbaum got up, seeming fatter, and escorted her to the darkened edge of the home-going tide of people.

*

She was soon swept along down Newgate Street and Cheapside amongst purposeful office legs whose escape schedules were timed to the second. Visions from the last few weeks spun in her head like the *Rouge et Noir's* reckless clattering game. Pigments of sea and sky, his clothes, his hair, her car, blurred together as they circled faster and faster, and she, the ball-bearing hurtled from hollow to hollow without rest.

Gripping some nearby railings, Catherine eased her breathing and closed her eyes. Thus she missed the elderly, square-shouldered man who stood close enough behind yesterday's *Financial Times*. Close enough to smell her perfume,

He could tell she was swollen with another life. After all, he wasn't *Herr Dokter* for nothing. The cut of her dress under the coat. Her breasts fuller beneath its woollen lapels, her complexion draining its blood to another. All giveaways. Besides, she was just another *Weibschen* now, like all the others from Villejuif and Vitry. Blanched like Carrara marble yet soft as cheese, and ripe for the melting...

The speeding, unfamiliar traffic harassed his thoughts and lashed his new English raincoat about his legs. She would cling. Ah yes, how she would cling, and her burden too, just as the Polymmatus Bellargus, or Adonis Blue butterflies suck from the clover. All in their Silent Phase, just like him, for whom time was noticeably running out. Waiting and watching under the winter skies, in sodium-lit suburban streets, had taken its toll. He was more stooped now, with old femurs and tibulae aching for the warm Mediterranean, and his head, despite a succession of hats, was permanently cold. Worse, the headaches had returned. Permanently, despite his pills. Even 'Arcadia's' demise was imminent, as Mrs. Robinson, wishing to increase her income, had already submitted plans to convert the hotel to a private, residential home, specialising in dementia care.

He watched the tall, auburn-haired young woman cross over Gracechurch Street, and this time, he followed even more closely, determined, as the city sky rapidly darkened, to put his house in order and efficiently solve his Final Problem. Now that the remaining '*Abschaum*' was deteriorating so well, his carefully researched his shortlist of gay bars in central London had become ever more important. It lay neatly folded in his palm, together with the detailed ground plan of the Church of the Knights Templar, just off the Strand.

XXVIII

'En rassemblance que nous sommes cendres et en cendres retournerons... '
(La litanie du mercredi des Cendres pour les frères Templiers.)

"After equally abominable and detestable acts they deliver themselves one to another without refusal-and from this time they are required by this vice to enter into an horrible concubinage; and that is why the wrath of God has fallen upon these sons of infidelity... "

Three months and ten days after his forced confession to the young Philippe de Marigny, new Archbishop of Paris, Mordiern Guyon revoked his account. Tortured into lies by his finder and deliverer Robert Sagan, now a wealthy man, despite the thrice-devalued currency. His one-time *'hommet'* could neither sit nor rest on his feet. In his sepulchral cell, the former farmer had calmly removed his nails and hung weights from his sinning cock, all the while listening to how Druide has vanished after Corbichon's fire in La Baume. But even this inquisition couldn't break the short man from Manorcastle, so on June 15th 1310, together with fifty-three brother knights, he was 'relaxed to the secular arm for burning' as a 'relapsed' heretic on the *Île aux Juifs* set in the River Seine in Paris. Free once more as the pale horse, while his old mother sung the songs that Marthe Roland had sent her, and the vast, limpid orange sunset below the busy city's horizon.

"... For when you wish to be this side of the sea, you will be beyond it... "

XXVIX

In a new atmosphere of cordiality and understanding, Daniel Madox sat back to enjoy watching Catherine's preparation for their big night out, for Clement's cantankerous manoeuvrings with his Will had been finally quashed by Greenbaum's persistent pressure. Cleared of any collusion, penance for the former choirmaster had nevertheless begun. His helper lymphocytes had welcomed like an eager host, the *Pneumocystis carinii* pneumonia, and now, slowly and subtly, as is its wont, an evil had consumed him.

She started by brushing out her hair, and now, just as when he'd first caught sight of her, he couldn't believe so much beauty could spring from so little. She stroked it, tossed it, sometimes turning, knowingly, to donate a smile. For charity. Then lipstick spread sweetly lustrous, to overlap each curving edge, and tightly sealed to last the night. Deft fingers next, smeared silver eye shadow close up in the mirror and her breath misted the glass.

"Gorgeous," he said, croakily. "What a lovely mother you'd make."

She started, then composed herself.

"You look O.K. too." She leant forward to check her mouth, seeing his reflection, darkly elegant in a hired morning suit. What else could she say to the man with fungus in his lungs who was dying in front of her? He lounged on the couch, like some *louche* young man in a Victorian painting. Legs splayed. No shoes, with two cartons of party streamers lying in his lap. Hermes of Praxiteles whittled to the bone by a tireless chisel, yet still noble in profile. His face still strong.

"Get your shoes on. Serena'll be here soon," she said. Then,

"Damn!" having remembered he couldn't, and his head, although free of lint and bandages, was still tricky. Catherine knelt to carefully begin lacing up each of his shoes, her soft, washed hair falling on both her hands. He reached over and touched it.

"I really used to love this... when you were walking home after choir... I won't say I was never tempted... Oh God, Catherine," he turned away, choking on sorrow as the bell chime on the front wall rang out, accompanied by a loud "Coooeee!"

She snatched her dressing gown together over her stomach and opened the door to Serena's over-made up face peering in. Eyes set in gaudy, emerald caves. A mouth too big.

"Hi there!" Serena beamed. "Have I got a surprise for you." Her layered, taffeta dress rustled forwards. "Someone who's been absolutely longing to meet you again. A blast from the past. Hope you don't mind... "

The old man was revealed, lit by two sets of outside lights. A smile on that dry, lascivious mouth.

"Jesus Christ!" Catherine recoiled. Her stomach suddenly heaving.

"I found him lurking around, so I naturally asked what he wanted." Her friend spoke with the confidence of not being fully understood. "He knew you in France, he says. Went into a lot of detail, so I thought, where's the harm?" She chortled as though she'd been drinking. "Actually, he's a bit like my ol' grandpa, and you know how I just adore little ol' men."

"Do come in." Daniel's voice seemed to come from a long way away. "*Bonsoir.*" He extended his hand to the stranger. "It's good to see you again, Monsieur Tavernier."

The Frenchman hesitantly responded; his expression barely concealing his distaste. Catherine stayed rooted to the spot, staring open-mouthed.

"What's up?" Serena whispered, exuding a sickly rich perfume. Her fluffed-up head nestling in its feathered collar resembled that of a chicken. "Tell me."

"Nothing. Nothing at all." Catherine pushed past the two men and slammed her bedroom door behind her.

"I see Madame Ash looks well." The visitor smiled after her, as Serena followed. All frills and stilettos. "Such a terrible tragedy about her husband... I am so sorry."

"We're living with it." Daniel opened one of the party poppers and it immediately ejaculated a froth of yellow foam on the carpet. He tried to laugh. "Do sit down."

The visitor arranged his houndstooth hat on his knees.

"Now I remember," said Daniel. "You came with us to... where?"

"Rougières." The other obliged, aware with every passing second that a force greater than life itself, and more exacting than any punishment he could mete out, had gained another hostage. Slower than the salts of hydrocyanic acid with which he'd come prepared. More callous than the beating, probing stick or the predacious soldier beetle. Monsieur Madox had now opened himself to far more deadly opportunists than ever he could become. Karposi's sarcoma would be the next to call, then the lymph glands would enlarge like his overgrown marrows, then pain, more pain with the bowels invaded and out of control...

"In retrospect, those small villas we showed you, weren't good value." Daniel tried to fill the embarrassing void without Catherine or Serena to help out. "People don't like to live quite so close to one another, despite what architects say." He coughed a series of dry, unrelieved barks and fumbled for his handkerchief.

"You must take care." The Doctor kept his eyes fixed on shut the bedroom door, which harboured two female voices. "Our health is all we have, and I am afraid to say that your London *Klima...* is, how shall I say, '*bosartig*'. It destroys. That is why I am not here long." He felt the little canister deep in his pocket and cradled its smoothness in his hand.

At that point, both young women emerged, almost conspiratorially, although Catherine now in a black, figure-concealing shift, looked far from happy. Serena perched blithely on the old man's chair arm, causing her dress to ride up and expose a pair of wide, white thighs.

"Gosh! Sorry folks!" She said, but there was no shame. She'd wanted him to see. "Look here," she decorously pulled on the hem with ten plump fingers each alight with green nail varnish. "We've decided that with 1993 upon us, we should strive for a little more *entente cordiale* and a little less of *la jalousie.effroyable*. What say you?" All eyes were on her. "We, therefore," she ignored Catherine, "suggest inviting Monsieur... ?"

"Léon Tavernier," he obliged.

"Monsieur Tavernier to accompany us tonight. Agreed?"

Catherine turned away, but the foreigner looked up. His interest piqued.

"Have you a ticket spare?"

"Sure. No problem. Dan here had extra for the choir, didn't you darling?"

The Doctor thought her lipstick disfiguring, like *une prostituée*, and like so many women of the streets she carried too much weight. Still, his sister had, during her best years, dealt well enough with those kind of imperfections.

"Ah. But please, you must allow me to pay... " He said, graciously.

"Put it away." Serena covered his hand hospitably with hers. "It's *our* treat! Right." She looked from one to the other. "Are we ready? Or does anyone need the loo?"

*

Catherine slung a black, fringed shawl around her shoulders and covered Daniel with a tartan blanket. His top hat lay underneath it. The Frenchman noticed she'd made no effort to hide her long legs. Dancer's limbs encased in sheer, dark hose with an arrow *motif* on each ankle. He'd also travelled far to their fusion; to that deep, moist virgin valley now bearing fruit.

"I don't know how to thank you." He said turning up his collar in the cold outside.

"Well don't try." Serena shouted from her car, all its doors open ready to receive. Daniel sneezed and shook convulsively as three pairs of arms lowered him on to its rear seat.

"Thanks," he managed to smile, and to the Doctor who sat alongside. "Nice car."

"Not bad." Serena slammed the boot on the folded-up wheelchair and pulled up the aerial. "I've always gone for Volvos." She revved in the still, evening air. "Though I've never cared for that slightly weird name."

A newly-installed Mrs. Jose from a flat further along, putting out milk bottles, thought it a strange foursome whose different voices carried her way.

"*Allez, allez!*" cried Miss Dicks moving into first gear before the white saloon set off, gliding like a wraith through the quiet, uneasy streets. The older man in the back angled himself so as not to touch the other passenger inadvertently during any change of direction, and whenever the choirmaster coughed or sneezed, he pressed his face against the window.

"You won't catch anything! Don't worry!" Serena teased. "Bless you, anyhow." She smiled at Daniel through her mirror. "There you are, I've blessed you ten times already, so you'll be alright."

Past Hyde Park corner amongst increasing traffic. Everything bathed in a bright, orange light. Joggers, late shoppers, the odd dog. Even the orange cones lined along Rutland Gate looked vulgarly festive.

"Don't get so many of these in France, do you?" Daniel tried to distract his companion away from the glass. But the old man was not easily baited with trivia. His distance remained fixed.

"We have far worse problems than the inconvenience of cones."

Serena glanced round, surprised. "Well, we'll try and have a jolly evening, anyhow." She found a space in Ennismore Gardens, and skilfully manoeuvred the big car between two vans. People walked by in pairs, in groups, singing snatches of 'Rule Britannia' and carrying little Union Jack flags and various mascots from their toy cupboards. Grown-up desires on purloined childhood innocence. The Doctor found it repulsive, more so when someone chanted whisky breath into the open car.

"We're having a party can you come? Bring your own cup and saucer and a bun... " before strutting away in a comical gait, coat tails flapping. Others followed. Each more outrageous than the last, in surreal contrast to the sepulchrally quiet street. Several curtains nearby moved in curiosity then eventually closed on the hilarity.

"*Merci*." The old man got out, quickly freeing himself from Serena's helping hand. His expression had changed to annoyance.

"Where are you staying, by the way?" Serena asked, knowing how to flirt.

"Russell Square." He lied quickly. "No gay bars there."

"What?"

A glance at Catherine yielded nothing. "Come again?"

"I have meetings at the British Museum." His headache had started again. He must be far more circumspect, he told himself. And no more

German words out loud. "For two weeks."

"Oh." She locked up the car and helped get Daniel organised. "What about afterwards?"

Afterwards? What afterwards? When the applause had faded and the last coat and bag had been collected? He didn't know. The canister was warm now and as comforting as Rosary beads to his doubting mind. These people were close and pressing closer. He could smell their clothes through the artificial perfumes to their bodies. Even the soap they'd used was distinct to his trained nose. *'Mein gut schnuffeln Hund'* was always one of *Hauptscharführer* Bilharz's favourite expressions. Not without cause, and like a faithful hound, he had herded *Das Ungeziefer* to poison.

It had taken fifteen minutes with properly sealed airways. Longer with carelessness. More than they deserved for blighting his life and, despite the choirmaster's fatal condition, revenge was incomplete. His fingers locked tight around the steel carton. Conjoined until the right moment.

"Thank you all, but I can't go in." Those cracked lips now in greater detail under the bright foyer lights. "There is first something I must do."

"Oh come on!" Serena gaily forced her arm into his. "Don't be such an old fogey. We've come all this way... " She eased him into the queue of revellers and kept him there, while Catherine and Daniel searched for any sign of wheelchair access.

Meanwhile, a group of music students piped their way through Vivaldi's 'Four Seasons' as the crowd moved forward good-humouredly for the baggage check.

"Do they have this palaver in France?" Serena asked, hoping others nearby would notice his accent in reply.

"It is many years since I have been to any performance." He was sulking. He had better things to do.

"This'll make up for it." Serena kissed his cheek affectionately.

Then the brightness overhead suddenly increased, illuminating them all like a gilded, heavenly host amongst the resplendent trappings of carved panels and iconographic photographs set between them, in homage to both the creators and purveyors of music. Catherine remembered the *Notre Dame des Anges* in Collioure where the same flood of light from darkness had seemed a benediction. Daniel too felt suddenly blessed, for those songs of love, those symphonies, cantatas, scores from every gamut of human experience, born of the temporal world full of misery and wickedness, had delivered Heaven to earth. Such courage, others said, seeing him smile, and how he basked, absolved, in the warmth of their sympathy.

The queue was beginning to move. Excitement growing.

"Might even get on the telly." Serena laughed from somewhere behind him. "Did you notice the outside broadcast vans?! If I see a camera I'm going to go like this!" Up went her skirt again with a *Folies Bergère* flurry and a twist of her ample hips. "What d'you think? Get me noticed?" She was unspeakably coarse, yet some people seemed to find it amusing.

"*Untermenschen.*"

After the box office, came a parting of the ways, with a huge galley staircase leading off. *Recht und link*s – right and left - with the Red Cross truck nearby in attendance. It was tempting, but how to choose for the best? On this occasion, it was the tickets that decided. Daniel and Catherine to the right, while Serena and the Frenchman were obliged to take the left, thereby joining the younger element already thronging the rowdy stalls.

His special device efficient, but not infallible.

"Come on." The interior designer took his hand. She liked him more and more, her little old man.

"*Just look at that pair. How cute.*" She knew that's what people were saying. She could tell. All the while, her predatory eyes scoured the crowds hoping to perhaps find one of her many acquaintances. Someone to show him off to. But he held back, like an uncooperative child in harness whose whims won't be denied.

"Catherine." He whispered in her hair as she drew alongside. Like the sound of the sea in a shell, his voice was an echo she'd not dared remember. "You are carrying my child. But you knew that already, don't you?" Then he was gone, borne away like picnickers' junk in the *Crique de la Moulade*.

Her hands left the wheelchair as though electrocuted. She left it for someone else to push through the tightening crush towards the mezzanine. Daniel saw Serena and the old man pressed together. Doctor and harlot, beige and emerald combined, finally to disappear beyond the dark, oblong doorway.

His deep, dry cough started again, and un-summoned tears blurred his vision as he was parked at the end of a row that looked down over the vast circular sea of celebration below.

"You O.K?" Someone enquired. A young woman.

"Catherine!"

"No. It's Julia, actually. I've got some tissues." She put the lightweight box in his lap. "I like your top hat." She gave it a playful push.

"Funny old boy, that Monsieur." Daniel mused absently. "Don't you think?"

"Who now?"

But the City of London Symphony Orchestra was already beginning to tune up in a discordant cacophony, while she tried to extract the tiny binoculars from the seat in front.

"Look! They're down there!" He craned forward. Tension in his every move.

"How can you see, silly?" The one called Julia passed the binoculars over, but its two small lenses showed nothing.

"Doesn't matter anyhow. We've got each other," he muttered distractedly. "And the baby. Which reminds me... "

"Of what?"

"I'm seeing Louisa next weekend. Geraldine's bringing her over... "

*

Meanwhile, the conductor, Sir Clifford Dawson had stretched up his arms to the lofty dome, and the tiered sky of boxed-in faces rained cheers and whistles as his baton fell. Then balloons, bright worlds of whisky breath, floated down on the *melée* below. On party hats and streamers, on girls who'd changed clothes at the office, and more young, top-hatted men, sombre as pall bearers were it not for the array of newsagents' novelties between their lips.

As Daniel hummed and moved his conducting hand in rhythm, the orchestra began the slow introduction, while Mary Donnelly, mezzo-soprano, a bleached blond complete with a round, uncovered turkey breast, advanced regally through their ranks. Through the masts of stroking bows the pride of Eniskillen came, towards the frail conductor standing amidst the ferns and floribunda heaped around his rostrum. The Maestro's *toupée* sat slightly askew on his smooth head, and a drop of mucus fell from his nose as momentum increased. The arm-locking bodies below began to sway to the familiar opening bars of Thomas Arne's 'Rule Brittania.'

The singer's white flesh glistened, newly basted, as her bejewelled hair and heavy, blue cloak dazzled sharply under the lights. More sweat, more streamers - one caught above an ear - more purpose now, more breath... She burst into song, flinging her arms wide, whereupon the cloak collapsed to the floor revealing a Union Jack dress, plumply padded from neck to ankle, resplendent for all to see.

"When Britain... fir... ir... rst at Heaven's command...ro... o... ose out of the azure main... "

However, her lilting, Irish voice was soon lost amongst the singing that swelled from three thousand other throats. Smothered by the fervour and moist, crying eyes of partying patriots.

The massive explosion took just two seconds.

Two seconds to crack the building's sturdy walls and tear too many balcony cradles free. From the sudden, terrible stillness came small tongues of flame nourished on the thickening air of human cries filled the hall. The furnace devoured the soft, silk flowers, the plastic greenery, the waving flags and the fleeing fancy dresses, many with no way of escape.

Then the deadly crystals met the air. Pretty blue chalk pellets that Doktor Pierre Arnajon had kept so well for so long, years past the DEGESCH corporation's use-by date. Hydrogen-cyanide, the ultimate fumigator, and no discriminator of persons or pestilence, added its lingering smell of bitter almonds to the final smoke.

XXX

"I hope my death will be accepted as atonement for all my sins, and as an expiatory sacrifice. By this sacrifice, our time's distance from God may be shortened by some small measure... We want to kindle a torch of life; a sea of flames surrounds us."
(Farewell letter of Count Peter Yorke von Wartenburg.Member of the Kreisau resistance circle. Tortured and hanged by the Gestapo in the Plotzenzee prison. 1945.)

The winter sunlight danced a dappled pattern along the dusty Embankment, and the Thames like a liquid ribbon, trailed slowly by, above the parapet's edge. Catherine's hair had lightened since the birth of her son to match the sallow sky. And now she pulled his pram to and fro in mindless rhythm as Serena stared blindly, blankly at the water, locked in thought. More time for that now of course, without work. More time to be ungrateful that she, Catherine Vitello Ash and her child had survived intact; for the barricade of resentment to thicken.

Her breathing came quick and shallow. Small, anxious gasps which forbade any laughter. Not that she had much to laugh about during those shortened, chilly days at the cusp of the year. Like others similarly handicapped, the blind have little cause to celebrate.

"Sing to Adam, Serena." Catherine encouraged absently. "He always loves a song."

"You know I can't, you stupid cow."

"God, I'm sorry. I can't seem to say anything right anymore."

"Got it in one."

"So I have to pay when I've already paid. And still paying,

alright?"

"That's up to you. I don't care."

Adam Vitello Ash, sensing discord from his blanket nest, began to whimper. Softly as those timid birds who, having stayed too far north, succumb. Softly, as the last leaves fall like petals for the dead. Catherine shivered. For a moment the sun was lost behind huge clouds weighing in from the east, pushed from the open sea by a stiffening breeze. Kinetic, ever changing. Here a hand, there a face, now a galloping horse, a pale gold-edged creature escaped from the fire, his head and tail arched in symmetry spreading over London Bridge.

"Look!" She cried. Forgetting her friend couldn't see. But the Doctor's red-haired child obeyed, to witness with his big, grey eyes how sweetly and fluently the pale, *Boulonnais* stallion ran across the sky.

*

After weeks of outrage and grief, with reports and diagnoses still un-sated, the medically re-constructed head of an elderly, white Caucasian male was beamed across the world with every television news bulletin. This cryptogenic, unclaimed creation had an immediately sobering effect on children in the midst of play, vulnerable women alone, and the bedridden who quickly changed TV channels whenever it appeared.

All except the one, whose view took in the brown, harvested vineyards layered bare beyond the outskirts of the out-of-season town. Larger than life, the plastic clay more fleshy than flesh under studio lights, modelled smooth where it should have been rough. Younger, before his *Milice* days and his abandoned Hippocratic oath. Before the sun and the wind had claimed him. Fifteen kilograms of red terracotta; rock sediment tinted by iron, now formed a nose, a mouth, and a big, clever forehead, that swivelled slowly, clockwise in perpetual motion.

When Estelle Arnajon could look at 'The Man from Nowhere' no longer, she got up, dressed herself in the first, unfamiliar moth-balled clothes that came to hand, and made her way through the deserted house in the Avenue Victor Hugo to find the telephone.

*

Some nine hundred miles north in an evening street of London's East End, a dark-haired youth, tall for his age, managed to find a public phone booth that was working.

"Me mum says I might 'ave something wot might be of interest." As the ten pence he'd shoved into the slot, rattled out of sight.

"May we have your name please?" The police station's duty sergeant asked amid confusing background noise.

"Yeah. Sean. Sean Steiner... She'e been goin' on abaht it ever since she found it. Says it's the spit of that face on the telly."

"What is?"

"This photo. Some Frog man. On a sort of card."

"A frogman?"

"I dunno. I'm only doin' this 'cos she made me. It don't 'arf pen an' ink in 'ere!"

"Address?"

"Do I 'ave to?"

"Yes."

"Shit. Me money's runnin' out. Five Albion Street... Mile End... "

"We'll be along."

Mrs. Steiner patted her son's gelled head as he emerged.

"You did right, Sean. You know I'm no good on them things. Anyhow," she pulled Léon Tavernier's face from her pocket, "I bet you they'll make it worth our while... if it *is* 'im, that is."

"What'yer mean?"

"A reward, son. Just think! It'll pay for that new three piece suite wot yer Dad's kept on about for bloody ages."

EPILOGUE

Catherine sneezes again, causing little Adam Vitello Ash to drop the large, furry brick he's been earnestly contemplating in his baby hands. He lies on the thick, white carpet, no longer delicately premature, but stoutly compact. His strengthening limbs akimbo.

"Serves you right." Serena says to her sourly, guiding a full wineglass to her lips. "It's too bloody cold out there now. It's a wonder he's not caught something."

"No harm in fresh air, that's what my mother... " Catherine stops herself. She's not had a mother in years. Nor a father. She turns up the TV's sound for the news on a set big enough to fill the room. Bought in case Serena's sight improves.

Jesus...

That head's there again. The sculpted one. Then something different, which changes everything. A photograph. Catherine listens, suddenly unable to breathe...

Her scream tears at her throat.

"What on earth?" Serena's bewilderment soon turns to fear. She drops her empty glass, and her white stick falls to the floor as the newsreader's voice surfaces again.

"... Dr. Joseph Weiss, Nazi hunter, who survived the horrors of Birkenau has confirmed that this is the very same Doctor Pierre Arnajon, *alias* Léon Tavernier, the notorious *Doktor 'Käfer.'* Perpetrator of unspeakable crimes against Jewish homosexuals from Nice during Alois Brunner's purge of the French Riviera. Adolf Eichmann had trucks to fill and discovered another willing collaborator. He later became involved in embryo research to prove how low levels of testosterone in the male foetal brain can create a preternatural homosexual. Dr. Weiss also claims Pierre Arnajon aborted many foetuses of women destined to perish, to aid this research. It's also believed this led to work with Thilo and Mengele selecting victims for the gas chambers and thus he must have learned how to preserve his supply of Zyklon B, which was normally only effective for three months... Further investigations show that contrary to earlier statements made by him and his younger sister while in Collioure, there was no author of that name. Nor cousins in Bavaria, and certainly no schooling in German."

Catherine clutches her stomach, feeling the vomit rising within. She's hysterical now. Immune to the shocking story's other embellishments. How the Doktor's hermitic wife had waited all those years to betray him. How their daughter, Agathe, a 'stranger' to her father and a recluse in America, had just succumbed to an overdose of painkillers in her freezing apartment. How Michel Villaine, a secular Jewish builder from Collioure bore witness and the sly priest did not. How Fritz Koppel once with Aktion-Reinheardt in Vienna, had gone to earth like *'Das Ungezeifer'*- the vermin - he so loathed, soon perhaps to break new ground in other places. Wherever he is needed.

And what else of the sister? *Der Osche*? The Ox? Who seems more colourful now. Smoother under lights, on the screen. Daily doses of her own piss have purged the fat from her body but that gaunt, cadaverous face remains the same. Now she and her hanging meat are reflected on the walls nearby. Almost God-like. All powerful, in slow motion, barely moving. Six black hooks protrude from a central ceiling beam followed by flickering black and white film of men wriggling like worms in a dazzlingly blinding light. A small table nearby is set with glasses of wine from Libourne for witnesses to watch them die.

Catherine picks up baby Adam and flings him at blind Serena's passive arms. "Take him!" she shrieks at her. "Son of the Devil!"

She's already by the door, not caring if he's fallen, or that the fruit of the Garden of Eden lies still and composed, following her with a quizzical, orphaned gaze. His pale eyes unblinking.

*

'... *to the woman were given two wings of a great eagle that she might fly...* '

And so she flies. Out into the street, awash since dawn, headlong towards the yellow, swollen Limehouse Canal, as martyred cries of the Apocalypse thunder in her ears, drowning another's desperate plea for love which she already knows by heart.

'Vous ay encheri
Tresdont que premiers
Vous vi
Jusqu'au morir
Vostres demour... '

'In the end is the beginning... '

GLOSSARY

FRENCH

cave – cellar
grenier – attic
charet – cart
messuage – dwelling house and curtilage
hommet – dwarf (derog.)
appentis – shed
mercredi prochaine – next Wednesday
"À toute à l'heure, mon papillon." – "Until then, my butterfly."
chef des troupeaux – flock leader
doulz – gentle (Occitan)
carrelage - tiling
croque-morts - undertaker
'la malchance' – bad luck

GERMAN

Ausdauer – persistence
Himmel färht block – Ascension block
Teilhaber – partner
diese Schunde – this trash
gebrechlich Hundin – weak bitch
Käfer – beetle
Mein gut scholruffeln hund – my good sniffer dog
Abschaum – scum
Gehenweg! – Go away!
Weibschen – female animal
gefärhlich - dangerous
Untermenschen – subhuman

www.publishandprint.co.uk

Printed in Great Britain
by Amazon